Pra
C

The

"A light and e
ance between the murder mystery and the intricacy of
human relationships. . . . The South Carolina setting teems
with Southern hospitality, the scenes [are] action-packed,
and there is romance and humor, as well. I give this book
four paws up!"   —MyShelf.com

"[An] amusing and enthralling regional amateur sleuth
tale starring an eccentric cast led by the likable, peace-
making heroine."   —Genre Go Round Reviews

The Cat, the Lady and the Liar

"A lighthearted, fun cozy starring an engaging cast of
characters. . . . Feline frolic fans will enjoy."
                                          —The Best Reviews

"Tightly plotted, with likable characters, and filled with
cat trivia, this entertaining mystery will become a favorite for cozy and cat lovers alike."   —The Conscious Cat

The Cat, the Professor and the Poison

"A fun, entertaining story . . . the mystery will keep the
reader guessing, and the conclusion is satisfying and will
leave readers looking forward to Jillian's next adventure.
I enjoyed this story so much."   —Fresh Fiction

"Sure to please the cat and cozy fans of the world. . . .
After reading the first book, I just knew I was going to
fall in love with this series and [I] have."
                                —Feathered Quill Book Reviews

"The characters and friends Jillian makes along the way,
and the care she gives to the cats she encounters, will
make her a fast favorite."   —The Mystery Reader

continued . . .

The Cat, the Quilt and the Corpse

"A solid start to a cozy mystery series." —CA Reviews

"The first installment of what promises to be a delightful cozy series. . . . Leann Sweeney presents readers with a solid mystery that kept this reader guessing through all of the plot twists and turns. Plenty of cat trivia adds to the richness of the narrative . . . highly recommended!"
—The Romance Readers Connection

"The cats are entertaining four-legged assistants . . . [and] kitty lovers will enjoy the feline trivia."
—*Publishers Weekly*

"Great fun for cat lovers . . . a lot of hometown charm."
—The Mystery Reader

"Fans will enjoy her amateur sleuth investigation."
—The Best Reviews

"[Leann Sweeney's] brand-new series about adorable cats that just can't stay out of trouble is bound to be a hit!"
—Fantastic Fiction

"Sweet but not syrupy, sharply written, and brimming with heart."
—Cozy Library

Praise for the Yellow Rose Mysteries

"As Texas as a Dr Pepper–swigging armadillo at the Alamo. A rip-roaring read!"
—Carolyn Hart, national bestselling author of *Death Comes Silently*

"*Pick Your Poison* goes down sweet."
—Rick Riordan, *New York Times* bestselling and Edgar® Award–winning author

"Full of emotions! Anger, sadness, fear, happiness, laughter, joy, and tears . . . they are all there, and you will feel them along with the characters in this book!"
—Armchair Interviews

"A welcome new voice in mystery fiction."
—Jeff Abbott, national bestselling author of *Collision*

Other Novels by Leann Sweeney

The Cats in Trouble Mysteries

The Cat, the Wife and the Weapon
The Cat, the Lady and the Liar
The Cat, the Professor and the Poison
The Cat, the Quilt and the Corpse

The Yellow Rose Mysteries

Pushing Up Bluebonnets
Shoot from the Lip
Dead Giveaway
A Wedding to Die For
Pick Your Poison

THE CAT, THE MILL AND THE MURDER

A CATS IN TROUBLE MYSTERY

LEANN SWEENEY

AN OBSIDIAN MYSTERY

OBSIDIAN
Published by the Penguin Group
Penguin Group (USA) Inc., 375 Hudson Street,
New York, New York 10014, USA

USA | Canada | UK | Ireland | Australia | New Zealand | India | South Africa | China

Penguin Books Ltd., Registered Offices: 80 Strand, London WC2R 0RL, England
For more information about the Penguin Group visit penguin.com.

First published by Obsidian, an imprint of New American Library,
a division of Penguin Group (USA) Inc.

First Printing, May 2013
10   9   8   7   6   5   4   3   2   1

ISBN 978-0-451-41541-7

Printed in the United States of America

*This book is dedicated to my own three amigos,
who left me for the Rainbow Bridge in the last year and
a half. Indigo, Archie and Agatha, I miss your
inspiration and I will hold you in my heart forever.*

Acknowledgments

This book came to life with the help of many friends, both of the human and feline variety. I would like to thank my writers group—Kay, Bob, Amy, Laura, Dean, Heather, Millie, Charlie, Susie, Isabella and Curry. My online support comes from dear friends Lorraine and Jenn as well as the many followers of the Cozy Chicks blog— www.cozychicksblog.com—and the other Cozy Chicks: Kate, Maggie, Deb, Heather and Julie. The cozyarmchair friends on Yahoo are always there for me, as well as my dear husband and my fur friends, Rosie the Labradoodle and Wexford the Ragdoll cat. Many thanks to my agent, Carol Mann, and my editor, Claire. Each and every one of you makes me a better writer.

If you stared deep into a cat's eyes, you would be able to see into the world of spirits.

ENGLISH PROVERB

One

Dustin Gray, the young man charged with taking Shawn Cuddahee and me into the abandoned Lorraine Stanley Textile Mill, put a key into the padlock on the metal gate. Dark clouds hung low, hovering above the three-story building on this cold January morning.

Chain-link fencing surrounded the entire ten-acre property, in many places topped with anti-climbing spikes. In other spots on the fence, time and neglect had taken their toll. It would have been easy to scale had I been a teenager looking to get into trouble. But I'm Jillian Hart, in my mid-forties and not inclined to climb anything other than the occasional ladder when one of my three cats accidentally sneaks outside and ends up on the roof.

While Dustin struggled with the rusty lock, Shawn and I stared at the caution sign posted on the hurricane fencing. He started reading the words aloud and I followed along: "'Cleanup project in cooperation with the South Carolina Department of Health and Environmental Control,'" he whispered. The admonition talked about a contract number and finished with the promise that "soil and groundwater will be tested for hazardous substances."

I'd once stopped here to take pictures of the burnt-orange brick mill, maybe a few months back, and this sign had been added since that time. *Hazardous substances, huh?* I wondered about the feral cats inside the mill—the cats who were the reason Shawn and I accompanied structural engineer Dustin Gray this morning. Were the cats sick? Would we find the bodies of those who hadn't survived living around toxins from fabric dyes that had leaked into the groundwater? I couldn't stand to even think about such a thing, so I turned my gaze back to the building.

This old mill had once hummed with activity and was a place where fabric had been made for nearly a century. Cotton fabric I dearly loved—beautiful woven fabric put together through American ingenuity and by American hands. I am a quilter. I have stacks of fabric at my home on Mercy Lake, here in South Carolina. But none of it is made in the United States anymore.

Behind us, a train chugged along. Trains once carried in new cotton and carried away fabric. Now all the railcars still passing through were probably filled with chemicals or oil. We stood before the graveyard of an industry—a broken building begging for our help. I felt a sense of urgency to begin the job of preparing this place for its future. And I felt a great responsibility, too. The same responsibility Shawn, animal rescuer extraordinaire, felt.

This gigantic place, with its old buildings and vast, grassy surrounding land, was now home to a colony of feral cats. I considered it ironic that these cats—so misunderstood and maligned by most of society—were the gatekeepers here. They had invaded the buildings probably years ago and taken on the task of ridding the structures of rats, mice and snakes.

We were planning to displace them from their home in the coming weeks. The sadness I felt was tempered by knowing the relocation of the feral cats would be done the right way. They would not be exterminated, as one town council member had suggested. I felt anger heat my cheeks as I remembered hearing the man's words at the council meeting ten days ago. He'd said, "Why can't we just shoot them all?"

"Tough old lock, but I got it," Dustin said as he pushed open the tall gate so we could access the property. Winter winds pushed us along as we made our way across the desolate acreage leading to the main building. I admired the handsome arched windows with their lovely brickwork, but I was puzzled, too. All the windows were bricked over—with much shoddier-looking work than had been used on the original building. *Why would they close off all the windows and leave no open eyes to the outside world for this mill?* I wondered.

A strong gust hit us and I had to hang on to my yellow hard hat. It was the first time ever for me to wear a hard hat, but Dustin had insisted we all wear them. He was a civil engineer who couldn't be more than twenty-five, if that. He wore a flannel shirt, faded jeans and a tool belt that seemed to carry enough equipment to weigh down even a person as strong as Shawn. Despite Dustin's slim build and pale face, his gait was sure and confident. Still, I couldn't help thinking someone like this young man, with his wire rim glasses and serious expression, seemed like an anomaly in rural Mercy, South Carolina. He looked as if he should be sitting in a lecture hall at Harvard.

He'd done his homework, that's for sure. When we'd met up with him at Belle's Beans, the local coffee shop, before driving across town to this spot, he'd shared his knowledge of the mill. Though not a local—he'd recently moved to nearby Greenville from the Northeast—he knew that the building had been abandoned for more than a decade. Though the structure stood mostly intact, it had been built in the late 1800s. He warned us that safety was definitely a concern, and Shawn shared cryptically that Dustin might be surprised at just how big a concern. Shawn was talking about the cats, of course. Dustin had no clue, but he might in a few minutes.

Dustin's job here was different from our mission. He was an impartial employee, hired by the Mercy town council to decide how best to rehabilitate this mill into a sound and usable space. Two sets of investors with very different ideas had offered up plans. Would the Lorraine Stanley Textile Mill become an "urban village" clustered around a mill museum? Or would it become a collection of open-space condos with a large central common area? Initial proposals had been readied and Dustin would of-fer his input after his evaluation. At this point, no one knew which concept would work better. First, the condi-tion of the mill would have to be assessed.

But even before any cleanup and rehabilitation could happen, Shawn was to check out the feral cat population—to see how many cats lived here and if there were any feline health issues—and then come up with a solution to deal with them.

"Like I said back at Belle's Beans," Shawn said to Dustin as we stopped in front of the main mill entrance, "these cats we're about to encounter are *not* your friends."

Shawn had begun his lecture on the topic of feral cats versus stray cats back at Belle's Beans and he couldn't leave it alone. Sure enough, he continued on, adding, "All feral cats are strays, but not all strays are feral. The cat who ends up at your back door meowing for food and longing for human touch? He's a stray. Strays make amazing and wonderful pets. But a feral cat will hide under your deck and never come close to you. He will eventually breed and you will consider him a nuisance. Ferals don't trust humans. Since people domesticated cats centuries ago, then some folks decided they could be discarded like garbage, ferals have been a group lost in limbo. They aren't wild and yet they cannot live with humans. They aren't pack animals, so they don't comfort one another much. It's our responsibility to find solutions, to care—"

I placed a hand on Shawn's upper arm and softly said, "And that's why we're here. We'll save these guys."

Shawn's face had gone beet red with agitation. "Yeah. Sorry. I've got strong feelings about this topic, if you hadn't figured that out."

Dustin, looking a little shell-shocked, mumbled, "I get it, man." He fingered through the keys on the ring he still held and now unlocked the double doors to the mill building so we could enter. The old wood, mildewed and faded by time, had cracked in places near its iron hinges. Dustin pushed one door with his shoulder and it creaked open in protest. He said, "These cats won't attack us, will they?"

Shawn walked through the door first, saying, "Not unless you try to initiate contact—as in corner them. You might not get so lucky with the rats."

I stifled a smile when Dustin's brown eyes widened. He said, "You're kidding, right?"

"Nope." Shawn walked into the darkness ahead, his Maglite leading the way.

As Dustin and I followed, I said, "Why did they brick up all these windows? This place is as dark as a dungeon."

Dustin pulled a flashlight from his utility belt and switched it on. The farther we moved from the open door, the darker and mustier it became. He said, "Mills like these went through many transformations for their power supply. Coal, steam and finally electric heat. When the air-conditioning was added, the windows were bricked up to save money on the electricity bills."

"How awful to work in a place without windows," I

said. "I didn't get a chance to tell you before, but my degree is in textile arts. That's why I volunteered to help you and Shawn with this project. I love fabric and learned the history of these mills in college. One of my courses had a boring title—History of Textile Production on the Eastern Seaboard. We never got to the part about the business of heating and cooling such gigantic places. But thanks to the course, I am familiar with spindles and weaving—that and the culture surrounding every big mill like this one."

Dustin didn't respond and I felt a little silly then. I guess I wanted to justify my presence. In truth, I was here for the cats more than for a forsaken culture. They still lived and breathed, after all. Textile production in America was dead.

Dustin stopped and swept his beam upward, downward and beyond us. Since Shawn had disappeared into the pitch-black space ahead, I thought Dustin was trying to find him. Then he stomped his booted foot and the sound echoed around us.

He probably didn't realize he'd scared a few cats by making such a loud noise. Shawn would not be happy if the kitties fled to hide inside the walls or were able to get up into the ceilings. If that was the case, we'd have a hard time figuring out how many cats lived here.

But Dustin has a job to do, too, I thought. If he made a lot of noise again, I'd say something. Now was not the time. Instead, I said, "I'll bet these wood floors will be beautiful once they're refinished."

Dustin still wasn't talking. He'd taken several steps farther into the abyss and now focused his light on one of the many support pillars.

"Wow." He sounded awed as he rested a hand on the pillar. Then he ran his hand up and down.

I stepped closer so I could see what had grabbed his

attention. The round support had some kind of metal sleeve that went about halfway up. I touched it and realized the metal was thick. I could feel gouges and scratches beneath my fingers. I said, "I've never seen anything constructed like this. Why did they put metal around the supports?"

"There are two stories above us, not to mention a basement below." Dustin put his face close to the metal and held the light so he could see better. "In a building this big, that's a lot of weight to sustain a structure as large as this building. They had to use strong materials like cement and cast iron."

As I touched the beam, my fingers found something etched into the metal. "Can you focus the light right here?" I tapped a spot at my eye level.

We both moved our faces close to see what was written and I smiled as I made out the words "Rosie loves Joe." The building suddenly seemed less empty. Three little words told so much.

Dustin stepped away from the support, apparently uninterested in this newfound touch of humanity. He was all about metal and wood and load-bearing beams. "Where did Shawn go?"

"To find the cats. Probably toward the walls and those bricked-up windows," I said. "He'll be looking for spots where the cats are getting in and out of here."

We walked side by side in the direction Shawn seemed to have gone—*seemed to* being the key words.

Dustin said, "We'll have to set up some kind of light source, probably halogens. Either that or knock out some of those bricks that obscure the windows."

"Getting rid of those bricks would be a wonderful idea." I could see Shawn's light up ahead and to our right. "There he is."

We picked up our pace and I whispered, "Best to keep

quiet now. The cats have probably already gone into hiding, but we don't want to spook them any more than we have just by coming inside the building."

Dustin whispered back, saying, "Got it."

Shawn was standing by old machinery that had been pushed against one wall. He was focusing his light inside what looked like an old twisting machine. Since twisting machines were no longer used in the textile process, the foreigners, mostly the Chinese and the Indians, who'd bought up most of the spinners, combers and other mill equipment, had apparently left these behind. I might not know about bricked-up windows, but I knew my textile machinery.

Shawn whispered harshly, "What *is* this piece of crap? How can I get any kind of cat count with this kind of junk all over the place? I see at least a dozen pairs of eyes staring up at me in just this one piece of machinery."

"All over the place?" Dustin said, sounding confused.

Shawn extended his arm and his Maglite illuminated an entire row of old equipment.

"But this is wonderful," I said, wishing I'd known we'd need flashlights and brought one for myself. "This is part of our history, Shawn. Maybe some of this machinery can be put in the museum if that's what the town council decides."

"Wonderful?" Shawn said. "Are you *kidding* me? There's a gazillion places for cats to hide in these damn machines. I thought this building was empty."

"Why don't we skip the machinery for now and take a look at the offices and the boiler room?" Dustin said. "No doubt there was a break room and bathrooms, too. Might be easier to find cats hiding in there."

"Yeah, let's get all the bad news out of the way so I can come up with a plan," Shawn said. "I can tell you right now, in a building this big, I'm gonna need a whole lot of feral cat portable structures. And they aren't cheap."

I swore it took us a good five minutes to walk to the far end of the ground floor. My exhilaration at being in such a historic place was wearing off. The darkness and the chill were sinking in and I felt my heart pounding a little faster. What would light reveal about this old place? I wasn't sure I wanted to know.

At one point in our trek, Shawn stumbled over something and swore. He said, "Not a dead cat, I hope," a hint of anguish in his tone.

I immediately looked down to where Shawn had trained his flashlight, my heart thrumming with dread. I saw a cheese cone. This odd name was slang for the extra-large bobbins used to hold wound cotton yarn. I wanted to pick it up and take it with me, but I figured there was probably plenty of time to collect souvenirs later. We'd be back here often in the next few weeks.

"What other kind of junk will we fall over in this place?" Shawn kicked the cone, sending it out of sight.

I heard no cats meowing or hissing during our walk, not even the mewling of newborn kittens—though I was sure we'd find some of those in the near future. Meanwhile, Shawn was mumbling under his breath about how this would be a lot tougher job than he'd thought.

We came to a wide hallway. To our left, a stone staircase curved up into darkness, so sturdy it probably hadn't needed to be repaired in the past one hundred thirty years. To our right was a tall, closed door, its paint so deteriorated it was impossible to tell what color the door had been. Shawn put a finger to his lips and quietly twisted the ornate and tarnished brass knob Dustin illuminated for him. Though he was hoping not to disturb any cats that might be hiding beyond this door, I was certain if they were inside this room, they'd already heard us. A cat's hearing is at least a hundred times more acute than a human being's.

I saw a hint of light coming from inside the room.

Faint. Dull. Was there an actual unbricked window beyond?

But when a woman's voice yelled, "What you think you're doin' in here?" I jumped back and got a taste of my own heart.

Two

I froze, more than a little startled at the sound of a woman's voice. Shawn immediately pushed the door completely open.

Dull light emanated from a candle sitting in what appeared to be a pie plate on the floor. I pressed my hand to my mouth and whispered, "Oh my goodness," between my fingers.

The clouded eyes of a woman stared up at us. The odor hit me then, the unpleasant combination of spoiled food and an unwashed body.

Shawn didn't whisper when *he* spoke. "What in hell are you doing here?"

"I asked first," the woman said.

"This place is dangerous, lady," Shawn replied. "Plus, I'm thinkin' you don't have a key."

Dustin cleared his throat. "This isn't a healthy place to be ... staying."

The woman drew her legs up to her chest, wrapped them with her arms and began to rock.

I felt a swell of emotion seeing her withdraw. I approached her, moving slowly so as not to upset her any more than she already was. When I reached her side, I knelt and saw she was wearing what could only be described as rags. Filthy ones at that.

"Are you all right?" I said.

She turned her face to me. "Right as rain," she answered. "You one of *them*?"

"One of whom?" I asked, taking in the objects surrounding her. I saw a saucer of curdled milk, a few chicken bones, a roll of paper towels, an old glass milk bottle full of water and a cellophane package of powdered sugar donuts.

"The ones that comes in the night," she said before burying her head in her knees again. More rocking.

"This is the first time I've been here," I said in a soft tone, hoping to calm her obvious fear. Before she hid her face, I'd seen her features more clearly—the road map of wrinkles and scars, the frizzy gray hair spilling over her shoulders and surrounding her face like a kinky woolen hat. She appeared to be a few decades older than me.

Shawn hovered over us. "You don't belong here, lady. Why are you here?"

She lifted her head and met his stare. "I don't have to tell you nothin'." Her mouth puckered into a childlike pout.

I held up a hand to Shawn, hoping he'd keep quiet. "I'm Jillian. What's your name?"

"Clara Jeanne if you'd met my mama, but I was always Jeannie to the rest of my kin." She squinted, looked up at the high ceiling. "Course Mama's been gone so long, I can be Jeannie, period. Just Jeannie." She looked toward the saucer on the floor. "Ain't that right, Boots?"

"Boots?" I said.

"My kitty. She's pretty, huh?" Jeannie smiled, revealing her rotting teeth.

An invisible cat. My heart ached with sympathy and concern. This woman definitely needed our help.

Dustin cleared his throat again before speaking. "We do have a job to do here, Mrs. Hart."

I turned to him and in a calm tone said, "We have a problem, though, don't we? One that needs to be handled first."

"I—I guess you're right," he replied.

Shawn offered a disgruntled "Great," under his breath.

"Boots *is* great," Jeannie said with a nod.

"I don't see Boots," I said.

"That's 'cause you don't believe. Most folks don't." She reached out with an arthritic hand and made a stroking motion, as if petting a cat.

"Ah," I said. "Boots is your pet. Do you both live here?"

"Yup. Gotta guard the door, you know. Never knew the creepers would come in the day. Never happened before." She stopped her hand movement and said, "Okay, my baby girl. You go on then. I'm kinda scared myself."

"Don't be afraid, Jeannie. This is Shawn, by the way. He likes cats, too." I gestured up at him and then pointed toward the open door where Dustin stood. "That's Dustin. No one will hurt you. I promise."

"Then you can just take your own selves right back out the way you came. Shut the door, too. Boots might get out and those mean cats will get after her. They's always stealin' her food."

"Mean cats?" Shawn said, his interest suddenly piqued. "Where are they?"

"All over the dern place," Jeannie said. "They do take care of the critters, though. Boots ain't such a great mouser. Never was."

"Maybe if we had invisible mice to go with the invisible cat, she'd do a better job," Shawn said.

"You might be right about that," Jeannie said, the sarcasm lost on her.

"Jeannie, we have a job to do here," I said. "Those

mean cats, as you called them? They don't come near you, do they?"

"Nope. They just steal food when I'm sleepin'." She glanced toward an old fireplace across the room.

I could see more objects now that my eyes had gotten used to the dim light. Several unlit candles sat on either side of the big fireplace. A wooden desk stood in the corner along with a pile of cheese cones. I also noted a large trash bag filled to near bursting with who knew what.

Dustin started toward the bag and Jeannie startled me by springing to her feet and racing across the room. She planted herself between Dustin and the bag, legs spread, arms folded.

"You leave my belongin's alone, you hear?" She lifted her chin and stared up at him.

Dustin, palms facing her in surrender, took a few steps back. "I—I promise not to touch anything."

But while this action was taking place, Shawn had gone to the fireplace and crouched. He was scanning the opening with his Maglite.

"You stay away from there, too, Mister Shawn. Don't be disturbin' nothin'." Jeannie, clearly agitated now, was glancing back and forth between Dustin and Shawn.

Shawn got down, pressed his cheek against the wood floor and trained his light inside the fireplace. "This could be one spot where the cats are coming and going. I can see daylight beyond all the hunks of concrete and loose bricks in this old fireplace."

Jeannie abandoned her spot in front of the trash bag, scrambled across the room and kicked Shawn's backside. "You stay away. Just stay away. That there is a holy place."

Shawn rose and looked up at her, unperturbed by this frail woman's attempt at an assault. "Sorry, but if you'd like those mean cats removed, I'm your man."

"How's that?" she said, taking a step back, her arms folded.

Each movement she made filled the already dank air with her sour odor. I wondered when she'd last bathed. Years ago, maybe?

"We plan to take them to another place. Take them away from here where they'll be fed and cared for," Shawn said.

"Maybe we can do the same for you, Jeannie," I said quietly. But I knew there was no maybe about it. She would have to leave. None of us had planned on finding a human being living here. Solving this problem took priority now. She could be ill. She might have family looking for her.

Jeannie backed into a corner of the room. She wasn't about to go—at least not now. "This is a holy place, I tell you. I ain't goin' nowhere."

"That simply won't work, um ... Miss Jeannie," Dustin said. "This structure could be unsound and—"

"Oh, there's sounds, plenty of 'em," Jeannie said, defiance in her tone. "Don't you be tellin' me somethin' you know nothin' about."

But I was tuned in to what Jeannie had said not once, but twice. "You say this place is holy. What does that mean?"

"Oh, come on," Shawn said, rising. "We do not have time for this crap, Jillian."

Shawn preferred dealing with animals over people every time, so I wasn't surprised at his impatience.

"Give me a moment, okay?" I edged closer to Jeannie. "How is it holy?"

She raised her chin. "It just is. This is where I belong. Don't need nothin' from the likes of y'all, neither."

I nodded. "Okay. We'll leave. But Jeannie, we have to come back. Do you understand?"

"Wait a minute," Shawn said. "Leave?"

I stared at him and I saw his expression change from stubbornness to understanding. He knew better than to argue.

"I—I think that's wise," Dustin said. "We should go."

Jeannie remained in the corner, her arms wrapped tightly around her. "You do that and don't bother comin' back."

Shawn led us out of the room with his Maglite and then shut the door behind us.

"Didn't expect to find a—a *person*," Dustin said. He said this as if we'd just stumbled upon Martians.

"We need help on this one," I said, half to myself. I looked at Dustin. "And not from the town council. Can you keep quiet about this to Councilwoman Webber?"

"I—I don't know. She's the chairwoman of the council and expects a report from me soon, so—"

Shawn closed the space between himself and Dustin. "You want these cats out of here fast?"

Despite the lack of light, I could tell poor Dustin was completely intimidated by Shawn and upset by our surprise discovery.

"Y-yes. Of course we need to deal with all the ... problems," Dustin said, nodding.

"Then do what Jillian says. She's good with *problems*. And, dude," said Shawn, tossing his head in the direction of the closed room, "that lady in there is one *big* problem."

Three

Since Shawn had driven us to the mill in his truck, he dropped Dustin and me off at Belle's Beans so we could pick up our cars. Shawn said he trusted me to solve the "Jeannie problem," as he called it, and solve it fast. For now, he had work to do at his Mercy Animal Sanctuary. Dustin agreed to follow me to my house to help me with the "solving."

On the five-minute drive home, I called my best friend, Deputy Candace Carson of the Mercy Police Department.

"Hey there," she answered. "You still at the mill?"

"We had to leave sooner than expected and we need your help," I said.

"Uh-oh. Were there . . . dead cats? Because I don't think I can deal—"

"No. Gosh, no," I said quickly, not wanting to even think about the possibility. "We ran into an unforeseen problem. When you have time, could you swing by my place so I can explain?"

"How about now?" she said. "This town is so quiet, I swear I can hear my fingernails growing." Candace didn't wait for me to respond before saying she would join me at my house in a few minutes.

I felt a smidgen of relief after I disconnected. I wanted

to brainstorm with Candace before getting social services involved in relocating Jeannie. In our county, the system was not known for its speedy action. Overworked, understaffed and underpaid, the social workers stayed too busy. My guess was they stayed too busy all over the country.

After Dustin pulled into the driveway behind me, I got out of my van and he exited his yellow VW Bug. His car looked vintage, not one of the newer models, but it gleamed, even in the gloom of the late-winter morning.

As we walked along the side of my house toward the back door, I said, "I have three cats, just so you know. And they won't hide like those in the mill. In fact, they're very friendly."

While I said this, I glanced at Dustin's chestnut hair. Because I have one cat allergic to human dander, this was routine for me — checking new visitors for dandruff. His hair looked as perfectly clean and flake-free as his car seemed to be. Chablis — my funny allergic cat — wouldn't need a dose of Benadryl, thank goodness.

As we walked around to the back of the house, Dustin stopped abruptly. He looked out at the lake beyond and said, "Wow. What a view. I hope to live on a lake like this one day. I love anything to do with water — skiing, boating, fishing." He nodded. "Yup, I want to wake up and see something like this every morning."

"It's peaceful here," I said. Despite the overcast weather, the lake shimmered. I loved how mysterious Mercy Lake seemed in the dead of winter. "I not only love this lake; I love this town."

Dustin said, "From what little I've seen and heard, the South sure is different from New York, where I grew up. But I've been with the company such a short time, I don't even have an apartment in Greenville yet. That's why I'm staying in town for this job."

"You're just out of school?" I said as we climbed the deck stairs.

"I graduated in December," he answered. "If your town council wanted a more experienced engineer, my bosses would have charged twice my hourly rate. That doesn't mean I can't do the job, though. I'm excited to get started."

"From what I've seen so far, you'll do just fine." I disarmed the security system and we entered the mudroom. I gestured at my three cats in waiting. "There's my family. Merlot, Syrah and Chablis."

They sat in a row, ready to greet us—the red Maine Coon, Merlot; the amber Abyssinian, Syrah; and Chablis, the seal point Himalayan. I felt a calm settle over me when I saw their precious, curious faces. All Hurricane Katrina rescues, these three cats meant the world to me.

Dustin knelt and extended a hand. "They're not afraid of strangers?"

Syrah answered by starting toward Dustin, but all of a sudden he stopped, arched his back and hissed. Strange thing was, he didn't seem to be hissing at Dustin. The cat was focused on something behind me and I wondered if a bug or a little lizard had come in the door behind us. I turned and looked at the floor. Nothing.

The little green chameleons so prevalent in the summer usually hid under stones in the winter. But maybe one of them had come inside. They move so fast, I could have missed one sneaking in the door. No matter what, any bug or other creature coming in here chose the wrong place. My cats could be relentless in their pursuit of small intruders.

Chablis, meanwhile, about-faced and hurried into the kitchen, ready for a treat—her usual routine when I came home. Merlot continued to sit and stare in the direction of my right calf. What was wrong with my boy cats? They were usually so friendly when I brought a new person into their home.

"I apologize for their rude behavior," I said to Dustin. "Maybe they're hearing something we can't."

Dustin still had his hand outstretched in Merlot's direction. "What's this big one's name again?"

"Merlot. Syrah is the one with the amber fur and big ears."

At the mention of his name, Syrah finally walked up to Dustin and rubbed his head against my visitor's knee.

Merlot chattered as he did when he spotted a bird, but he didn't move. His gaze was still focused beyond me.

After petting Syrah, Dustin rose and approached Merlot. He put his fingers down near Merlot's face. My big boy swiped his face against Dustin's hand.

"They're a pretty good judge of character and I believe you just passed muster," I said with a laugh. "Though I'm not sure what's with the hissing and the chattering. We'll chalk it up to weird, feline behavior."

Dustin followed me into the kitchen. First order of business was treats for my fur babies. After I doled out several pieces of salmon-flavored goodies, I said, "Can I get you a drink? Sweet tea? Coffee?" I wanted to add milk as a choice since Dustin, with his boyish, dimpled face, seemed so young.

"Sweet tea," he said with a smile. "Since arriving in this state I've become addicted to the stuff."

"Popular choice in this house," I said. "You went to school in New York and from your accent I'm guessing you are a complete Yankee."

"Complete. I'm from Niagara Falls," he said, still watching the cats.

I followed his gaze. Though Chablis had finished her treats, neither Syrah nor Merlot had touched theirs. They stood stock-still, staring at the window seat in the breakfast nook. *What in the heck?* They never passed up treats.

No sooner had I handed Dustin his tea than Candace rapped on the back door and stepped inside.

She wore her forest green uniform and her blond hair had this lovely side braid to show off the magenta highlights she'd recently added. The braid was pulled back and pinned up at the nape of her neck.

She smiled at Dustin. "Deputy Candace Carson, Mercy PD. Don't believe I've made your acquaintance."

Dustin seemed frozen for an instant, his mouth slightly agape. "D-Dustin Gray." He strode toward her, hand out, never taking his eyes from hers. As they greeted each other, I noticed Dustin held on to her hand.

Candace gently pulled her hand free, cheeks brightening. "Nice to meet you, Dustin. You're the engineer the town hired, right?"

His head bobbed in agreement.

Gosh. The kid is smitten, I thought.

Candace helped herself to a glass of tea and we headed for the living area adjacent to the kitchen. Dustin waited until Candace and I sat before taking the easy chair opposite the sofa. I expected the cats to join us since they hadn't properly greeted Candace. They do adore her—and like to sniff for traces of her own cat. But all the felines remained in the kitchen. I'd obviously allowed an invisible-to-me creature—maybe even an ant—into the house. Their job was to stalk and dispose of any non-human invaders.

Candace said, "Since Mr. Gray is here—"

"Dustin," he said quickly. "Please call me Dustin."

"Sure. And I'm Candace. Never Candy, always Candace. Anyway, since you're here, I assume Jillian called me because whatever help she wants has something to do with your new job."

"Always the good detective, huh?" I said. "We ran into a little problem at the mill. But first, for this conversation, can you simply be my friend and not a police officer?"

Unsmiling, she said, "Police officers are always on duty, Jillian. You know that."

I knew Candace took her job seriously, and usually I respected and appreciated her for it. But this seemed like a special situation, and I wanted her to trust me on that. So I offered my best pleading look. "Please?"

Candace sighed heavily. "Let's call this *off the record*. Doesn't mean—"

"Off the record," I said. "Sounds perfect. See, there's a woman who seems to be living inside the mill. From talking to her, I'm sure relocating her will be difficult. She insists the mill is a holy place and—"

"*What?*" Candace's already flushed cheeks flamed even more. "How the heck did she get inside? We put up warning signs; there's a tall fence with spikes; we patrol. Sorry, but *off the record* just went out the window."

"*Please* hear me out?" I said.

Dustin was watching our exchange with intense interest. I was certain he would love to have Jeannie removed from the mill as soon as possible and perhaps saw an ally in Candace. But I considered the woman in the mill like the feral cats—she needed to be handled with great care and compassion.

"Go on," Candace said, sounding exasperated. Over time, I'd learned that her first reaction to almost anything was usually based on a black-and-white police view of the world. Beneath that façade, however, I knew Candace well. Nothing to her was as black and white as her new acquaintance Dustin might be led to believe.

"Social service people are overworked," I said. "What will they do with her? Ask you to put her in jail while they clear their calendar?"

"Of course not. She'd go to a shelter." She paused, seeming to consider this option further. "Although I have to say, it's hard to find a decent one in this part of the state. Most of them are overcrowded. I give. You probably have a different idea. Tell me."

"I work with several charities." I looked at Dustin. "See, I'm a quilter and I donate quilts to several organizations. I know people who might help." I returned my focus to Candace. "Let me make a few calls before you drag Jeannie out of the mill, okay?"

Candace's eyes widened in surprise. "Jeannie? Does Jeannie have a last name?"

"She said her name was Clara Jeanne, but everyone calls her Jeannie. We forgot to ask her for a last name."

"Oh. My. Gosh. Clara Jeanne Sloan." Candace appeared more than a tad stunned. "She disappeared years ago. Rumor was she went off to look for her daughter, Kay Ellen. The teenager went missing and a few months later, Jeannie was gone, too. Morris knows the details. He talked about all the unsolved cases when I first joined Mercy PD. Said I should read about the missing mother and daughter as well as all the other old files for future reference. Now I wish I'd examined the case more closely."

"You're saying there was an investigation?" I said.

"I know they tried to find those two, but they were never found—until now. Was the daughter there, too?" Her fair skin had almost returned to its normal pink, though color remained high on her cheeks.

Dustin said, "We didn't get farther than the office where we discovered . . . the lady. There could be more people inside the mill, though."

"Great," Candace said. "Why didn't I listen to that old coot Morris for once and pay more attention to those files?"

"Who's Morris?" Dustin said.

"He's Candace's partner," I said. "Kind of a bristly guy, but once you get to know him, he's not so bad."

Candace checked her watch and stood. Dustin quickly rose, too, never taking his eyes off her.

She said, "Okay, here's the deal. I need to re-read the file before we take action. We keep them in a storage unit, so I'll have to get the key, find the files. Might take a couple hours."

"You want to call me after you're done?" I said.

She nodded. "Meet me at the station around the end of my shift—about four." She glanced at Dustin. "See, we need to know as much as possible about this woman before we go charging into that old mill like gangbusters."

My turn to stand and meet her gaze. "Wait a minute. *Charging in?* What are you talking about?"

"Right now I have to entertain the possibility that Jeannie's daughter *didn't* go missing." Candace said. "Maybe Kay Ellen is with her. Or what if Jeannie went into hiding because she did wrong by that girl?"

"I said, "Could the reason she went into hiding be because she was heartbroken about losing her daughter?"

Candace's gaze went to the ceiling as she considered this possibility. Then she said, "Plausible, but I do recall Morris mentioning talk of foul play—at least as far as the girl was concerned. Gotta go back over the file." She hit her forehead with the heel of her hand. "Why didn't I pay more attention to the details?"

"You were a brand-new officer—how old were you five years ago? Twenty? You thought—"

"That's not an excuse. I was supposed to examine those cold cases and see if anything had been missed. And obviously I screwed up." She looked at Dustin. "Nice meeting you. Welcome to Mercy."

She got up, hurried through the kitchen and out the back door.

Dustin's "Bye" came too late for Candace to hear.

Wow. Candace seemed pretty upset with herself. I understood she felt the need to be perfect, to have the answers before anyone else, but obviously dismissing Morris's suggestion bothered her—a lot.

I smiled at Dustin. "Can we keep this business to ourselves until we see what Candace digs up? See, this town generates enough gossip to run a power plant. I want to call in a few favors from the charities I've worked with."

"Whatever Candace wants," he said. "She seems to know what she's doing even if she's being hard on herself."

"She does know what she's doing," I said, smiling to myself. "We'll give her a chance before the whole town council gets up in arms about more than feral cats."

Seemed I now had more leverage with Dustin Gray than I did prior to Candace's visit.

Nice.

Four

I didn't need to tell Dustin that head Councilwoman Penelope Webber was the interfering type. He'd witnessed her behavior firsthand in several meetings. So before he left my house, he asked what he should say if she phoned for an update about our visit to the mill.

I suggested he let his calls go to voicemail for the next several hours. Meanwhile, if I had news for him, I'd make a direct call to the Pink House, the local bed-and-breakfast where he was staying.

Only Chablis joined me when I settled on the couch with my phone and my charity contact list. She loved when my lap was free for her—and since no boy cats were hanging around, she settled right down. Merlot and Syrah had journeyed down to the basement in pursuit of whatever creature I must have let inside earlier.

I immediately started phoning people connected to the organizations where I donated my time and my quilts. Most of my contacts were with people who helped pets, children or returning soldiers. But I figured six degrees of separation applied here. Turned out it was only three degrees of separation. A friend of a friend gave me the name of a gentleman named Harry Williams who ran the Upstate Homeless Partnership—better known as "UHP."

Unfortunately, Dustin wasn't the only person letting his calls go to voicemail. Forced to leave a message, I hoped Mr. Williams would get back to me before Candace made a decision on how best to help Jeannie. I wanted the chance to offer resources other than the local social services.

My task completed, I gently lifted a sleeping Chablis off my lap and set her on the quilted throw at the other end of the couch. I decided this gloomy day required tomato soup and a grilled cheese sandwich. But before I was done preparing lunch, my friend Tom Stewart called and said he was on the way over. I added two more sandwiches to the frying pan.

Truth be told, Tom and I were more than friends. I cared for him deeply and he'd recently told me he was in love with me. But though I had strong feelings for him, I still couldn't get past the memory of my late husband. He had died of a heart attack only four years ago, and I still felt as if beginning a new relationship with another man was a betrayal. John had been the love of my life, the man I'd thought I would grow old with, and I still missed him every day. I couldn't say "I love you" back to Tom. Not yet. The words stuck in my throat like a wad of cotton. Did I love him? Maybe. But I needed more time to understand my tangled emotions of grief and loss, not to mention quit feeling guilty over my newfound joy with Tom. Fortunately for me, Tom seemed to understand perfectly and said he would wait for me as long as it took.

He arrived five minutes later and came into the kitchen. Before he could say a word, I turned and smiled. "Sorry. I didn't lock the door. No lectures, okay?"

He took me in his arms and kissed me. "No lectures. I will say this. My almost-perfect woman has one fault—she's too trusting."

"No. Forgetful, that's all." I asked Tom to handle the

soup in the microwave while I flipped the sandwiches over.

Soon, we were sitting at the small table in the breakfast nook with a view of the lake, enjoying a little comfort food.

"Does Finn have class today?" I asked. Finn was Tom's stepson and had been living in Mercy since only last fall. He'd started community college a week ago and was glad Tom supported his dreams since his parents hadn't seemed to think college was important.

Tom nodded. "Since he took on a full load of courses," he said around a mouthful of grilled cheese, "he won't be home until late."

"He's making up for lost time now that he's living with you rather than your ex. He's only one semester behind and he's smart enough to ace every one of those classes. I'll bet Yoshi misses him, though." Yoshi was Finn's rat terrier—a dog almost as smart as my cats. Almost.

"Yoshi has plenty of company. He goes fishing with Ed almost every morning."

"With Ed? Go figure." I shook my head and smiled. "The guy who swore he was afraid of dogs. What a liar." Ed Duffy lived with Tom's mother and owned Ed's Swap Shop.

"How did it go at the mill today?" Tom crumbled a handful of Ritz crackers into his soup.

"Interesting. You won't believe—" I was interrupted by a serious cat chase. Syrah, my speedster, raced through the kitchen with Merlot hot on his tail. I shook my head, saying, "I have no idea what's going on with those two. Before you arrived, they seemed to be stalking a bug or a lizard. Now they're burning energy. But they have certainly forgotten their manners."

"Yeah," Tom said. "They didn't even say hello. What's with that?"

"Cat business, I guess. Anyway, let me tell you about

the mill—and who we found living among the feral cats."
I went on to tell him about Jeannie and my efforts to
delay yanking her out of a place she considered home.
"You say Candace has heard of this woman?" Tom
wiped the remnants of lunch from his mouth with his
napkin.

I did the same and as we carried our dishes to the
sink, I said, "Apparently her story is well-known. I'm betting Ed knows plenty since he's lived in Mercy all his
life—unlike you or me."

"Ed knows almost as much stuff about Mercy as he
has objects crammed into his junk shop," he said. "Can
you be a hoarder of information as well as a hoarder of,
well, *everything*?"

I laughed. "You can."

Tom faced me and held my arm. "Do that again," he
whispered.

"Do what?" Gosh, I could get lost in his brilliant blue
eyes.

"Laugh. I love to hear you laugh."

Our kiss was interrupted by a cat chase headed in
the opposite direction, one that continued down the
basement stairs.

"I hope they catch whatever it is they're chasing. I
don't want any midnight visitor with eight legs or moth
wings," I said.

I'd put on coffee when Tom had said he was coming
over and now we both took mugs of hot brew into the
living room. We sat on the sofa and I cuddled next to him
like Merlot often cuddled next to me.

"Aside from the homeless woman, what was the mill
like inside?" Tom said.

"Kind of spooky in the dark," I said. "I'll be excited to
see the place once they turn on the electricity. When I
met with the town council, Penelope Webber told us
they're working on getting power to the building, but the

town will have to give a giant down payment to Upstate Energy because of how huge the place is. The mill went bankrupt and became a tax foreclosure, so there are no utilities."

Tom swallowed a gulp of coffee. "A tax foreclosure. Sounds like an event I never want to face in my life. Anything with the word *tax* in it scares the crap out of me."

I laughed. "Me, too. But your business is doing great. In fact, why aren't you out on a job?"

"Just wanted to see you. Next appointment isn't until this evening. Your friend Penelope Webber, by the way."

"She's an acquaintance. But doesn't she have a state-of-the-art security system already?" I asked.

"You know how I put those new features on your phone—the four-screen view for your cat cam and the remote app for arming your security system?"

I nodded. "Love the four screens at once, by the way. I can find the cats immediately now while I'm off running errands."

"Knew you'd love it. Anyway, Ms. Webber heard through someone in town that she can check on all the rooms in her fancy house while she's having lunch at the country club."

"First I knew that Mercy had a country club," I said.

"There isn't one," he said with a laugh. "I guess I mean she can see her house from wherever women like her go in the afternoon to show off their new shoes."

I smiled at Tom. "Women like *her*? Really, Tom?"

"Sorry. That sounded bad. I get tired of entitled, rich people like her, is all. Believe me, you would, too, if you had to deal with as many of them as I do. If she were a guy, I would have said, 'Wherever men like him go to show off their Cuban cigars.'" He lifted his eyebrows. "Sound better?"

"I was just giving you a hard time. Truth is, I don't care for her, either. Why can't she be like Ritaestelle Longworth? She's filthy rich and yet she's so sweet and kind and giving. Did you know she's the reason Shawn can relocate all those ferals in the mill?"

"How's that?" He drained his mug.

I said, "Using the money she gave him, Shawn bought up the acreage surrounding the Mercy Animal Sanctuary. He's been investigating new techniques used to give ferals a safer environment. Maybe you can help him with the future heavy lifting that will be involved in the project. See, he'll have to move these new portable structures inside the mill. They kind of look like Dumpsters."

"I'm not sure I understand," Tom said.

"Maybe I can show you a picture on your phone," I said.

He pulled it out of his pocket and I gave him the name of the website dedicated to rescuing ferals.

Tom nodded as we both looked at the pictures on the site. "They do look like miniature Dumpsters."

"Using food," I said, "Shawn will lure the cats into these things. They're a nice kind of trap with everything inside that the cats need. Food, a litter area, a sleeping spot with quilts I made. At first, the cats can go in and out. Then Shawn will fix it so they have to stay inside the shelter. After the cats calm down, he can—"

"Calm down is right," Tom said. "A *nice* trap is still a trap."

"I know. The idea didn't sit right with me at first. But Shawn convinced me that this is the best way to handle the problem. Once the cats settle down, he'll move the traps onto his property. Then, after they're spayed or neutered, he'll let them out a few at a time and they'll be off and smelling the same kind of food set out on his property. Apparently, feral cats captured like this keep coming back to their shelters on and off for the consistent source of food. It's such a great way to save these guys."

"I take it Shawn needs help lifting these shelters," Tom said. "Glad to help. Finn's nearly nineteen and since he's put on some muscle since he's moved in with me, I'll get him involved, too."

"That would be great. Thank you. But first things first. Before we can move cats, we have to help Jeannie. If I knew more about her, maybe I'd be better equipped to talk her into leaving the mill. I'm betting Ed knows her story in detail."

"All we can do is ask him. He's at the shop. Want to run over there?" he said.

"Yes." I hopped up, forgetting I held a nearly full mug. Coffee sloshed over the rim, spilled onto my shirt and splashed onto the coffee table. I set the mug down and started for the kitchen to grab a towel. "Call me your Klutz of the Day."

Tom laughed. "Okay, Klutz. I'll clean this up while you change. And I'll give Ed a call, too. For all I know, maybe he closed up the shop. Went fishing or went out looking for junk. You know how he is."

"Indeed I do." I thanked Tom, gave him a quick kiss and hurried off to change.

And no cats followed me. I wondered why.

Five

Ed's Swap Shop sat on a piece of property right off Main Street. The place was once a small house, but now each room was crammed with items Ed had found—everything from old computers to true antiques. He rescued old magazines, newspapers, dishes, clothing—you name it. For Ed, everything was recyclable.

The cold morning had segued into an even colder afternoon, so after I'd doused myself with coffee, I'd changed clothes and added two new layers. Now I wore a Henley and a cardigan under my wool jacket.

We heard Yoshi barking the minute Tom turned the doorknob to enter the shop. When we walked in, the little brown and white dog began to jump as if he had springs on his feet. Tom held out his arms and Yoshi leapt into them and began licking his face.

Tom smiled broadly and set the dog down. I knelt before the jumping could start again and Yoshi slathered me with doggy kisses, too.

"Hey there," Ed called. He'd appeared in the small hallway beyond this most cluttered part of his shop and waved Tom and me to the back of the house.

Yoshi bounded ahead of us and we all joined Ed in what had once been the kitchen. It was now used as a break room. There was no stove, but there was a small round table in the corner opposite the refrigerator. The old pink fridge was a recent find; I guessed it was maybe circa 1960. Though Ed probably could have sold it for a pretty penny in this day of shabby-chic decorating, he'd decided to hang on to it.

Ed had recently trimmed back his long gray beard to stubble because Yoshi had gotten his feet tangled in the beard a few times too many. Ed was compensating by growing out his wiry silver hair to shoulder length.

I smelled coffee and hoped I could actually drink the stuff rather than spill it all over again. Ed poured us each a cup in jadeite mugs. We then sat and doctored our coffee with the cream and sugar sitting in the center of the table. Yoshi picked up a rawhide bone almost as big as he was and settled at our feet.

"Good to see you two," Ed said, and then fixed on me. "What's this about Jeannie Sloan? She's been gone from here a good ten years."

"Maybe not." I went on to explain about my morning at the mill.

"I'll be a second cousin to a monkey," Ed said when I'd finished. "You think she's been livin' in that old building all this time?"

"Hard to tell," I said. "From what I saw, I'd guess she's been there awhile."

Ed slowly shook his head. "I thought she was long gone. Her daughter went and disappeared and Jeannie was beside herself. The woman wandered the streets, bothered the heck out of Morris Ebeling to keep lookin' for her daughter. After she got put in the clink a couple times for loitering, she started turnin' up at the police station. She'd just sit on them old benches in the corridor hoping to hear word about her Kay Ellen."

"How sad." I thought about Candace's theory that Jeannie might have hurt her daughter, but from what Ed said, that didn't seem likely. "Does Jeannie have any family in town? Someone who could help her out of this situation?"

"All she had was Kay Ellen. They'd been foreclosed on—once had a little brick house in the mill village," Ed said.

Mill villages consisted of streets and streets of identical houses surrounding the hundreds of mills all over the South. They were originally built by mill owners for the workers. The villages usually included churches, stores and sometimes even post offices. The Lorraine Stanley Textile Mill must have had a wealthy owner because the village in Mercy consisted of all-brick construction—a rarity. The houses elsewhere across the South were mostly clapboard.

"They owned the house at one time?" I said. "From what I understood, the mill owners owned the houses in villages."

"Nope," Ed said. "Ward Stanley sold them houses. Offered the mill workers a pretty good deal, too. Probably the only nice thing that old coot ever done in his life."

"Ward Stanley owned the mill?" Tom asked.

"He did. And his daddy before and his daddy's daddy before that. All of them are dead now except the last Ward Stanley and who knows what he's up to. Anyways, once the bank kicked Jeannie and her girl out of their house, Kay Ellen got herself a job at Red Top—you know, that fallin'-down hamburger joint on the other side of town? Don't know how the place stays in business. Anyways, they was livin' at the church for a while 'cause minimum wage don't pay anyone's rent. Then Kay Ellen up and left. Don't blame a sixteen-year-old for wantin' to quit and leave a life such as she had."

"Did she stay at the church in the mill village—or somewhere else?" I asked.

"Mill Village Baptist," he answered. "I know 'cause the preacher came in here once askin' to swap me firewood for a phone. Said with a teenager stayin' in the pastorium, they needed another telephone."

"That means Kay Ellen had friends—or at least one friend," Tom said.

"Good thinkin.'" Ed nodded and smiled. "You can string things together like nobody I ever known—you and Tom, that is. A phone means the child was talkin' to someone. Got to say, I never knew much about Kay Ellen. But Jeannie? Knew her better than most people did. She'd bring in junk she'd collected every other day and I'd give her a dollar or two."

"Tell me more about her," I said.

Ed rubbed a stubbled cheek. "She'd be about my age—maybe mid-sixties. Had her baby late in life. See, Jeannie was slow-witted. More like a kid than a grown woman. There was whispers someone took advantage of her after she showed up pregnant. I don't think she even knew what happened to her. The daughter was a pretty thing and by the time she was ten, she was takin' care of Jeannie. I once heard her explainin' to her mama something about how to buy the best fruit in the Piggly Wiggly. Made me think she was a nice girl. Respectful. Maybe a little protective of Jeannie, too."

"Jeannie never had a job?" Tom said.

Ed smiled. "Oh, she did. Worked in that mill since she was young. Us kids in town called her and the others like her lintheads. They'd be covered with cotton pieces when they came off a shift. Looked like they'd been snowed on." His smile faded. "I'm not proud of how we treated the village kids. Not proud of how we treated the blacks, neither. It was a different time. Not an excuse, mind you. Wrong thinkin' is all."

"Ed, you are a wealth of information concerning this town," Tom said, sounding amazed. "But the truth is, not everyone else has realized how wrong-thinking those times were. The people who live near the mill still don't

mingle much in town. I've heard plenty of unkind re-
marks about the residents."

Ed said, "Prejudice is for dumbasses and we got a lot
of dumbasses left in Mercy."

I'd learned about how towns treated the village residents from my college course work about the textile
industry—not Mercy, per se, but the textile towns in general. It was a sad part of our history that few people today seemed to know about. But though I felt exactly the
same as Ed, I wanted to get back to why we'd come today. I said, "What did Jeannie do after the mill closed?"

"Her parents was older than dirt by then and she'd
been carin' for them. I'm thinkin' there was some kind of
severance they lived on—plus their social security. Jeannie buried her parents and not long after she and Kay
Ellen got kicked to the curb by the bank. Pretty cold how
we treat some folks in this country, them who's worked
hard all their lives."

"Do you know anything about the police investigation?" Tom said. "Did they believe from the get-go Kay
Ellen ran off? Or were there indications she met foul
play?"

Ed grinned. "Listen to you soundin' like a cop again.
You'd have to get with Morris on the particulars, but Kay
Ellen didn't take a damn thing with her when she ran off.
Not even her purse, or so I heard. What young thing
leaves without her purse?"

"You're right," I said, half to myself. I looked at Ed.
"Does the same preacher still work at Mill Village Baptist?"

"He does. Name's Mitchell Truman. You probably
seen him around town. Tall black man with the shiniest
skull I ever did see."

Tom stood. "Guess I know where we're headed."

Six

During the ride to the outskirts of town and the Mill Village Baptist Church in Tom's brand-new Prius—loved the new car smell—I took a moment to check on my cats. They had to be exhausted after all their running around this morning. But though Chablis lay sound asleep on the sofa, Syrah and Merlot were not on any of my four screens. I guessed they'd taken their chase to the basement and perhaps decided to nap down there.

The church sat one block from the mill, and the pastorium next door was set farther back on the property. Both structures were the same red brick as the rows of identical mill village houses lining the streets.

"I never noticed that the preacher's house is almost as big as the church itself," Tom said. "Not to say either building is all that large—unless you compare them to the village houses."

"Quiet neighborhood," I said, glancing up and down the street.

"Too bad we hardly ever see people from this part of town on Main Street," Tom said.

"It does seem a little like a ghost town," I said. "Maybe most of these houses are empty."

"Yards look too tidy. People *are* living here," he answered.

As we walked hand in hand up the brick sidewalk, the church's steeple looked regal against the dreary sky. Great care had been taken in this building's construction. Arched stained-glass windows and ornate double doors beckoned. We climbed the few steps to the entrance and I reflected on how much I adored old churches—and the South had plenty of them to admire.

The sanctuary, with its wooden pews and simple altar, was deserted. We found Mitchell Truman in the church office, sitting at a desk dwarfed by the large man.

When I gently tapped on the frame of his open door, he looked up and smiled.

"Good afternoon." He stood and I guessed he had to be six feet four. "I'm Pastor Mitch. So glad you stopped by our church." His voice was deep and the rich baritone made him seem even bigger. I was willing to bet he gave powerful sermons.

Tom strode into the office, hand outstretched in greeting. "Tom Stewart. Nice to meet you, Pastor."

They shook hands.

Then the pastor smiled at me, eyebrows raised.

"Nice to meet you, Pastor. I'm Jillian Hart and I'm so glad we found you—but if you're busy—"

"Jillian Hart? The lady with the smart cats?" he said.

I smiled. "Why yes, but how—"

"Can I see them? The cats, I mean?" He sounded genuinely excited. "Several of my parishioners tell me you watch your cats on your phone."

People do talk in Mercy, but I was surprised to learn they were apparently discussing *my* small life. I took my phone out of my jeans pocket and we spent a few minutes observing Chablis sleep on the sofa. When Syrah and Merlot finally sauntered into the kitchen, Pastor Mitchell laughed and sat down.

"What mellow cats," he said.

"You can say that now," I said. "You should have seen them earlier." Just then, I felt pressure against my calf, same as when Syrah rubs against me. I looked down. Nothing. I glanced behind me, wondering if the pastor had a sneaky cat of his own. "You seem to love cats. Do you have one or two lurking around here?"

"No. I'd love a cat to keep me company, but my wife is worried about allergic parishioners who might have problems if we had animals in the church," he said.

"I understand, but cats and dogs can be therapeutic and I am sure you counsel troubled souls in this very office. If you ever get her to change her mind, please go to the animal shelter run by Shawn and Allison Cuddahee and adopt," I said.

"I will do just that." The pastor looked back and forth between Tom and me. "Are you two looking for a new church home?"

"Not right now. We've come to ask about someone you know," I said.

His face grew serious. "You understand if this person shared a confidence, I cannot speak with you about such matters." Though his tone was formal, I sensed he was a warm and caring man.

"Clara Jeanne Sloan? Remember her?" Tom said, sounding a little too coplike. It made me uncomfortable and I wondered if the pastor felt the same way.

"Oh my, indeed I do," he said, seemingly nonplussed by Tom's official tone. "She left Mercy a long time ago."

"We found her living in the mill this morning," I said.

"What?" If a person could be *plussed*, the pastor was now. "Oh no. Are you saying she's . . . homeless? That she came back to Mercy and couldn't call on us to—"

"We're not sure how long she's been there," I said. "We could use your help before we . . . Well, we need to understand her better. Can you help us?"

"Most certainly I'll help. We could go over to the mill

right this minute. We should. We need to help the poor lady." He started to rise.

Tom held up a hand. "Hang on, Pastor. From what Jillian tells me, we can't barge in like the savior patrol."

"He's right," I added, hoping the crack about the *savior* patrol would be forgotten. Still, I couldn't help but like how passionate Tom was about helping Jeannie.

"Do you have a plan, then?" Pastor Mitch eased back into his chair.

"Can you tell us about her history?" I said. "When we do go in and assist her to leave, I want her to feel we understand her."

The pastor nodded. "You seem like a wise woman. All right. Before we get started, would you two care for tea? I was just about to ask my wife to bring a pitcher over from the pastorium. If you'd prefer hot tea, we can arrange that. It is chilly today."

"I am a confirmed iced tea addict," I said.

Pastor Mitchell smiled broadly and asked Tom, "What can I offer you?"

"Whatever you two are having," Tom said.

"Iced tea it is. Meanwhile, please have a seat." He made a sweeping gesture toward the two leather padded chairs facing his desk.

Tom helped me take off my coat while the pastor made the call to his wife.

As we waited for the tea, Pastor Mitch filled the time by asking more questions about my cats, about Tom's job and about my stepdaughter, Kara. Apparently he had met her when she did a piece about rural churches for the small local paper. Kara was editor-in-chief and owner of the *Mercy Messenger*.

When Mrs. Truman finally wheeled in an old-fashioned tea cart, Pastor Mitch knew far more about Tom and me than we knew about him.

The pastor stood and smiled warmly at his wife. She

was smartly dressed in gray wool. I even caught a hint of pearls beneath her coat. Her skin was a good two shades lighter than her husband's and the mahogany-colored wig she wore beautifully accented her creamy skin tone.

After introductions, Mrs. Truman said, "So nice to make your acquaintance." Then she turned to her husband. "I am glad you caught me, Mitchell. I have a meeting of the Pastors' Wives Association in Greenville, if you've forgotten." She looked at me. "Pastors' wives have a lot to talk about."

"These folks have come to ask questions about our Jeannie," the pastor said.

She looked surprised. "But she's been gone for so long. Why would you be asking about her now?"

"Because she's not gone anymore," I said. "She's been living in the old mill."

A wide-eyed Mrs. Truman said, "Oh no. Who would have thought anyone could live in that place? Is she all right?"

"Hard to say. We only met her briefly," I said. "But I think she needs to be checked out by a doctor. If she's been living in that dungeon-like atmosphere, I'm sure she has a few health problems."

"You're probably right," the pastor said.

"Bless poor Jeannie's heart. This is simply unbelievable. What are you waiting for, Mitchell? We need to get over there right now," Mrs. Truman said.

The pastor explained how we wanted to approach the problem and Mrs. Truman, after some argument, agreed. "She was always a very stubborn soul. But Lord knows I cared for that woman. I tried to find her and her daughter a permanent home. We couldn't continue to let them live with us. Our mission is to uplift the downtrodden. Give them hope as well as charity. I offered to relocate Jeannie to a place in the middle of the state near Columbia."

"A shelter?" I said.

"Not exactly," Pastor Mitch answered. "So many folks were displaced as the mills closed up in South Carolina. We learned of several retraining opportunities—sent dozens of our parishioners to these programs."

Mrs. Truman nodded in agreement. "I found a nice, clean group home where Jeannie could be trained for a new position. Her job at the mill had been a simple one. Cutting loose threads from some kind of loom. Problem was, Kay Ellen would have had to go elsewhere."

"I'm guessing Jeannie didn't go for that," Tom said.

"They packed up and left the pastorium the minute after I presented her with the opportunity to move," the pastor said.

"Kay Ellen wanted to finish up at Mercy High School," Mrs. Truman said. "The child had friends she'd gone all through school with, so I couldn't blame her. Plus, she adamantly refused to be separated from her mother."

"And yet," I said, thinking out loud, "Kay Ellen ran away before she ever finished high school and left her mother behind? That doesn't make sense."

Mrs. Truman pursed her lips and nodded in agreement. "That's *exactly* what I told Morris Ebeling when he came here asking about the two of them. I was not impressed with his *investigation* into their disappearance." She checked her watch. "I could cancel my trip to Greenville. I would like to help in any way I can."

I said, "Oh, don't do that. There's time. See, we have a meeting scheduled with Deputy Carson to discuss the options concerning Jeannie. Plus, I have put in some calls to friends who know of charitable organizations that might help. I'm waiting on them to call me back."

Elizabeth Truman smiled. "I do believe Jeannie's fate is in good hands. But please know we will be right beside you. Call us for any help you need. Truth be told, I am so relieved Jeannie is alive and it gives us hope for Kay Ellen. Perhaps she is in that mill somewhere, too." She turned to her husband. "Please text me if I'm needed and I'll hurry back from Greenville. At any rate, I'll be home by seven." She said her good-byes and left.

Candace had also wondered if Kay Ellen was somewhere in that mill, too. She certainly could be. The place was huge and we'd only seen a tiny portion of the building.

The pastor told us to help ourselves to glasses of tea—and to wonderful-looking cookies shaped like flowers.

Once we were settled with our drinks and the melt-in-your-mouth lemony cookies, I said, "There is one thing Jeannie said about the mill. She said it was a *holy* place and she wasn't leaving. Maybe if we know what she means, it'll be easier to convince her to leave. Can you help us understand?"

The pastor tilted his bald head, considering the question. Finally he said, "People like Jeannie—folks without many skills, without an average IQ—how can I put this?" His brow furrowed. "They have a connection to the earth and to God and to their own instincts about what is right and wrong for them. Jeannie may not be the most brilliant person by modern standards, but she is brilliant in other ways. She understands where she needs to be, what her life is about. She probably believes she is in her own special and holy church. Am I making sense?"

"Yup. Makes sense," Tom said. "She's so strongly connected to the mill, she won't leave willingly."

"Or," I said, "she believes she has to stay because that's where her purpose lies?"

The pastor smiled. "I believe you're both right. But I'm not sure how much these insights will help you solve the problem. Bottom line, I don't believe she'll leave without a fight."

"If we can't convince her, you'll be available to help?" I asked.

"Certainly," he said. "But you need to know that when Jeannie left our care, she was angry. She thought we were casting her off on others because we didn't care. As my wife mentioned, she is a stubborn soul and might dig her heels in even more if she sees my face."

My disappointment must have been evident, because the pastor went on, saying, "Let me tell you one thing that might work. Jeannie is like a child in many ways. She believes in magic and fairy tales. If you bring her options as if you're telling a story about someone else, about this poor person who lives alone in an old house, and how you need Jeannie's help to save this person, she might leave with you."

Tom said, "In other words, lie to her?" He stood and I got the sense Pastor Mitch had just taken Tom right out of his comfort zone with the storytelling idea. "We have that meeting with Deputy Carson, but thanks so much for taking time to talk to us."

The pastor smiled. "I would not consider such a story to be a lie. You asked for my help, so allow me to give you a bit more. You've involved the police and that might make your efforts more difficult."

"Is Jeannie afraid of the police?" I asked.

"Not afraid. She was more upset with Mercy PD than she was with my wife and me," he said. "She haunted that police station after her daughter disappeared. Bothered Morris Ebeling to death. I heard she even sat outside his house at times. In Jeannie's defense, she didn't know how to get things done in, shall we call it, a *socially acceptable* way."

"Her girl was missing," I said. "Sounds like she was beside herself."

"Oh, we all understood. We knew Jeannie well. We sympathized. But in the eyes of the law, a teenager ran off. Happens all the time. I believe Morris did what he thought he could."

Now Tom was the one checking the time—on his phone. But I had another question.

"How about when Jeannie herself disappeared? Did anyone search for *her*?" I asked.

The pastor looked about as comfortable as Tom seemed to feel. "I say this as a man of God who is compelled to be honest. Jeannie's absence went unnoticed for weeks. I feel guilty about that. Morris did make inquiries after I mentioned to him that I hadn't seen Jeannie in quite some time. But when all was said and done, I believe there was a certain . . . *relief* that she was gone. To many in Mercy, she had become nothing more than a nuisance. We here in the church gathered people and searched for her, just as we had done when Kay Ellen disappeared months before—but I feared we'd acted too late. I am so very relieved she is alive." He smiled—a smile filled with regret.

"At least you and your congregation were kind enough to make an effort," I said softly.

"When she leaves the mill, I do want to see her—if she agrees, of course."

"I will tell her myself," I said. "Thank you for your time."

After I put on my coat, Tom and I walked out through a side door the pastor pointed out in the hallway.

He let out a sigh of relief the minute we were outside. "Didn't all that stuff about magic and fairies and stories bother you?"

"Nope," I said with a grin. "But then, I'm not a guy."

"And I am so glad you're not." He grabbed my hand and we started for his car.

But before we'd gotten ten feet, it happened again.

I felt as if a cat had sideswiped my leg.

Seven

Tom and I stopped at Belle's Beans and picked up coffee for Candace. We got some for us as well since I needed more caffeine than the iced tea had provided. This busy day had started a little too early for me.

We headed for Mercy PD, located in the back of the courthouse. I saw only two of the six squad cars in the lot. Candace's RAV4 was there as well. With the police offices in the back of the building and the jail in the basement, it sure streamlined the trip through the justice system for anyone caught drunk and disorderly or defacing property. Most crime in Mercy consisted of those two offenses.

Candace hugged me when she saw we'd brought coffee from Belle's. As she led us through the squeaky gate separating the waiting area from the offices and interrogation rooms, I waved a hello at B.J., the gawky college student and part-time dispatcher. Since he was talking on the phone, he simply waved back.

We entered the break room with its scuffed-up table, small fridge and vending machine. The drafty room sent a chill through me and I was glad we'd stopped for hot drinks.

Candace hungrily eyed the coffee Tom carried in a cardboard tray. "Which one is mine?"

Tom nodded at the cup on the left. "Just how you like it."

Candace gripped the coffee with two hands and stared up at the ceiling. "Praise the Lord for decent coffee. And thank you both for bringing it." She looked at me and said, "My mind needs a kick start after trying to piece together Kay Ellen Sloan's disappearance and then her mother's a few months later. Morris would never win any cursive awards. These reports are not typed. Even now he makes me do all the computer work since he hates 'the machines.' And at times a *machine* can even be a cell phone to him."

"That sounds like Morris," I said.

Tom put the tray on the table and when he offered to help me with my coat, I told him I'd leave it on.

We took seats around the table and Candace filled us in on what she'd learned from Morris's case notes. He'd spent about a week questioning people in Kay Ellen's old neighborhood as well as her high school classmates. The girl left without any of her belongings—and that raised a red flag. Plus Kay Ellen adored their cat, but she left it behind with her mother.

However, when Jeannie went missing a few months later, Morris conducted only two interviews in the woman's neighborhood. These people speculated Jeannie heard from her daughter and joined her in another town. Morris seemed to accept this because he never investigated further.

Candace finished her coffee and tossed the cup in the wastebasket behind her. "Thousands of people disappear every week in this country. Unless it's a small child or we find a puddle of blood where the person was last seen, not much happens. Adults are free to come and go. Every cop knows that making the assumption a person has gone missing because they wanted to might cause problems down the line. But the sheer volume of disappearances makes following up on every single case impossible."

Tom said, "And when there's no pressure from family to look for the missing person, those cases are shelved pretty quickly. Unfortunately, both Jeannie's and Kay Ellen's investigations went cold almost at once."

Candace nodded her head in agreement. "No one looked too hard for either of them."

"We talked to a minister today who took Jeannie and her daughter in when they lost their home," I said. "He told us the church did a search for both of them. Gathered folks from the congregation and tried their best."

"Really?" Candace said. "Morris didn't mention any searches other than the ones he and his partner back then did. They checked along the creeks that feed into the lake. Made a few searches along Mercy Lake. What church are you talking about, by the way?"

"Mill Village Baptist Church. The preacher is Pastor Mitchell Truman," I said.

"Ah. The mill village. Figures. Why is it that whenever I have to go down to the mill neighborhood to find out who stole someone's bicycle or to respond to a domestic disturbance call, no one will talk to me? Same holds true for Mercy residents outside the village. Town folk always tell me they don't know anything about what happens in the village. There's some kind of divide, but I don't know what it's all about."

I said, "That's because no one talks about prejudice— and there's a long history of it when it comes to mill villagers all over the South." I went on to explain a little of the history, how most textile workers were considered poor white trash, called names like linthead and worse, and had been discriminated against for generations. But, like blacks who'd suffered even worse discrimination, mill villagers remained a proud bunch. They'd learned to walk tall but say little.

Candace, who'd been sitting back and sipping her coffee, leaned forward, realization evident in her expression. She said, "Now I get it. Nobody comes right out and says stuff like what you just told me, so I had no idea. See, I was about fourteen when they put the padlocks on those mill fences. My parents never spoke about the mill villagers, but now I understand. Jeez. Wounds inflicted by prejudice heal slowly, if at all. But as a cop, if I can go into a situation with a certain understanding . . . well, it can make all the difference in an investigation."

"Sad to say we don't have a complete understanding about our history because we stay silent," I said.

Tom cleared his throat. "This is good conversation, but back to the matter at hand. Did you happen to tell Morris about Jeannie's reappearance?" Tom said.

"I promised to look into the case files *first*, before we did anything about the Jeannie situation. That said, are you kidding me?" Her eyes had gone wide. "The man gets riled if his coffee isn't the right temperature. Hearing about the woman squatting in an abandoned building would probably have him driving over to that mill faster than you can say Jeannie Sloan. He'd want to deliver her a lecture about how she wasted his time ten years ago." Candace smiled at me. "Think I'll let you tell him. He likes you."

"Um, no. Not gonna happen," I said. "Let Chief Baca tell him."

Candace nodded. "Since Morris couldn't locate Jeannie way back when, and since the town council won't be thrilled about this state of affairs, Morris becomes the perfect scapegoat. Yup, I do believe this is a job for Chief Baca. Meanwhile, did you get in touch with anyone to help us convince Jeannie to leave the mill willingly?"

"I'm waiting on a call from the Upstate Homeless Partnership," I said. "I've heard it's a wonderful organization and I'm hoping they'll step in."

Candace glanced up at the clock above the fridge. "Sorry. It's been hours since you told me about Jeannie.

We can't wait. She's trespassing and if I know about it and don't do anything before I call it quits for today, I'm in trouble. Phone your friend Dustin and tell him to meet us at the mill with the keys. We've got to talk that woman out of there."

I sighed heavily. She was right, of course. "But where will you take her? Not to jail, I hope."

Tom stood. "I say she needs to be checked out at a hospital. By then, maybe your contact at UHP will call with a solution. Or Pastor Mitch might take her in. Wish I could go to the mill with you, but I have to meet with Penelope Webber about her security system. At least I can keep one council member busy while y'all work on the problem."

Candace stood, apparently ready to roll.

"Wait," I said, looking up at both of them. "Pastor Mitch said Jeannie dislikes the police—a lot. Maybe you need to change out of your uniform before we try to convince her of anything."

"I will happily do that," she said. "After you phone Dustin, would you mind calling the Main Street Diner and ordering a bunch of burgers and chili dogs? I'm starving. Then we can meet up at the mill, fill our bellies and bring in a bag of food for Jeannie. She's more likely to cooperate if she's not hungry."

"Good idea." I took out my phone and as we all walked out to the waiting area, I asked B.J. to give me the number for the Pink House. I then punched the numbers B.J. gave me into my contact list and couldn't help but sneak a peek at my cat cam. My three amigos were all sleeping, but they would soon awaken. Dusk and dawn are the most active times of day for felines.

As we walked toward Tom's car, I called the new owner of the Pink House, a sweet woman named Laura. Mercy draws a few tourists thanks to plentiful antiques and quaint shops, but nothing like Asheville to the northeast. Most people choose to stay there when visiting the area. But Laura was eager to succeed in the B and B business where others had failed.

"Hi, Laura. This is Jillian Hart. Is Dustin Gray in his room?"

"Um, no. That young man has been pacing the floors, goin' up and down the stairs, waiting for I don't know what. Let me get him."

Soon Dustin was on the line and I explained we wanted him to meet us at the mill so we could talk Jeannie into leaving. "Meet us in thirty minutes. We're bringing food since—"

"Oh, Laura made this awesome beef bourguignon for an early supper," he said. "I'm stuffed. See you there."

Beef bourguignon, huh? I thought, as I climbed in the car beside Tom. I might have to spend the night at the Pink House one of these days just for a decent meal.

Tom dropped me at my place. I turned on Animal Planet for the kitties and gave them a quick pet, found a flashlight and then went by the diner to pick up the food. Soon Dustin, Candace and I sat in her RAV4 outside the mill fence and ate. Well, Candace and I ate. Dustin just stared at Candace, his expression similar to one my cats wore when they were fixing on a bird out the window— as if he'd love to pounce but knew he didn't dare.

Candace, now dressed in blue jeans and a short down jacket, held a wad of French fries close to her mouth and said, "You should do the talking at first, Jillian. You can get anyone to sing off your song sheet."

Puzzled by her remark, I said, "I can?"

She shoved the French fries in her mouth and chewed a few seconds before saying, "You're nice. Me? I tend to get a little pushy when I want something done in a hurry."

I looked at Dustin and nodded. "She *can* be pushy."

He smiled.

"Any which way," Candace said, "that woman is coming out of that mill tonight. But I am deferring to you to encourage her to leave. At first."

"Promise not to rush me, okay?" I said.

"My mama always told me the most important words she ever spoke were 'Hang on a minute, Candace.' She says she did manage to teach me a little bit of patience." She grinned. "Now let's get this show on the road." She grabbed the sack containing a burger and fries for Jeannie and got out of the car.

With winter darkness well upon us, the mill loomed like an overpowering shadow as we passed through the gate and up the walkway. Our flashlights did little to penetrate the night. My heart sped up the closer we got to the door.

"Yikes!" I stopped suddenly. It felt as if I'd brushed up against something.

Candace and Dustin halted and she pointed her light at me. "What's wrong? Did you trip?"

Dustin swept the brick path with his Maglite. "I don't see any debris. You okay?"

"It's nothing," I said. "Let's hurry and get in there." But it *was* something—that feeling again, the brief touch against my leg. I'd heard back problems can cause strange sensations in the legs, but as far as I knew, my back was fine. Maybe this creepy place and Jeannie's belief she had a companion cat no one else could see had seeped into my mind, because it definitely felt as though a cat had just touched me.

If the mill had seemed as dark as night in the daytime, it was even worse now. As we walked into the expansive old factory, I heard a scurrying noise and turned quickly enough with my flashlight to catch a glimpse of cats racing along the wall to our right.

"Shawn spoke at the town council meeting and said

those aren't friendly cats," Candace said. "But they look just like mine and yours."

"They are definitely *not* friendly. They do not trust people," I said. "And please keep your voice down or you'll frighten them even more than they already are."

"Sorry," Candace whispered.

Meanwhile, Dustin forged ahead toward the hallway that led to the office where we'd found Jeannie this morning.

But we all froze when we heard a loud moan. All our flashlights veered in unison toward the sound. I could make out the silhouette of what looked like a mound on the floor.

But then the mound moved and cried, "Help me."

We all rushed over and found Jeannie lying on the old plank floor.

Candace got there first and knelt beside her. Dustin and I followed right behind.

"Where are you hurt?" Candace's flashlight spread an eerie glow over Jeannie's anguished face.

"I—I busted somethin'," she said.

I got on my knees beside Candace. "Jeannie, it's Jillian. What happened?"

"I—I fell. They was chasin' me and I fell." Her eyes closed and I could tell the poor woman was in serious pain.

Candace stood and pulled out her phone. She tapped a few buttons and then sighed in frustration. "No signal. I'm headed closer to the door to call B.J."

"Okay." I rubbed Jeannie's upper arm. The fabric of her shirt was thin. Looking up at Dustin I said, "She's so cold." I worried she might be in shock and not just freezing because it was so chilly in this building.

Dustin took off his jacket and laid it gently over the woman.

"Where does it hurt?" I asked.

"Here." She rested a hand on her left hip. "Can't get up and they're gonna get me." But her frightened expression vanished when her gaze fell away and she focused on the floor next to me. "She came back. I knew she would."

"What are you talking about?" Dustin said, training his light on the empty space at my side.

"Boots is here. My sweet Boots," Jeannie said.

Eight

Boots? I blinked several times. Jeannie said Boots came back. Had I been so touched by this poor woman and her predicament that I'd been subconsciously sensing her long-gone kitty's presence? *Yes. That must be it.* Still, the touch of a cat against me had felt so real.

Candace returned and said, "Help is on the way." Then she bent and whispered in my ear. "Better warn her about what will happen in a few minutes."

I nodded and looked at Jeannie. "You're hurt and we need to help you. What that means is you will have to go to the hospital."

Jeannie, who was lying on her right side, covered her ear with a blue-veined hand. "No, don't you be tellin' me that. No. They don't let cats in the hospital. When my mama died, I found that out right quick. Now that Boots is back, I can't leave her. And I can't leave here. Who will do the watchin' out?"

I tugged Jeannie's hand away from her face and held it in both of my own. "I promise you, Candace and I will make sure nothing bad happens while you're gone. And I'm betting they'll let Boots go with you." It wasn't really a lie; the hospital didn't allow cats, but they couldn't stop a cat they couldn't see from coming in. The poor woman needed to calm down, so why not offer what little reassurance I could?

She gripped my hand and said, "You think they will?"

"I'm pretty sure. And just so you know, they'll take special pictures of your hip where it hurts. You might need it fixed."

"How they gonna fix it?" she asked.

Thank goodness I didn't have to get into an explanation of surgery if indeed her hip was broken, because just at that moment the two Mercy paramedics, Marcy and Jake, wheeled a stretcher our way. These two had been smart enough to put lights on their caps, freeing up their hands.

"Are they cops?" a panicked Jeannie said. "They look like cops and I don't want nothin' to do with them."

"They're not cops. They work for the hospital and they came to help you." I held her hand tighter when she tried to pull away. "Let them, okay?"

She looked up at Marcy and Jake, then back at me. "You swear they're not cops?"

Candace took a step back farther into the shadows. She was a young woman who had a hard time not coming out with the blunt truth, so she must have figured she'd remain out of this part of the conversation.

Marcy smiled down at Jeannie. "We are not the police. I'm Marcy and this is Jake. We'll be talking to the doctors on this radio." She pointed to her shoulder. "That way we can help them figure out how to help you."

Jeannie said, "Somethin's busted. How's that gonna get fixed?"

Marcy knelt beside me, so I stood, allowing her room to work. She snapped on gloves and Jake knelt opposite his partner, Jeannie between them. He opened his medical kit.

I turned to talk to Dustin and Candace, but Dustin seemed to have disappeared. I couldn't blame him. The guy came here to do a job and I'd had him cooling his jets all day at the Pink House. And now we had a medical emergency. Bet he wished he'd never been assigned to this job.

I heard Marcy asking Jeannie what hurt, but she kept saying, "It's busted," over and over.

"Her left hip," I said. "She fell."

"Said she was running from someone," Candace added. "Y'all got this under control? Dustin took off and if someone is lurking around like the woman told us, there might be trouble."

"We're on this," Jake said. "Go."

Candace disappeared into the darkness beyond.

Jake mumbled into his radio and a staticky reply I couldn't make out had him nodding. He stretched out IV tubing while Marcy began her examination. When she touched Jeannie's hip, the older woman's cry echoed through the building.

"Jeannie," Jake said, rubbing a thumb on the woman's hand, "can you tell me the last time you ate or drank?"

She ignored him and looked at me when she replied. "Had water a couple hours ago. Don't go out for food until the night—after the Piggly Wiggly closes. I was thinkin' today is the day they usually toss the cinnamon rolls and donuts. Was lookin' forward to that."

Marcy held up a blood pressure cuff and raised her eyebrows at me.

I'd become the conveyor of information and said, "Marcy has to take your blood pressure," I said. "Do you know what that means?"

"I ain't stupid," Jeannie said. "I know there's talk I'm dumb, but I ain't."

"Then you'll let Marcy take your blood pressure?" I said.

"It's my leg that hurts. Ain't nothin' wrong with my blood."

We went on like this as Jake and Marcy ran through all the steps of their medical evaluation. Jeannie never looked at them, but she did allow them to check her blood pressure and take her pulse. She didn't even flinch when Jake started her IV and she actually seemed fascinated at first, but fear again clouded her expression.

"Am I gonna die? 'Cause they was runnin' water through tubes like this into my mama when she was in the hospital and then she up and died."

Marcy said, "You'll be fine. We want to put medicine in this tube to help with your pain. Are you allergic to anything?"

Jeannie looked up at me. "What's she talkin' about?"

I explained what an allergy was and Jeannie denied ever having a reaction to any medicines or foods. Jake injected a syringeful of what I assumed was morphine into Jeannie's IV tubing. He told her how they planned to move Jeannie onto the stretcher hoping to cause as little pain as possible, but I had to repeat the steps of this process after she looked up at me in fear.

I held her hand as the paramedics expertly transferred her. Despite the pain medicine, she hollered, all the while gripping my hand so tightly I thought I might lose circulation. But once this ordeal was over, she let out a sigh of relief—and so did I. They raised the stretcher and made another radio call to let the hospital know they were on the way.

"I can't see her no more. Where is she?" Jeannie mumbled as the morphine began to take effect. "Where'd she go?"

"Are you talking about Boots?" I said.

She nodded, her eyelids heavy.

"She's probably waiting at the door and she'll jump on the stretcher when they take you out," I said.

As they moved her along, Jeannie clung to my hand

like a child. I felt tears burn behind my eyes when I saw she was crying.

"Boots ain't comin' with me. She's more scared than me."

Marcy said, "Jeannie, Mrs. Hart is gonna walk with us to the door and then—"

She was interrupted by the loud arrival of two volunteer firemen dragging in portable halogens. "How about some light, Jake?" Billy Cranor called.

"Who's that?" Jeannie said, her speech slurred. "Them creepers? I don't like them."

"Not creepers. I know these folks and they're here to help you, too," I said.

"If they ain't villagers . . ." Her eyes closed. "I ain't talking to them."

Marcy and Jake directed the stretcher more quickly toward the exit now that the area was brightened by the lights. I hurried to keep up.

By the time we reached the door, the questions about her cat were moot. Jeannie appeared to be asleep.

Once they took her out, I turned to Billy and the newest volunteer fireman, the burly, rusty-haired Grant Jamison. I'd met him at the Fourth of July fund-raiser for the fire department. He'd just graduated from high school last June.

I said, "Candace is here somewhere—with the engineer the town hired. They could probably use these lights."

"Where the heck are they?" Billy peered past me.

"I can lead you to where I *think* they are, but let me call Candace to make sure." But I couldn't get a signal.

"Too much cast iron, brick and concrete in here," Grant said. "Let's head where you think they went, Mrs. Hart."

So we did. The halogens saved me, because despite what I said about knowing where they were, I *am* directionally challenged. But now I could actually see the hallway leading to the office where we'd found Jeannie this morning.

"I always wondered what this place looked like inside," Billy said as we walked side by side. "It's like a gigantic barn minus the hay and dried corn."

Soon, I heard the sound of voices and Candace must have seen the bright lights coming her way because she stepped into the hallway.

Hands on hips, she said, "Look what the invisible cat dragged in."

Candace greeted Billy and Grant with fist bumps while I sneaked around them and into the office Jeannie had been calling home.

The room smelled just as sour as it had this morning, despite Jeannie's absence. Dustin, who'd been kneeling in front of the fireplace, stood.

"What's up?" I asked.

"I found out how she gets in and out." Dustin nodded toward the wall to his right. "Over there. That bricked-up window? There's no mortar. She removes the bricks when she wants to leave. I'm sure we'll find a broken fence outside, too."

I peered at the window. "Look at that. For an old woman, she must be strong to climb in and out. Who knows how long she's been surviving here or somewhere else without a home or anyone to help her."

Dustin knelt down in front of the fireplace again. "After I figured out about the window, this old chimney caught my eye. It's packed with hunks of concrete and old bricks, but the way it's been done doesn't seem right."

"What do you mean?" I got down on my knees beside him.

"See here on the left?" He played his light over the debris. "This side seems far more organized with more old bricks used. I'm guessing they were piled high, almost to the top of the fireplace arch, but most have fallen away. Plus, I may be wrong, but I believe I see a canvas tarp back in there." He leaned back on his heels. "Why a tarp?"

"Maybe they hauled in these bricks on a tarp and saw no reason to remove it," I said.

"Maybe," he said. "The canvas seems to be all twisted up." He pushed aside the fallen bricks and began to tunnel toward the tarp.

That was when I felt the pressure against my leg, as if one of my cats were sitting next to me to watch what Dustin was doing. My heart skipped. This time, the touch wasn't brief and seemed familiar, almost loving.

Dustin said, "What the heck?" as he dragged out a foot-long stretch of frayed and nibbled-on jute twine. He dropped it and reached back in. He started to reach in again and Candace must have noticed from where she was standing in the hall.

She said, "You want to grab hold of a bunch of roaches or dead mice, you might want to put on a glove." She walked in and handed him a latex glove she'd pulled from her pocket.

"Thanks," he said as he snapped it on. He slipped his hand into the narrow space again and pulled it back out quickly. "What *is* this?"

He held an object in his open palm and I shined my light above it.

I gasped.

Dustin's face drained of color and he whispered, "Oh no."

And I thought I heard a small, plaintive meow coming from right beside me.

Nine

Dustin and I both stared in horror at what appeared to be a skeletal hand—pulled off cleanly at the wrist.

Candace knelt next to Dustin. She seemed fascinated and said, "Try not to disturb it any more than you already have."

Meanwhile, I felt panic constricting my throat. These bones belonged to a person. What else was in that fireplace?

Then the invisible presence beside me pushed against my leg as if to comfort me. I couldn't ignore this strange feeling any more than I could ignore the bones in Dustin's hand.

Grant and Billy sauntered in and the bright light they brought with them made the thin, frail bones almost fluoresce.

"L-look," I said, nodding at Dustin's outstretched palm.

Candace continued to stare at the hand for a good ten seconds before switching her focus to Dustin's pale face. "You feel anything else in there?"

His voice wavering, he said, "Yes. I—I think there's more."

"Guys, bring those lights closer right quick," Candace said.

Soon five pairs of eyes gaped at what Dustin held. His hand was trembling and Candace gripped his wrist and quietly said, "I want you to keep your palm open while I hold your wrist steady, okay?"

Dustin said, "Sure. Of course. S-sorry."

"Nothing to be sorry about." Candace set her flashlight down and reached in her jeans pocket with her free hand. She held up her car keys and said, "Billy, run out to my RAV and get my evidence kit. I need to bag this. While you're out there, I want you to call the chief. Tell him we got skeletal remains in the old mill. He'll know what to do. Use your cell, not your radio. I don't want every Mercyite comin' this way and hanging around the fence to gawk."

"I'm on it, Candace," he said.

"You don't want me to move my hand?" Dustin said.

"No," Candace said brusquely.

Meanwhile, Grant busied himself setting the halogens up so they shed excellent light on the fireplace.

Dustin was in an awkward crouch and I could tell by his expression he was uncomfortable.

I said, "You all right?"

"If I could sit on the floor, I'd be less likely to drop this—this . . . person's hand," he said.

"Do it," Candace said. "Just go real slow."

She gripped his shoulder as he eased himself into a cross-legged position. He sighed with relief.

Candace cocked her head as she refocused on the bones. "Small hand. Woman, I'm guessing. But I'm no skeleton expert."

I sat on the floor, too, but when what *had* to be a hallucination curled into the space created by my crossed legs, a shiver ran up my spine. I peeked down at my lap. Nothing there. Yet I felt as if I could stroke this invisible cat—she seemed that real. But I didn't dare. If I was losing my mind, I wanted to be the first and the last person to know.

We soon heard Billy's running steps echoing through the building and as they grew closer, two feral cats who must have been hiding under the old desk scrambled out into the hallway.

Dustin jerked and Candace said, "Hang on, cowboy. Not much longer."

"What *was* that over there?" Dustin said.

"A couple cats," I said. "They're gone now." But the cat on my lap didn't budge. *Listen up, Jillian. There is* no *cat.*

Billy burst into the office a second later, flashlight in one hand and Candace's evidence kit in the other. Soon, Dustin was gripping his own wrist while Candace carefully eased the bones into an evidence bag. She looked around the room. "I need something firm to rest this on and then secure it."

Grant said, "I saw several loose planks in the hallway."

"Get one for me, would you?" she said.

He hurried from the room.

Dustin's gaze was still fixed on his open and now-empty palm. "I never held the hand of a dead person before."

"Let's hope you never do again," I said.

He nodded solemnly and closed his hand into a fist, then let his arm drop.

Billy told us the chief would be here as quickly as possible. Grant then brought in the plank and Candace taped the evidence bag to it.

While we all watched her, I was thinking how those bones once belonged to a living, breathing human being. These thoughts were interrupted by Grant.

He said, "If I'm not mistaken, I saw tool marks along

the baseboard where I found the plank. Someone loosened a few floorboards."

"Interesting," Candace said as she set the plank on the old desk. "I'll have a look later." She asked Grant to stay next to the bagged and secured hand so anyone else who arrived wouldn't accidentally disturb it. Then she sent Billy to wait for the chief and guide him in here.

Candace turned her flashlight back on and addressed Dustin. "Point the light to exactly where you found the bones."

He held up the piece of twine. "You might need this, too. Found it first."

"Ah, good." She smiled. "Thanks for being so conscientious about this evidence, Dustin." She turned to Grant. "You're pretty observant, too. I like that."

Candace had both young men blushing.

After the twine was also placed into an evidence bag and labeled, Candace looked through the small tunnel where Dustin found the hand.

"Can't see much except wadded tarp," she said.

Dustin moved his flashlight beam over the bricks now sitting on the hearth. "I took those bricks out after I saw that tarp crammed back in there."

"I guess I should have noticed someone was trying to hide something," Candace said. "Why else fill a fireplace up like this?"

"Oh, it's not unusual," Dustin said. "See, they fill these old, tall chimneys with bricks and cement hunks to stabilize them. Don't want them falling down during high winds. A chimney collapse of this size could hurt or even kill someone."

"If it's not unusual, what made you go looking in there?" Candace asked.

"It caught my eye because the packing wasn't done the way I've seen in pictures," he answered. "Too many bricks neatly stacked on one side."

"Guess your training gives you a good eye for detail." Candace took her camera from her evidence bag and snapped pictures.

Though I was interested in what she was doing and what secrets the fireplace would reveal, I was distracted by the phenomenon in my lap. I not only continued to feel the light pressure of what seemed to be a small cat, but now I swore I heard purring. If I moved, would all this stop? Did I want it to stop? Was it supposed to stop? I had no idea, so I continued to sit and feel comforted by this . . . this *presence*.

Chief Mike Baca and Deputy Morris Ebeling arrived within fifteen minutes. I could tell Morris was stewing by the glare he fixed on Candace. He remained tight-lipped as Candace detailed the situation, spilling everything from this morning on. But then the mention of Jeannie Sloan turned his skin a tad ashen.

Mike Baca asked Billy and Grant to wait outside and make sure anyone who noticed all the cars by the fence didn't wander in here—and they weren't to give out any information.

After they left, he turned to Candace. "You made the decision to gather old case files, read them and come out here to this mill with your only backup a friend and a civil engineer?" Mike looked her up and down and by the fire in his eyes, he was as angry as I'd ever seen him. "And without your uniform? What were you thinking? That you were on a little scavenger hunt in an old building?"

Candace examined her Nikes. "I made a mistake, sir."

"I should take you off this case," he said.

Morris nodded, almost smiling.

"But you're my best officer," he said, though still grim. "You're special, Deputy Carson. But don't you *ever* do anything like this again."

"You gotta be kidding me." Morris's color had changed again—to an unhealthy shade of red. "This is *my* case."

"With all respect for your years of service to Mercy PD," the chief said, "you closed a missing person's case maybe you shouldn't have closed. *Maybe*. Time will tell whether Jeannie Sloan has been holed up here for ten years or ten days. No matter what, you're on this as a loyal partner to Deputy Carson. Am I clear?"

"Clear as day," a seething Morris said.

"Good." Chief Baca ran a hand through his hair and focused on me. "Why am I not surprised to see you here?"

His accusatory tone made me feel as if I needed to defend myself. "I was asked to help because of my knowledge of textile mills, Mike. If I remember right, you were at the council meeting when the decision was made." My imaginary cat nudged my hand just like one of my own would do knowing I was upset. *Imaginary, Jillian. Keep that in mind.*

"Yes, you were invited to help," he said. "But a homeless woman seems out of your range of expertise, wouldn't you agree?" But his focus was now on the fireplace—the one Candace and Dustin stood in front of like sentries. Dustin's gaze remained on the floor and I guessed he wanted to be as invisible as the cat in my lap.

"Not completely out of my range, Mike," I said. "Jeannie's a former mill villager and I know about her roots and—"

"I get it. I respect your knowledge." Mike sighed heavily. "Sorry if I sounded rude, but a squatter and now a skeleton will not be easy to explain to a council eager to shed this mill from the town's fiscal responsibility. See where I'm coming from?"

I nodded, but I felt disappointed in Mike's reaction. Dustin found the hand of a dead person. Finding out whom those bones belonged to seemed far more important than small-town politics.

Mike must have read my mind or come to his senses, because he said, "I'm sorry. Our priority is to find out who died, how they died and why."

Morris cleared his throat. "How we gonna do that, Chief?"

"For starters, I've made a few friends at the many workshops and conferences I attend. One of those friends happens to be a forensic anthropologist."

"A *what*?" Morris's bushy brows came together.

"Skeleton expert," Candace said.

"She's a university professor," Mike said.

"How long before she gets here?" I said, resisting the urge to stroke an imaginary cat.

"Tomorrow," Mike said. "Meanwhile, this room could be a crime scene." His expression changed from concern to consternation. "Heck, this whole mill could be a crime scene."

"We don't have enough crime scene tape, then," Morris said.

Dustin found his voice. "I haven't even gotten to the upper levels of this building to assess the structural integrity. If you plan on bringing people in here, can I finish my evaluation first?"

"What if you find another skeleton?" Candace said. "You'd want one of us with you, right?"

Dustin paled. *"Another one?"*

"Yeah, kid," Morris said. "Word in town is that this old place is haunted. Could be a bone factory for all we know. Serial killer dumping ground."

Knowing Morris, I understood he was kidding, but from the look on Dustin's face, he was buying every word.

He said, "I—I guess a police presence would be needed, then."

"You guessed right," Candace said. "Chief? You want Dustin and me to check this place out?"

"I'll go with you." Mike turned to Morris. "You're on guard duty. I don't want any unauthorized people in or out of this place. Park your squad car at the gate and stay there."

Morris checked his watch. "How long? I ain't even had my supper."

"As long as it takes. Go on. Get out there." Mike waved his hand toward the door.

Morris's ears grew scarlet to match his already ruddy cheeks. "Whatever you say, Chief."

Dustin and Candace slipped out the door and I heard them start up the stairs that lay just beyond this office door to begin their search of the upper levels. Morris stomped out and we heard his heavy steps for several seconds—but then they stopped.

A female voice echoed in the distance.

"Maybe the professor was able to get away sooner than she thought." Mike started for the door.

But he didn't make it.

Councilwoman Penelope Webber stormed into the room and stopped, hands on hips. "Just what in heck is going on here?"

The invisible Boots hissed.

Ten

Mike Baca said, "Hello, Penelope. As you seem to have heard, we've run into a small snag here." He laughed nervously.

She glanced down at me where I sat on the floor. I was a little afraid to get up, first because this cat—or my own failing mental health—seemed to be holding me hostage. I also feared I might disturb anything in what I now considered a tomb. And then there was Penelope herself. I had to admit, the woman, with her ageless beauty and tall, commanding presence, intimidated me.

But Penelope's tone softened when she addressed me. "I heard about the paramedics and the ambulance, though I'm not sure why *you* are here so late in the day."

"Kind of a long story," I said.

She cocked her head and fiddled with the loosely knotted cashmere scarf at her neck. "Fill me in. I'm all ears."

"I can do that." Mike looked pointedly at me. "Mrs. Hart was just leaving."

I placed my hands behind me on the dirty floor so I could get up and as soon as I made a move to rise, the pressure on my lap disappeared. Mike offered me a hand and I stood. I started to brush the dust off but then thought better of it. Candace had taught me about the importance of every piece of evidence and I didn't want dirt off my hands or jeans contaminating anything.

"Can you find your way out or do you need help?" Mike said.

I pulled my trusty flashlight from my coat pocket. "I'll be fine—probably right on Morris's heels."

I hurried past Penelope, whose heavy perfume, combined with the dust and mold in this place, made my nose itch. By the time I was halfway out of the mill, I was capturing sneezes in the crook of my arm.

Guess Tom wasn't able to keep Penelope occupied, I thought as I walked out into the night.

Morris, Grant and Billy were gathered outside the fence and Billy opened the gate for me.

He said, "Trouble came calling, huh? As if a skeleton's hand weren't enough. I tried to call Candace to warn you about Ms. Webber, but I couldn't get through."

I smiled. "Thanks for thinking of us. Would you mind telling Candace I went home?" I felt Morris's stare and turned to him. "I'm sorry the chief was so hard on you."

"Been there, done that," he said. "Chief has his favored child to do his work now. Time was, I'd be the one he'd turn to. Not your fault. You go on home and take care, Miss Jillian."

He sounded sad and resigned, and for some reason I still felt partly to blame. Maybe we could talk about all this later, without Grant and Billy paying such close attention. "Good night, y'all," I said, and started for my van.

I put my phone on speaker and called Tom the minute I left the mill village. "Can you meet me at my house?" I said.

"Sure. Penelope Webber showed up, didn't she?" he said.

"Oh yes," I replied.

"Sorry about that. She got a phone call and suddenly

that woman was ablaze. Sent me packing because she said there was an incident at the mill and her presence was necessary. What happened?"

"I'll tell you all about it in person. I should be home in five," I said.

"Meet you there," he said.

We disconnected and I tossed my phone onto the seat beside me.

And I heard a tiny mew of displeasure.

I blinked several times, keeping my eyes on the road and my hold on the steering wheel tight. *This is all in your head, Jillian, so don't even look over to that passenger seat.*

I sped up and after I pulled into my driveway and parked, I reached for my phone, keeping my eyes straight ahead. I found it right away. And that was all I felt. *Thank goodness.*

Just as I was getting out of my van, Tom pulled up behind me. His headlights offered a little illumination and I couldn't help but take a peek beside me.

See? Nothing there, silly.

I got out, shut my van door and greeted Tom. The hug we shared felt wonderful. I definitely needed a hug.

Gripping my upper arms, he held me back so he could look at me. "You're upset. I mean, every muscle is tense. Let's talk."

With his arm around me, we went inside.

Three cats waited in the kitchen when we walked in. Chablis arched her back and squinted up at me, almost smiling, and I reached down to pet her. Syrah and Merlot sat stock-still, however.

"What's with them?" Tom stepped around the cats and into the kitchen.

"They've been acting strange today," I said.

But with their gazes fully engaged on a spot beyond me, I was putting the pieces together. My logical, grounded side wanted to reject the explanation, but because of what I'd been experiencing all day, coupled with their reactions, another part of my brain started to believe the illogical. The spirit of Jeannie's cat was with me—and Syrah and Merlot knew it. I shivered at the thought.

"I'm thinking hot chocolate. What about you?" Tom said. He was standing in front of the open pantry.

I didn't answer. I felt stuck to the floor. Stuck in my mind. This was ridiculous. And yet I watched as Merlot's and Syrah's stares moved in tandem, observing what could not be seen.

There it was again. The brush against my leg. The little nudge to remind me I had a visitor of a very different kind.

Tom looked at me around the pantry door. "Jilly? Hot chocolate or coffee?"

"Um . . ." I met his gaze. "Um . . ."

"Are you feeling sick?" I heard the concern in his voice and saw it in his eyes as he strode to me.

"No. No, I'm fine." I watched as Syrah and Merlot walked across the kitchen in their sauntering, "we're in charge here" style. They were following her. Following *Boots*.

"Take off your coat and sit down. You've gone an ugly shade of gray." He helped me slip out of my jacket.

"It's been a long day," I said.

He felt my forehead. "You look sick to me. You might have breathed something toxic in that mill." Tom took my elbow and led me into the living room.

Chablis followed, meowing the whole time in fear I'd forgotten her treat.

I sat in my usual spot on the sofa and it did feel good to be in familiar surroundings. I picked up the remote and turned off the muted episode on Animal Planet—a rerun of *Big Cat Diary*.

Tom looked down at me. "There's my Jilly. She's coming back to me. So, is it hot chocolate or coffee?"

"The dark hot chocolate I just bought sounds good," I said. "And would you mind giving Chablis a treat? But only one. She's already had more than her share today. Gobbled up Syrah's and Merlot's before they could blink earlier."

While Tom fixed our hot drinks, I watched what could only be described as a cat dance. No doubt in my mind that Merlot and Syrah saw what I could only feel — Boots's spirit. My two must have boxed her in, because they sat staring at the corner next to the entertainment center.

The mug of chocolate and its aroma soothed me, not to mention Chablis purring in my lap as we all sat on the sofa. Soon, I was relating everything that had gone on — Jeannie's injury, Dustin's finding bones from what Candace had said was probably a woman, Penelope's arrival, the summons of the anthropologist.

"Wow," Tom said after I'd poured everything out in rapid-fire fashion. "No wonder you look stressed out. The mill has bigger secrets than we thought."

"It sure does," I said. *Including a ghost cat.* I left that part out of the story, however. I didn't want Tom questioning my sanity. I was doing enough of that for both of us. I noticed how Merlot and Syrah still guarded the corner and I realized I found a bit of comfort at the sight. They saw what I felt. I wasn't completely nuts.

"I'll bet they find an entire skeleton in that fireplace, what with the tarp and all," Tom said.

"The mill office was a tomb," I said, half to myself. I turned to Tom, whose shoulder was touching mine. "A *holy place.* Jeannie knew what was in the fireplace, Tom. I'm sure of it."

Tom nodded in agreement. "Question is, *how* did she know?"

Eleven

The next morning, I woke to my cell phone's ringing. I fumbled around on my nightstand, found it and squinted at the display. *Candace.*

I connected but barely got out a hello before she started talking. "I need your help, Jillian. The woman needs an operation but won't sign the consent before she talks to you."

"Jeannie needs surgery?" I said.

"Broken hip," she said. "Can you go with me to the hospital? Please?"

I sat up and Chablis, who'd been sleeping next to me, rose and stretched. "Sure. She's at County?"

"Yup. I'll pick you up in twenty." She disconnected.

I stared at the phone. *Twenty minutes? Jeez.*

Before Candace arrived, I'd managed to wash my face, dress in jeans and a sweatshirt and eat a blueberry yogurt. I sensed all my activities were being watched by not only my three cats, but by Boots as well.

Gosh, how would I explain this to anyone? I wouldn't. No one would believe me anyway. But I did realize that during the night, a peace must have been forged. My three fur friends sat waiting as I poured kibble into bowls, but there was a space between Merlot and Syrah.

Did ghost cats eat? I didn't want to find out, so I set only three dishes on the floor and turned away.

No time to brew coffee because I heard Candace's car pulling into the driveway. But I needn't have worried. She brought me a vanilla latte from Belle's Beans. I went out the back door and engaged the security system before Candace could even knock.

She was in uniform and we drove in her squad car to the county hospital—about a forty-five-minute drive for regular folks. We made it in thirty. I still had a full cup of coffee when we arrived because drinking anything with Candace behind the wheel was like trying to down a milkshake on a roller coaster.

During the drive, I managed to relay my suspicion that Jeannie might have known about the skeleton in the fireplace and, taking it one step further, perhaps suspected the skeleton was that of her missing daughter.

Candace silently took this theory in during our ride, but after we got out of the squad car in the hospital parking lot, she popped the trunk and strode around to the back. "You could be right about that skeleton." She scrounged around in her evidence kit. "That means we'll need Jeannie's DNA." She held up a tube and long cotton swab packaged in paper and cellophane. "Your job will be to convince her to let me swipe inside her cheek." She started toward the hospital entrance.

"Um, okay—I guess." I hurried to catch up with Candace while unsealing the drink opening on my coffee cup. Surely I could steal a few sips before we reached Jeannie's room.

We rode in the elevator to the fourth floor and no one asked any questions of a uniformed officer and her harried companion as we hurried along the corridor toward room 410.

Jeannie's wild hair was spread out like a giant gray

halo on the white pillow surrounding her pale face. She looked like a different person here in this well-lit room — younger and more peaceful at first glance. Then her eyes popped open and she focused immediately on Candace. The uniform. She'd forgotten how Jeannie felt about cops and so had I.

"I didn't do nothin' wrong," Jeannie said immediately, defiance in her voice. "I was protectin' the holy place and makin' sure those creepers didn't steal nothin'."

"No one said you did anything wrong," Candace said in a quiet and soothing tone. "I have a few questions, is all."

But Jeannie switched her focus to me. "And you. You stole my cat."

"I-I'm sorry." What else could I say? I wasn't about to admit in front of Candace that perhaps Jeannie wasn't wrong.

Candace must have taken my response as meaning I wanted to placate Jeannie, because she said, "You'll get your cat back when you're well again."

"Is that why you asked for me to be here?" I said. "So you could tell me how angry you are about Boots?"

"Nothin' like that," Jeannie said, turning her face toward the window. "Cats'll do as they please." She faced me again. "Tell me just how they're gonna fix a busted leg? 'Cause I need to get back to the mill right quick."

Candace started to speak and then shut her mouth when I sent her a sharp look. We knew Jeannie was never returning to the mill, but now was not the time to tell her.

"May we sit down?" I approached the bed.

"No one's stoppin' you," she said.

I set my coffee on the bedside table and Candace and I pulled up two chairs. I sat closer to the head of the bed. I noticed Jeannie was clinging to one of those buttons that administered pain medicine through her IV tubing.

"I don't have to tell no one when it starts to hurtin'," she said when she saw I was staring at her hand. "New-fangled way, but I like it. Less folks to deal with."

"Does it hurt much?" I asked.

"Not no more," Jeannie said with a grin. For the first time I noticed her teeth. No decay, no tobacco stains. She actually had a nice smile.

I smiled back. "They'll be taking you to the operating room. The next thing you know, you'll be back here in this room with your hip all fixed. Of course, you'll have to stay here a few days so they can help you heal. Doctors do this kind of thing all the time, so you'll be fine."

"I don't like that doctor. He's a smarty-pants," Jeannie said.

"Are you talking about me?" came a voice from the doorway.

We turned to see a short man, perhaps in his fifties, wearing a white lab coat over an expensive-looking tailored shirt and silk tie.

"I am." Jeannie faced the window.

Candace rose and extended her hand. "Deputy Candace Carson, Mercy PD."

The two shook hands and I looked up with a smile. "I'm Jillian Hart."

"Ah. You're the one Miss Sloan has been asking for. I'm Dr. Worthy, the surgeon on this case. Are you related to my patient?"

Jeannie's head jerked in his direction. "I ain't got no relations. Not no more. And not Miss Jillian, and surely not the likes of her—" She waved a hand at Candace. "None of you but Miss Jillian seems to care anyways."

She sounded so fierce and yet beneath her harsh words, I understood her pain wasn't all physical.

"You know what, Miss Sloan?" Dr. Worthy said. "You don't have to like me, you don't have to believe I care, but I am taking your case free of charge. I'm taking it because you need your hip fixed. And you need it done as soon as possible before a large blood clot causes you more problems. Will you sign the paper to let me help you get back on your feet?"

Jeannie suddenly looked more relaxed than I'd seen her in the last two days. "Now there's a man who knows how to take charge. No pussyfootin' around. Maybe you ain't so bad after all."

"Good. I've scheduled your surgery for this afternoon. My nurse practitioner will be round with the paperwork. See you this afternoon." He smiled curtly, turned on his heel and left.

"You've made the right decision," I said.

"I was gonna sign anyways. Only way I got a chance of walkin' outta here. Still, I got you here, didn't I?" Jeannie gave me a sly look.

Candace cleared her throat and I knew that her packaged cotton swab was burning a hole in her pocket.

"I would have come anyway," I said. "And so would Candace. She helped you last night—called 9-1-1."

"She never said she was no cop, though," Jeannie said.

"I understand you've had your issues with Mercy PD in the past," Candace said. "But—"

"You don't understand nothin'," came Jeannie's harsh reply. "My daughter went missin' and not one of your kind gives a rat's ass."

"I heard what you said to the doctor," Candace said. "I can tell you want the straight story about your daughter—good, bad or ugly. Am I right?"

"Maybe so," Jeannie said begrudgingly.

Candace had made progress, because Jeannie was speaking directly to her now. But my heart sped up at what Candace was about to say. How would this poor woman handle what she was about to hear?

"You believe your daughter is dead. Am I right?" Candace said.

Jeannie's lips tightened and she nodded.

"And you're sure that mill has something to do with her death." Thank goodness Candace's tone showed her compassion and showed she cared. "Isn't that right, Jeannie?"

"It's a holy place now," Jeannie said softly. Tears filled her eyes.

I reached for Jeannie's hand. "Candace is a different kind of officer than you're used to. She'll find out what happened to your daughter. But you need to help her do that."

"How'm I supposed to do that from this place?" Jeannie said, regaining her composure.

Candace pulled out the DNA kit. "With this. All I need is for you to open your mouth and let me touch your cheek with this long stick."

Jeannie's brow furrowed in confusion. "Huh?"

"You and your daughter share the same blood," I said. "You get that, right?"

"Course we do. But what does a long stick have to do with our blood?" she replied.

"Blood and spit and bone are made of the same stuff," I said. "Candace will get some of your spit on that cotton swab and . . . and—"

"And then," Candace went on, "when we find your daughter's body, we can test her against what I collect on this swab, just to be sure it's her."

The silence that ensued made my heart speed up. Then my stomach tightened as I searched Jeannie's face for clues as to what she understood.

"You found her, didn't you?" Jeannie's lower lip quivered.

When Candace didn't answer right away, she said, "Go on. Tell me, girl."

Candace took a deep breath. "We found bones. They might belong to Kay Ellen."

Twelve

Candace and I remained mostly quiet on the drive home to Mercy. Back at the hospital, we'd helped Jeannie understand how the bones or maybe even any traces left on the tarp could be compared to her saliva. She'd let Candace take the DNA sample then.

When I told Jeannie I would return tomorrow and check on her, she'd asked me to bring Boots. I said I'd try, all the while wondering how I would communicate with a ghost cat. Then, on the way to the elevator, Candace had asked if anyone could ever help Jeannie understand there was no cat—implying, of course, that I should be the one to present this reality to the woman. I told Candace I didn't think I was the person for the job—that maybe a therapist would be needed down the road. We'd left it at that. I mean, how could I convince Jeannie no cat existed when I myself believed Boots might still be around in a different form?

As Candace drove up next to the back door of my house, both our cell phones rang. I got out of the car and spoke with Shawn, who told me a shipment of portable feral cat shelters had arrived and he was directing the truck to the mill. He wanted me to meet him there and help talk the police into allowing him to unload the shelters so the driver wouldn't have to be paid to wait around. He'd heard that something was going on inside the mill and there might be a problem. I agreed to meet him there but told him I wasn't sure how much influence I would have getting him inside the place.

When I disconnected, Candace stepped out of the squad car, her phone pressed to her ear. She said, "I'm on my way," then hung up and looked at me. "The bone doctor is at the mill. But she wants Dustin there to help pull the bricks out. She figures he'll know how best to do the job without disturbing any remains. Apparently she's never excavated from a chimney full of cement before. Can you phone him to come or even bring him to the mill?"

"Sure." I explained about Shawn's request—okay, his *demand*—that I meet him at the mill because of the arrival of the shelters.

"Oh boy," Candace said as she slid behind the wheel. "That crime scene is gonna be like a three-ring circus today."

I waved good-bye as she pulled out of the driveway. Once I stepped inside my house, I saw the chase was on—presumably Syrah, Merlot and Boots being the ones involved. Poor Chablis apparently was as clueless about this little ghost as most everyone besides my boy cats and Jeannie. Chablis wanted treats and a lap and she'd be happy. I could provide the former, but no lap—not on what looked to be another busy day.

I opened the treat jar and took two out as I tapped the keypad on my phone with my other hand looking for Dustin's contact number.

He answered right away and said, "I'm so glad you called. I'm going crazy. I've worked up a few ideas from what I saw today on my iPad, but that's about all."

With Syrah and Merlot looking up at me, I explained he was needed at the mill and why. No doubt Boots was right beside my two living, breathing cats.

"That is *fantastic*," Dustin said. "Those bones may have creeped me out, but to actually be able to say I helped with a job like this? *Wow*. I'm on my way."

"I have to go there to meet Shawn, so I can pick you up," I offered.

"I'm finding my way around town without a problem," he said. "Meet you there."

"Sure." After I disconnected, I spoke to my onlookers, making sure to blink a lot. Cats respond to human blinks. "Well, friends, I made someone happy today. But Jeannie's in a hospital and she needs you, Boots." I closed my eyes. *Jillian, you just spoke to an invisible cat.* I shook my head and mentally prepared myself for the next encounter of the day—with an impatient Shawn.

Before I left, I grabbed a bagel and filled a travel cup with sweet tea. I was certain I would be playing referee between the police and Shawn. He'd want those expensive shelters inside the fence, if not inside the mill. That could be a problem if the entire mill was indeed a crime scene.

When I turned into the village and passed the church, I first noticed a yellow Penske moving van. Then I saw a crowd of people standing outside the mill fence. What was happening? Had my stepdaughter and editor-in-chief, Kara, gotten wind of the bones and played town crier in the *Mercy Messenger* this morning?

But as I drove up to the side street leading to the mill, I knew this wasn't about anything in the newspaper. This was all about town politics.

Penelope Webber, wearing a ruby red wool coat, stood between two groups of men in suits. After I slid from behind the wheel and approached them, I heard the men shouting questions at Penelope. But because they were all talking at once, I couldn't understand anything they were saying. I doubted Penelope could, either.

I didn't even hear Shawn come up beside me until he whispered, "Will you look at that?"

I stopped and faced him. "What's going on?"

"Bunch of idiots going at it," he said.

"A few faces look familiar. Where have I seen them?" I said.

"Probably at the town council meeting. To the right of Penelope Webber, you got Ward Stanley's group of investors. To the left, you got Lucas Bartlett's crew."

"Ah. Condos versus urban village," I said with a nod.

"That sums it up. Inside the mill is the woman who belongs to the SUV parked over there. I saw her go in with Chief Baca and Candace." Shawn nodded at a black Expedition parked near the gate. "Penelope unlocked the gate for them. And ignored me completely. I'm left here with fifty grand worth of donated cat shelters." He thumbed behind him at the rental truck. "And I've got to get that truck back by five this afternoon. Can you help me move these shelters beyond the fence so they won't get stolen?"

"Let me talk to the woman with the keys," I said.

As I walked toward the crowd filled with some people I knew but many I didn't, and all of them talking at once, Dustin pulled up in his Volkswagen. *Ah,* I thought. *Here's my ticket inside.*

He hurried toward me, pulling his jacket tightly around him in the stiff breeze. "Dumb me managed to get lost after all."

"These country roads can be confusing." I hooked his arm and whispered, "Come with me and follow my lead on this, okay?"

"But—"

"You'll understand in a minute," I said.

When we reached the little crowd, Penelope turned and said, "There you are, Dustin. So nice to see you again, too, Jillian. Have you met these wonderful people?"

Before I could get a word out, Penelope introduced Ward Stanley. "This mill was named after his great-grandmother, Lorraine, may she rest in peace. He's gathered this group of people hoping to get his mill back and change it into something amazing." She rattled off their names and each man nodded a greeting. Then she turned to Bartlett. "And Mr. Lucas Bartlett has a committed group of investors who hope to save this piece of history from destruction. We will have a difficult choice to make in the coming days and weeks." More introductions followed.

Oh boy, I thought. *We're having a town council meeting right here.*

The rather rumpled Ward Stanley stood in sharp contrast to Lucas Bartlett, whose manicured nails and sculpted eyebrows told me this guy was *not* from Mercy. The two men stared at each other wearing tight, fake smiles. Dustin shook hands all around, but when the thirty-something Stanley began to introduce the four men he'd brought with him, Dustin surprised me by interrupting.

He said, "I would love to meet all you people, but there's been a development inside the mill and I understand my help is needed."

Penelope's gaze swept across all the men surrounding her. "And we're sure this *development* won't interfere with any future plans for the Lorraine Stanley Textile Mill. It's just a little bump in the road." She laughed—a tittering laugh that sounded quite counterfeit to my ears.

How inappropriate, I thought. All she cared about was that one of these investor groups would produce a shiny new and profitable project, one that would relieve the town of Mercy of any obligation to care for this crumbling eyesore. Meanwhile, inside the mill, bones lay waiting to be identified. Human bones. To paraphrase Emily Dickinson, Penelope dropped very low in my regard right then.

I cleared my throat and said, "Since Dustin might need my help inside getting to the back office, he's asked me to go with him. Can you allow us room to get through the gate, Penelope?"

She looked at Dustin. "Why would you need help? You have blueprints and spent a good deal of time in there yesterday."

"Jillian is quite familiar with the layout of old mills," he said, looking down at me. He turned back to Penelope. "I could really use her expertise, if you don't mind."

"First professors and police officers and now the two of you." She turned to the suddenly silent crowd—who rather reminded me of those twelve angry men of movie fame. She gestured broadly and stepped back, her entourage following her lead. "Go right ahead."

Dustin fumbled with the lock, but finally we were through the gate and heading toward the mill. The stares of those we'd left behind seemed to pierce my back, but when I felt that familiar thing that cats do—jump dolphinlike against my leg and then surge ahead to lead the way—I knew Boots had come along. And somehow, this provided a kind of reassurance.

Before we reached the door, I heard Penelope call my name. I turned.

She gestured for me to come back, saying, "I need to ask you something, Jillian. It will only take a second."

Dustin sighed heavily. "Go on. She *is* my boss on all this. Let's make the woman happy."

I returned to the fence and Penelope didn't open the gate. She simply leaned against the chain links and whispered, "I understand there's a skeleton in there. Let's be clear. You're here as a volunteer and not connected in any official capacity to this mess. Don't say a word to anyone. This could be a PR nightmare. Everything goes through me? Understand?"

"If you believe I'd gossip about what we found, you don't know me very well." I forced a smile.

"Your stepdaughter works for the media. You cannot tell her about this . . . this *mess*."

"The mess you're referring to might be human remains," I said, my patience quickly fading. "And Kara runs a small-town newspaper. She's not a CNN producer or anything."

To her credit, she looked embarrassed. "I'm sorry if I sounded unsympathetic. Please, assist Dustin, if you would. Just remember what I said." She turned on one heather gray heel and walked back to the men vying for the mill.

I rejoined Dustin. Just inside the massive door, he'd left a box with hard hats and bulky leather protective gloves. We donned the gear and, with our flashlights leading the way, walked to the office, being careful to dodge the debris on the floor—cheese cones, reed hooks, heddle hooks, spools and scatterings of settled lint.

The halogens in the office shed their light well outside the office door and seemed to be summoning us. We heard voices and picked up our pace.

Mike Baca wore jeans, a zippered dark green jacket with the Mercy PD logo on the chest and a baseball cap with an identical logo—far more sensible clothes for this operation than the suits outside were wearing.

A plump woman was kneeling near the fireplace, her back to me. She wore a navy blue jumpsuit of some kind and her head was covered with what looked like the kind of hat worn by doctors in surgery. Candace stood looking down at her, but when we entered the room, surprise registered on her face. Surprise directed at me.

I felt silly in a hard hat when none of these people considered it necessary.

The chief said, "Jillian," with a nod. He then extended his hand to Dustin. "Good to see you again, Mr. Gray."

Dustin introduced himself to the kneeling woman, and she struggled to her feet. She seemed to be trying not to touch anything as she rose.

She wore latex gloves and said, "I'm Dr. Ruth Maddison. You don't want to shake my hand, Mr. Gray. I do need your assistance, sir. This is a tricky operation we got going, so let me ask your opinion on removing these bricks so we can see what we've got." She waved him toward her and he eagerly joined her.

Mike whispered, "You needed to hold the guy's hand or what?"

I said, "I came to collect a few of Jeannie's things, though that's not the story we offered the town council meeting that's going on outside the gate. Jeannie might feel more comfortable in the hospital if she has something familiar." I glanced around, ready to get to the most important reason I'd come in here. "Then there's the matter of the cat shelters. All Shawn wants to do is unload them, set them inside the gate, but away from anything that might be related to the . . . skeleton. He's worked hard to get those shelters donated and wants them stored in a safe place."

"So, you're a messenger." He looked at Candace, who was engrossed in the hushed conversation going on between Dustin and Dr. Maddison. "Deputy Carson. Any problem with Shawn bringing the shelters inside?"

Candace looked at us, seemingly perturbed. Then she sighed heavily. "If we do have a crime scene, I suppose we can't protect every inch of this property. It's just too big." She turned pensive. "But where to put them?"

Dustin glanced at her. "Can they stay outdoors?"

"From what Shawn told me," I answered, "they're meant to be outside eventually. But I know he'd prefer them to be locked up in this building. If that's impossible right now, we can find a place that's out of sight from the road."

Mike turned to leave, saying, "I'll take care of Shawn and his shelters."

He didn't ask me to go with him and I sighed with relief. I wanted to know what the professor would find in that fireplace. And apparently I wasn't the only one.

Sitting on the hearth, and watching with intense curiosity as Dr. Maddison and Dustin resumed their discussion, was a small black cat with white paws.

Oh boy. Now I could *see* her.

The cat glanced at me and quietly meowed while I swallowed a gasp.

Thirteen

"Are you okay?" Candace said to me. "You look as if you saw a ghost."

I blinked several times and Boots didn't completely disappear, but rather went translucent. "I-I'm simply worried about what they'll find." *And concerned I truly am losing my mind,* I added to myself.

"If you don't like skeletons, I suggest you leave," Candace said. "But even though I understand you want to help Jeannie, I can't let you take anything out of this room. Cat shelters are one thing, but this area will need to be searched for evidence."

"I understand. But I'd like to stay and watch them work." Even if I was taken aback by what I saw beyond Candace, I was still mesmerized.

Boots had found a way into the right side of the fireplace while Dustin and Dr. Maddison concentrated on the left. Only her tail was sticking out. I suppose ghost cats *could* travel right through brick. I stepped closer and said, "Perhaps the feral cats can give us a clue about this fireplace. Earlier we decided they seemed to be coming in and out through this room." I pointed to the small opening where I could still see the tip of Boots's tail. "Like right through there."

Dr. Maddison turned and looked up at me. "Feral cats?"

"I'll explain later." Candace, hands on her thighs, peered into the fireplace, glancing left and then right. "There is a space a few feet to the right of where Dustin pulled out that hand."

Dustin scrambled over and stuck tentative fingers into the opening. "Ah. This might give us a shot at removing bricks and concrete with minimal disturbance to what might . . . lie beyond." He looked up at me. "Good call, Jillian."

Thanks, Boots, I said to myself.

Dustin said, "If we can reach in through this opening and remove a few bricks, we might be able to see what we're dealing with. I'm sure you understand, Dr. Maddison, that this *structure* of debris began in the middle and then whoever filled this fireplace piled on to the outside. Sort of like a pyramid."

Dr. Maddison smiled for the first time. "If we pull the wrong brick, the whole thing could topple down and destroy what we're hoping to find. Simple common sense. But that's a pretty small opening. We'll need little hands to reach in and see what's loose enough to pull out." She stood with a groan. "Okay, everyone. Let's see your hands."

"Wait a minute," Candace said. "We could have an entire dead body in there and—"

"Or," Dr. Maddison said, "we could have nothing more than a piece of tarp inside this fireplace. The skeletal hand could have come from some prankster's anatomy lab."

Candace's jaw slackened and I could tell she'd realized the professor might be right. Finally she said, "I suppose that's possible. Might not be anything more criminal than that. Let's see whose hand will fit in that hole." She looked at me. "But I already know."

Sure enough, I had the thinnest hands and after I traded the leather gloves for a pair of latex ones from Candace's evidence kit, I swallowed hard. "Okay, Dustin. Guide me as best you can."

Dustin said, "I've already moved the loose bricks in front. I believe we have a large hunk of concrete that's pretty much supporting everything above it. Little chance you can budge it. But if you can reach in and loosen more bricks on the right side, maybe pull them out, we'll have a better view. I'll shine the Maglite in there for you."

I shed my coat and once I was down on my knees, Dustin focused the light through the small passage where I'd seen Boots disappear. Once I leaned my head to the side and looked into the hole, there she was, her little face offering me a pleading look. The light passed right through her black-and-white fur. Oh boy. I was learning way more about ghosts than I ever wanted to—like, for instance, that they do exist. I shuddered and decided to concentrate on my task.

Sure enough, I was able to pull out first one brick and then another, sliding them sideways through the opening Boots had pointed out. I also saw daylight filtering through a hole in the back of the fireplace on the right corner. *Must be how the ferals are getting in and out,* I thought.

Dustin, down on the floor with me, said, "Remember, we're hoping to remove just enough so we can angle a light to the left and get a good look at that tarp."

I could see the configuration—sort of like a Jenga tower. I saw what few bricks I could remove and did so carefully. I then squinted at what I saw inside the fireplace. Dustin was right. A big piece of concrete in the center seemed to be supporting most of the debris. I lay on the floor on my left side so I could get most of my arm in. I carefully withdrew two more loose bricks right in front of the monster hunk of concrete. The tarp was clearly visible from this angle with the help of the Maglite. Looking straight at it hadn't revealed what I could now see.

"Oh no," I whispered.

I yanked my arm out, tearing my Henley in the process. I pressed the back of my gloved hand against my mouth and mumbled, "Oh no," several more times.

Candace knelt beside me, her hand on my shoulder. "What is it?"

"H-hair spilling out of the tarp. Long dirty hair. And a s-skull." I looked up at the professor, who hadn't joined Dustin, Candace and me on the floor, even though her concern was evident.

I said, "This is no prank, Professor."

Since cell phone reception inside the mill was nonexistent, Candace had to leave to get reinforcements from outside. My presence, thank goodness, was no longer needed, so I walked out with her.

The crowd outside seemed to have grown, but Penelope Webber's red coat reminded me of a ball of fire in an ocean of gray. She started toward Candace while my friend dragged me along, hurrying to where Morris and Chief Baca stood. They both seemed winded as we approached and then I realized they must have helped Shawn unload the cat shelters. Yes, that must be what happened, because I caught a glimpse of the Penske truck driving away.

Keeping her voice low, Candace said, "We got trouble, Chief."

"Did you say trouble?" Penelope said. She'd swiftly closed in on us.

Candace whirled and faced her. "Ms. Webber, with all due respect, I need you to step back while I discuss an urgent matter with the chief."

Penelope looked past Candace at Chief Baca. "Mike,

if there's a problem, I need to be informed. The investor groups are both here and if I don't give them an update, we could lose them—and their revenue."

Candace's lips tightened and she turned back to face Mike. All she did was raise her eyebrows and widen her blue eyes. We all knew Candace well enough to know what that expression meant: *Get her out of here. Now.*

Mike smiled at Penelope and said, "I would guess there won't be any tour of the mill today. That is why you brought these folks here, am I right?"

"Yes," she said. "I promised them that since the engineer had gone in without incident, and since I am told halogen lights are in place, they could all have a peek at more than blueprints."

"You *shouldn't* have done that," Candace said.

Mike stepped between Penelope and Candace while I glanced over to where Morris stood. He seemed to be enjoying all this.

Mike said, "I need to talk to my officer, but I'm thinking a tour of the building is a bit premature. You're good with people, Penny. You can explain this as a miscommunication on my part. Tell them we found a woman living in the mill and we want to remove all her belongings before they see the place. How's that?"

Penelope's hazel eyes darkened. "Exactly *what* is the *real* problem?"

"I promise to call you as soon as I find out," Mike said, his voice like warm syrup. "Give us a little time and space to sort things out, would you?"

Penelope took a deep breath and exhaled slowly. She straightened her shoulders, put on her politician smile and walked back to join the curious onlookers.

When she was out of earshot, Candace whispered, "There's a body in there, Chief. And we're gonna need a jackhammer to get the bones out of that fireplace."

Fourteen

When I drove away from the mill property, I passed my stepdaughter, Kara, as she was arriving. I waved and sped on. Word that something was up had obviously gotten out, but the last thing I wanted was to talk to Kara about what I'd seen in that old fireplace. Besides, Candace had sworn me to secrecy and said she wasn't even putting up crime scene tape in hopes of keeping away the entire population of Mercy. With Kara's arrival, it would seem she was out of luck—but not because of me.

I arrived home hungry as well as fatigued by the stress of seeing that skull, but my three cats weren't the least bit tired. As soon as I made myself a PBJ and carried it, along with a huge glass of sweet tea, to the small table in the kitchen nook, three kitty faces stared up at me.

They wanted me to do normal things—like quilting—rather than deal with bones and ghosts. I did have kitty quilt orders pending. I made them to order for cat lovers and my business was building. It would be so nice to sit in the easy chair in my quilting room and pick up a project, allow the rocking of the needle through fabric to soothe me. Instead, I found myself glancing around, thinking about Boots. Apparently she'd stayed at the mill, because Syrah and Merlot showed no indication we had a mysterious feline visitor. Had her whole purpose been to lead me to where that body lay hidden? Would she disappear for good now? Had the whole ghost-cat thing been my imagination working overtime to help solve a problem? Perhaps. But deep down, I knew I'd seen Boots, felt her, sensed her—and so had two of my cats.

I was just putting my plate in the dishwasher when Tom arrived. His hug-and-kiss greeting was exactly what I needed and I clung to him, my head against his chest.

"Mmm. I smell peanut butter. But are you okay?" He lifted my chin so he could look at my face.

"There are more bones in that fireplace—and I saw them. It was awful." I felt tears burn behind my eyes and I blinked them back.

With his arm around my shoulders, we went into the living room and sat on the sofa, where I told him everything—except about Boots. I still wasn't sure what Tom would think of me if I mentioned a ghost cat—and what he thought of me was important. Yes, I was falling for this man, falling hard. And no talk of ghosts would get in the way of what we might have together.

"I heard nothing about the mill on my police scanner," he said. "So, I'm guessing Mike and Candace have succeeded in keeping this quiet—for now."

"I passed Kara on the way, so it won't be a secret for long. I can see the *Mercy Messenger* headlines already. Anyway, Candace says they have to come up with a plan to get the skeleton out of the fireplace—and they would like to do that with as little interference as possible. But we all know once odd pieces of excavating equipment begin showing up in town, the cat will be out of the bag." *Oh boy,* I thought. *Poor word choice.*

"This professor's appearance didn't stir up any grapevine interest?" he said.

"The anthropologist came early this morning, before Mercy got out of bed. Before I got out of bed," I said. "Kara's smart. She caught on pretty quick that something is up. I saw her arrive at the mill when I left. But I'm more concerned about the town council, now that I think about it. Will this *discovery* ruin any hopes of turning that old place into a useful, beautiful building again?"

"Actually, it might have a positive effect in terms of revenue. Curiosity seekers could be drawn to the place." Tom reached over and stroked Chablis, who had climbed into my lap the minute I sat down.

"Then there's Jeannie to worry about," I said. "I'll bet that skeleton belongs to her daughter."

"You're probably right. Maybe Jeannie put the body there—her idea of a burial in a place she knew well," he said.

"Burial?" I said. "How awful. Why would she do such a thing?"

"Well, we don't know if this was a murder," Tom said over Chablis's loud purrs. "Maybe her daughter died by accident or of natural causes and Jeannie had no other place to lay the poor girl to rest. She was at odds with Pastor Mitch and his wife, so she might have felt as if she couldn't turn to them for help to give her daughter a proper burial."

"Sad, if that's the case," I said. "How terrible to have no one's help at a time like that. I plan to help Jeannie any way I can. No one should have to live like she has—alone, in an abandoned building. I feel as if this whole town has let her down."

"Could be she was perfectly content where she was," he said. "Not everyone needs the company of others—although I know I surely do. I've been missing Finn. He's gone from sunup until sundown and when he is at home, he's studying. Yoshi spends most of his time with Ed."

"But I know you're proud of him," I said. "He was smart to come to Mercy and find you. But then, he's a smart kid."

Tom smiled. "He is that."

A knock sounded at the front door and I decided it must be a stranger since most of my friends all come to the back door. Turned out, it wasn't a stranger after all.

I saw the county assistant coroner, Lydia Monk, through the peephole and stifled a groan. I whispered back at Tom, who was still sitting on the couch. "It's Lydia. And I'm sure she's recognized your car. We're in trouble."

Tom stood. "No, we're not. That woman—oh, never mind. Let her in and let's see what crazy story she's dreamed up now that she's found us together."

I opened the door.

Lydia had chosen black today—with studs all over her leather pants and matching jacket. I mean, what coroner *anywhere* dressed like she belonged in a heavy metal rock video? But being a true Southern lady, I smiled and asked her to come in.

The look of fury on her face was not directed at me for once. She had her eye on Tom and marched into my living room, her stiletto boots probably making gouges in the wood floor. "I am not allowed at a crime scene. Me? The assistant coroner of this county *not allowed*?" She pointed a finger at Tom, the magenta paint blaringly bold. "*You* can do something about this."

Tom looked both confused and irritated. "What are you talking about, Lydia?"

I walked over and stood behind her, thinking she might shoot fire right through me if I got too close. Syrah, however, was undeterred. He couldn't stand Lydia and thus, being a feline, wanted to be as close to her as possible. For once, she didn't even notice him sitting by her right foot ready to use Lydia's leg as a scratching post.

"What I am talking about," Lydia said, enunciating every word, "is Mike Baca bringing in some professor from who knows where to do my job. Mike and I are not on the best of terms, but he can't shut me out. He has to allow me access to the body. Since he's *your* friend, you need to fix this."

"But it's a skeleton," I said softly, hoping my tone would bring Lydia down a notch. "And it's kind of wedged into a fireplace, so—"

Lydia whirled to face me. "Wouldn't you know Jillian Hart would be smack-dab in the middle of this? A skeleton is still a body."

Tom said, "Then what reason are they giving you for keeping you out of the mill?"

Lydia tossed her head with its overprocessed blond hair in my direction. "Does she have to be here? I came to talk to you because, of course, I knew this is where I'd find you."

"It is her house, Lydia. I'm betting she stays." I could tell Tom was fighting a grin. Lydia annoyed me but amused the heck out of him.

"Oh, all right. She can stay. She seems to know everything anyway. My point is, if they can allow Shawn to bring those Dumpster contraptions he calls cat shelters inside the building, why can't I be inside, too?"

"Perhaps because bones require special handling?" Tom said.

"I'm not good enough to touch bones? I've handled plenty of them. Bringing in this expert is all Mike Baca's doing. Political animal that he is, he wants to impress Penelope Webber. She wants this silly project to stay on schedule. Well, her silly project is a crime scene and I belong inside."

"Hold on. They're officially calling it a crime scene?" Tom asked.

Lydia was tapping her foot and Syrah found this interesting enough to paw at her boot. Lydia was too wound up to notice, but she might end up with a few scratches in the leather. I glanced around, wondering where the other two cats were hiding. They were nowhere in sight—and I didn't blame them.

"*I'm* calling it a crime scene," she said. "That's why I need to be involved. Did I see any yellow tape? No. Were there folks gathered around the fence wondering what was going on? Yes. Could bringing in those stupid cat contraptions destroy evidence? Yes."

"Those *stupid contraptions* will save cats' lives," I said.

"Who cares about that?" She finally looked down and noticed Syrah, who had indeed left a long scratch on her boot. She bent and waved a hand at Syrah, saying, "Look what you've done. Get away right now."

He didn't budge.

"Jillian, control your animal," she said. "It's the least you can do."

And then I saw her—Boots—sitting on Lydia's right side. She blinked as if she'd just awoken from a nap. Ghost cats napped? I supposed all cats needed their beauty rest, whether they were alive or dead.

Lydia said, "Jillian. *Your cat?*"

But by the time she spoke, Tom had picked Syrah up and held him close. He said, "I have no say in how Mike wants to handle the mill problem. You've wasted your time coming here, Lydia."

"I will *not* take no for an answer. You go over there and you tell him to let me in there and see what they're doing." She stomped her foot and said, "Right now."

I realized why Tom had picked up my cat. But Boots seemed unperturbed by the temper tantrum.

Tom shook his head, stroking Syrah, whom I could hear growling from where I stood, a good five feet away.

My cat wanted Lydia gone more than I did.

"Sorry," Tom said. "Maybe you can get your boss involved. You know—the coroner you report to? The one who just got re-elected?"

"He's more political than Mike Baca and you know

it." She sounded disgusted. "He'll side with Mercy PD. And here I thought we had something special enough that you'd do this *one* favor for me." Lydia waved a hand at me. "Maybe if your stalker here wasn't in the room, you'd see things my way."

The tips of Tom's ears reddened. "Lydia, you say one more negative thing about Jillian and I will throw you out of here."

I wanted to smile. In the past, Tom's approach to Lydia's ridiculous fantasy concerning her supposed relationship with him was to ignore her behavior—in hopes she'd give up one day. He'd always found the whole delusion funny. But there was nothing in his demeanor right now that indicated he was amused.

Meanwhile, Boots was sniffing Lydia's feet and then suddenly backed up and hissed. She looked up at Lydia and hissed again. Cats are such excellent judges of character.

Fifteen

After Lydia left in a dissatisfied huff, Tom waited awhile before he took off, concerned she might return. Not that I needed his protection from Lydia. She was harmless. But his concern felt like a warm shawl around my shoulders. I liked it.

I spent the next few hours catching up on the few online orders I'd received after Christmas. My customers would choose one of the designs on my Web site or send in their own ideas for what they'd like for their kitties. Today was a machine-piecing day with batik fabrics in earth tones for one small quilt and a black, white and red design for the second.

The cats surrounded me in the quilting room. Chablis took a spot in the easy chair while Merlot spread his long body over a stack of new fabrics. Syrah and, yes, Boots, sat on either side of the sewing table, staring at each other. For some reason, now that I could see her, Boots was a comforting presence. But she belonged to Jeannie, who probably needed her desperately right now. Why had she chosen to haunt me during this time?

I planned a visit to the hospital later today and I sure hoped Little Miss Ghost Cat would come along. It was not as though I could just pick her up and put her in my van.

I'd just started piecing the second quilt when I heard a loud rapping and realized someone was at the back door. I hurried to answer, a crew of cats on my heels. Then suddenly, Boots and Syrah raced ahead of me.

Candace said, "Took you long enough," when I opened the door. She came into the mudroom and stopped to pet each cat on the head before walking into the kitchen. "I hope you have tea made."

I opened the fridge and took out a half-full pitcher, saying, "You look like you've been working in a coal mine."

"I know." She swiped her forehead with the back of her hand but didn't come close to erasing the smears of gray soot on her face. "They had to get this special concrete saw—heavy son of a gun. This fireman who knows how to work the contraption came from Woodcrest and cut a big enough space through those bricks and cement that we were able to carefully remove the rest of the skeleton. Thank goodness he knew what he was doing and didn't send the whole debris tower crashing down."

"I guess that's good news," I said, pouring a glass of tea for Candace.

My cell rang and I pulled it from my jeans pocket and answered.

"This is Harry Williams from the Upstate Homeless Partnership," the man said.

"Oh, hello! Thank you so much for calling me back. I was hoping to hear from you," I said. "I'm in Mercy and we have a problem we hope you can help us with."

"That's what the Partnership is about. What can we do for you?"

I covered the mouthpiece of the phone and spoke to Candace. "This is about help for Jeannie, so I need to take this."

"And I need to make more tea. Go ahead." She walked to the fridge to find the cane syrup I'd made up. Homemade cane syrup made the best sweet tea.

I put the phone back to my ear and walked into the living room. The cats stayed behind to see what Candace was up to. Perhaps something that involved treats or toys.

"Let me explain the situation, Mr. Williams." I went on to tell him about Jeannie and how she was currently in the hospital with a broken hip.

"Unfortunately," he said, "we have no ability to care for medically compromised homeless folks. But when Miss Sloan has recovered from her injury, I hope you'll call me back and we can set up an evaluation. When we find out exactly what skills she might have, we can find a work-training program and a home that will suit her."

"I'm disappointed, but I surely understand. Jeannie once worked in the Lorraine Stanley Textile Mill, so she probably has abilities that I know nothing about. You'll be hearing from me again," I said. "And thanks again for calling."

I disconnected, feeling a little deflated. But I truly did understand. Jeannie would need continuing medical supervision and rehab once she was released from the hospital. I decided I would call the hospital and see when would be a good time to visit. But a nurse's aide answered the phone in her room. We did a little verbal dance as she said she wasn't supposed to tell me anything, but she finally told me that Jeannie was out of her room because she needed *something taken care of*. I took that to mean she'd gone to surgery. The aide did tell me that Miss Sloan would probably be back in her room this evening.

I went to the kitchen where Candace had just finished

making a fresh pitcher of tea. She said, "You look like you just lost a cat. What's wrong?"

I sighed. "Poor Jeannie went into surgery without anyone there to hold her hand and tell her everything would be all right. I feel terrible."

"You can be there when she wakes up, though," Candace said. "And that works out fine, considering the reason I came over."

"So it wasn't just for my wonderful tea?" I said with a smile.

"Well, that's always a reason to come over." She pulled a small clear bag from her uniform pocket. I recognized the yellow evidence tape that sealed it. Candace held up the bag, which contained a tarnished small ring with a dirt-encrusted purple stone. "We found this next to the skeleton. Think we can head to the hospital later and ask Jeannie if she recognizes it?"

"Today?" I said. "The woman is in surgery. She'll be in pain and drugged and afraid when she gets back to her room. If this ring does belong to her daughter ... well, can you imagine how she'll feel?" Sometimes the cases Candace worked consumed her so much that she forgot to consider the emotional impact on the people who were touched by the crimes.

Candace's features softened. "You're right, of course. Sorry. I'd just like to identify this victim as quickly as possible and get on with the business of finding a killer. See, she was murdered."

"How can you tell? I thought all you had was a skeleton," I said.

"The professor was able to give us plenty of information once she looked at the bones," Candace said. "Of course, those are preliminary findings that she'll have to confirm once she examines the skeleton in her laboratory."

"The ring is definitely small and feminine. But did she find a bullet hole? Or a fractured skull?" I said.

"Crushed hyoid bone." Candace touched her throat. "From manual strangulation."

I closed my eyes. "That's a horrible way to die. What else did the professor tell you?"

"Female, probably late teens," she answered. "Professor Maddison knew this because certain bones weren't fused. And from the shape of the skull and the dentition, she believes it was a white girl. This all fits the description of Jeannie's lost daughter."

I tried to swallow the lump that had formed in my throat—but it stayed there, perhaps to remind me that I was lucky enough to be alive. "I suppose it does. How sad. Jeannie camped out a few feet away from her dead daughter."

"You know me," Candace said. "I don't believe in coincidence. I'm willing to bet Jeannie knew exactly where her daughter was—maybe because she put her there." She swallowed what was left of her tea and put her glass in the dishwasher. "I need to wash my face. Got any less-than-your-best towels?"

"Um, sure," I said, concerned about Candace's assumption that Jeannie killed her own daughter.

After I handed Candace a washcloth and towel from the linen closet, she closed the door to the powder room and I heard her give a little screech and say, "My gosh, I look like a hobo."

I would have smiled if Candace hadn't just voiced her renewed suspicions about Jeannie. Coincidence or not, I was certain the woman hadn't hurt her daughter. There was so much we didn't know about Jeannie and Kay Ellen, so much we needed to learn before deciding Jeannie stuffed her daughter's body in a fireplace. While Candace followed the evidence, I promised myself I would learn more about both of them. In the meantime, I felt a strong need to protect the woman, at least for today—starting with that ring.

I had an idea, so when Candace came back into the kitchen, all fresh-faced with her blond hair pulled back neatly again, I said, "I know a person other than Jeannie who might recognize that ring."

Sixteen

Dusk muted the landscape as I drove behind Candace's patrol car back to the mill village. At least she was more careful driving the town's vehicle than when driving her own car. We first stopped at the mill so Candace could let the chief know she and I planned to get help with the identification from someone other than Jeannie.

The lack of crime scene tape that normally would have surrounded the area had apparently fooled no one in the Mercy grapevine. Plenty of gawkers had gathered outside the fence. In the mill village houses in the surrounding area, faces peeked from behind curtains and the children playing in their yards couldn't seem to keep their curious gazes off the crowd.

Apparently the investors decided they weren't leaving until they knew what was going on because Lucas Bartlett came up to Candace the minute she slid from behind the wheel. I actually took him in for the first time—things had been too crazy earlier for me to even pay much attention to those who were here only about money. Now I noted he was maybe late forties with graying temples and deeply creased worry lines on his forehead. Someone had made a coffee run at some point, because he held a Belle's Beans coffee. Steam swirled out of the drink opening.

"What is going on inside that mill, Deputy Carson?" he said. "No one will tell us anything."

"All in good time, Mr. Bartlett," Candace said, scanning the surrounding area for the chief.

"My investment group and I have money we're willing to spend to help this town get out of debt." He gestured pointedly with the hand holding the coffee. "Shouldn't that mean you'd have the courtesy to keep us informed?"

Candace, seemingly distracted by her hunt to find Mike Baca among the sea of faces, said, "I suggest you talk to Penelope Webber. We'll be funneling information through her."

His cheeks, burnished by the sharp winter wind, seemed to grow brighter. "Penelope Webber seems to have better things to do than hang around here. Should I send my fellow investors home? Or are we going to be able to talk to that engineer—or at least speak with the police chief about a new timeline? I am assuming whatever has happened will seriously disrupt the timeline as far as a vote on whose proposal wins."

I pulled my jacket more tightly around me. When Candace didn't answer—she was still hunting for Mike, I assumed—I said, "Mr. Bartlett, I can't speak for Ms. Webber, but I do have her phone number. Would you like me to give it to you so you can call her?"

He sighed, seemingly frustrated. "Don't you think I've called her a dozen times already? And who are you, anyway, to be so involved in all this? You make cat quilts, last I heard." He sounded angry—but then I knew there was fierce competition for this mill property and venting at me was about the only option he had right now.

"I'm simply a volunteer helping Shawn Cuddahee with the feral cats," I said evenly.

Candace must have spotted the chief, because she left

without a word, making a beeline into the center of that cluster of onlookers.

Bartlett rolled his eyes at the sky. "Where is she going? Why can't I get answers?"

In a quiet and I hoped soothing voice I said, "This must be upsetting. I guess you were told to come out here today and a circus broke out. Is that why you're here—because Penelope or someone—"

"There was talk." He swigged his coffee. "Once I heard Stanley was over here, that something big was going on, my fellow investors and I had to come, too. They've since left, but I've hung around waiting for answers and gotten nothing for my trouble."

"They did have to get the cat shelters inside," I said. "You know about the cat project, right?"

"Yes, yes, but whatever's going on isn't about the cats. I heard there might have been a squatter—or vandalism of some kind in that building. If it's vandalism, I can see why they won't tell us anything. But, even so, if there's damage inside, we need to know. We need a walk-through."

"It's getting late, Mr. Bartlett. Too late for you to go inside the mill today," I said.

But Lucas Bartlett didn't seem to hear a word I'd said. "Where's Stanley?" he said, looking around. "What if they let *him* inside? You understand he and his motley crew had to scrape and beg for enough money to take on a project like this—and they won't even be creating the kind of jobs I will." He pointed at the mill with his coffee cup. "I'm willing to put up good money for that ramshackle place—and I'm betting more funds than he's offered. What does Stanley want with it, anyway? His father had his chance—and *his* father before him—and they let it fall into ruin."

I said, "I don't know anything about the politics of—"

"This may be politics to Penny Webber and her best

buddy, Stanley, but it is important business to me. I want answers." He was shouting now and people around us were beginning to stare.

I took a chance that perhaps he needed a kind touch rather than a soothing voice and rested a hand on his arm. "If it's worth anything, with the feral shelters now in place, things are moving forward."

He was breathing fast and still staring at the mill. But he nodded.

"The timeline you're referring to hasn't been totally interrupted by whatever has happened inside the mill," I said. "That's good news for you if there's a deadline as far as funding your purchase."

He looked at me. "Sorry, but what's your name again? I've forgotten."

"Jillian Hart. Call me Jillian, though."

He nodded and at last seemed calmer. "Listen, funding isn't the issue." He really looked at me for the first time since we'd started talking. "I apologize for losing my temper, but I want answers. The Mercy town council has to understand that this isn't how to do business. We should be kept informed. For goodness' sake, they've brought in lights and equipment and there were firemen and, of course, the police presence."

"I can't argue with you, but I have no influence over the police or Penelope or . . . anyone. I'm just a volunteer," I said.

Neither of us seemed to notice Ward Stanley's approach, but suddenly he was right beside us. He looked as worn out as his brown winter coat. Stressed. Tired. And probably older than he actually was.

"What are you two cooking up?" he said.

"None of your business," Bartlett said.

What was it with these guys? Apparently the competition for the mill was far more intense than I'd realized. "Gentlemen, all I can say is that I know nothing about what's happening that I can share with you." I couldn't *share* anything I knew because Candace would want me to keep my mouth shut about the poor dead girl in the fireplace. "What about Councilwoman Webber? Have you spoken to her?" I asked Stanley.

"Nope," he said. "Doesn't want to answer questions, is my guess."

"Maybe I can find Chief Baca for you, then." All I cared about was that dead girl and the cats—cats who were probably totally freaked out by all the action inside the mill. Besides, I wasn't the competitive type and these two men definitely were. *Escape from these guys now, Jillian,* was all I could think.

I walked away, leaving the two men in a stare down. There had to be fifty people milling around, craning their necks to see what couldn't be seen through old red bricks. I caught a glimpse of Kara, talking to a cluster of people, notebook in hand, and then I spotted Candace's forest green uniform. I slipped between onlookers, hoping Bartlett and Stanley would continue their preoccupation with each other and not follow me.

When I reached Candace, she was with Mike, who said, "Good to see you, Jillian." He wasn't in uniform and that was probably the reason those two money men I'd just run from hadn't located the chief to hammer *him* with questions. Good thing his fatigued and drawn features had probably prevented them from recognizing him. Mike didn't need to be in the middle of their conflict over the mill right now.

"Ah, there you are," Candace said—as if *I* were the one who'd disappeared. "The chief thinks you had a good suggestion about getting an ID on the ring. Let's go."

"Best idea you've had all day," I said.

We weaved through the crowd with Candace ignoring the questions thrown at her from every direction. Me? I would have stopped and tried to answer every one of them if I had been in her shoes. Obviously I wasn't meant to be a cop.

We could have walked to the church, but Candace feared people might follow her—and she was probably right. I led the way in my van even though Candace no doubt knew exactly where we were headed.

We found the church itself deserted, so we walked over to the pastorium. Elizabeth Truman, not the pastor, answered the door. She invited us in and when I introduced her to Candace she said, "And it's Elizabeth, ladies. No need to be so formal. Follow me. Pastor Mitch is in his study."

"And I'm just Candace, not Deputy Carson," Candace called after her.

Elizabeth turned and smiled. "Oh, I know, dear girl. Your reputation precedes you."

Out of the side of her mouth, Candace whispered, "What does that mean?"

I shrugged in response and put a finger to my lips. I didn't want Elizabeth to think we were talking behind her back, no matter how innocuous the conversation.

The pastor's study was far warmer than the hallways we'd traveled through to get to this room. A fire glowed and the atmosphere alone was calming after my encounter with Lucas Bartlett and Ward Stanley. After Elizabeth introduced Candace to the pastor, she started to leave the room.

I said, "Perhaps you could stay?" In my experience, women tended to pay attention to jewelry more than men did.

"We need anyone and everyone's help," Candace said. "See, Jeannie is having surgery, and—"

"Oh my. What happened?" the pastor said. He'd stood up when he'd greeted us and now gripped his desk chair.

"She broke her hip," I said.

"That is most unfortunate," Elizabeth said. "We'll put

her on the prayer list—and if you'll give me the information, I will take a comforting gift to her when she's well enough to receive visitors. We have a woman in our congregation who makes the most beautiful afghans for the sick. Our parishioners will want to add their thoughts and prayers as well."

"There is another way you might help," Candace said. "See, we didn't want to upset Jeannie today—she's got enough on her plate—but I'm sure you've noticed the mob over at the mill."

"Indeed we have. Does it have to do with the new plans for renovation?" Pastor Mitch asked.

"In a roundabout way," I said. "But somehow word got out that the police were called here for a different issue and that's why there's a crowd hanging around."

Candace pulled the bag holding the ring from her pocket. "Do you recognize this?"

Elizabeth's sharp intake of air said it all.

I said, "Did it belong to—"

Candace quickly interrupted me. "Do you recognize this?" She glanced back and forth between the pastor and his wife.

"That ring belonged to Kay Ellen," Elizabeth said. She glanced at her husband, her eyes filled with tears. "She *didn't* run off then, did she?"

"No, ma'am," Candace said. "She didn't."

"Where did you find it?" the pastor said, walking to his wife's side and putting a comforting arm around her shoulder.

"We found this ring inside a mill office." Candace explained about the bones in the fireplace as the pastor and his wife stared at Candace in horror.

"Oh my. This is truly the most terrible news. As for that ring, Kay Ellen had a boyfriend. Her first. He gave it to her," Elizabeth said.

"What was his name?" Candace asked. I could hear

the excitement in her voice in anticipation of this first real clue in a decade-old cold case.

"I have no idea," Elizabeth said. "He wasn't a villager. That was all she would say about him."

"So, that was why you didn't tell Deputy Ebeling much about this boyfriend when Kay Ellen first disappeared?" Candace said.

"He was so certain she ran away, though he mentioned he'd asked a few young people at the high school about her," the pastor said.

"Would Jeannie have known who this kid was?" Candace asked.

"She never mentioned anything about him to me," Elizabeth said. "You understand Jeannie lives in her own world. She never shared much about herself except to talk about her old job in the mill or how pretty her daughter was."

I said, "Is it possible Jeannie didn't even know about this boyfriend?"

After I asked the question, I had to keep my eyes from going wide with surprise, because Boots had suddenly made an appearance. She sat by the pastor's side, but she was looking up at me, blinking slowly. She might have even nodded.

"It's very possible Jeannie knew nothing about Kay Ellen's friends," Elizabeth said.

Candace sighed. "I have a few names from Deputy Ebeling's report that I still have to follow up on. If you think of anything, remember even a tiny detail, please call me at Mercy PD. They'll get in touch with me immediately." She looked at me. "Let's go."

But the pastor said, "Wait. We need information about Jeannie. Where she is. And who will care for her after this operation."

I smiled sadly. "That's kind of a problem." I told him about the Upstate Homeless Partnership and how they could assist Jeannie only after she recovered from surgery. "I suppose there's a social worker at the hospital who might have resources."

"We have resources," Elizabeth said firmly. "If Jeannie agrees, we will bring her here."

"Indeed we will," the pastor said with a solemn nod.

I swore that invisible-to-everyone-but-me cat smiled.

Seventeen

Once we left the pastorium, Candace thanked me and said she'd call me later. But before either of us got to our cars, my phone rang.

"Jillian, this is Shawn," he said when I answered. "I need your help at the mill."

"Hang on," I said, then called to Candace to wait up. If I needed to get inside that mill, I'd require her help to let me inside the gate. She and Mike Baca now had keys to the place.

"Sorry, Shawn," I said into the phone. "What's up?"

"I'm at Doc Jensen's with one of the ferals. Found him lying outside the mill with a broken leg. Once I got here to the vet clinic, I realized I'd forgotten to bring the cat kibble to the mill. Can you pick it up at my shelter and take it over there? Allison has to stay at our place. Can't leave the rescues unattended, you know."

"Sure," I said. "Are there dishes to fill inside those feral shelters? And what about water?"

He told me Allison would explain exactly what to do and in true Shawn style, he abruptly disconnected.

I looked at my phone. "Okay, then."

Candace had been tapping her foot impatiently while Shawn and I talked, so I quickly explained that I would need her help getting back inside the mill in a while.

"Not a problem," she said. "I'll be over there having a little chat with my partner about the disappearance of Kay Ellen Sloan and whether he knows anything about a certain *boyfriend*." She took a deep breath. "And I'll be nicer to Morris than he'd ever be to me if I were in his shoes."

When she drove off, the patrol car's tires squealed as if Candace were in her own car. Maybe she'd blow off enough steam in her one-minute drive to follow through on being *kind* to Morris.

I climbed into my minivan and took a deep breath. The last two days had been unnerving to say the least. Before I pulled away from the curb, I hit the icon on my phone for the cat cam.

Merlot, stretched out on the sofa, practically took up two cushions. Syrah crouched on the sofa's back and Chablis was curled on top of a stack of quilting magazines on the floor. They all looked so peaceful and I could feel my shoulder and neck muscles ease immediately as I smiled at the images.

"Okay. Off to Mercy Animal Sanctuary," I said, setting down the phone on the seat next to me. Boots hadn't appeared on the seat and I wondered if she'd decided to ride with Candace for once. But I knew better. She was riding with me—somewhere.

Thirty minutes later, the back of my van loaded with bags of kibble, I was headed back to the mill when my phone rang again. It was Candace.

"Hey there," I said. "I'm on my way to the mill right now. You will let me drive this stuff in, right? Because carrying—"

"Do you have any idea where Penelope Webber is?" Candace interrupted.

"No. But she wouldn't keep *me* informed of her itinerary," I said.

"We need her here," Candace said, sounding more

than a little frustrated. "These self-important investor types who all skipped their fancy lunches and dinners are cranky. They want answers and the chief isn't giving any press conferences about what we've found. He's afraid he'll scare off the businessmen. He wants to tell Penelope enough information so she can act as a liaison. But she's not answering her phone."

"I talked to Lucas Bartlett earlier," I said, "and he couldn't reach her, either. If you're wondering whether I have some secret phone number for her that no one else has access to—"

"I need a favor. And then I promise I'll be waiting at the gate to let you in with the cat food. I'll even help you carry the stuff inside. See, we have to wait here on the professor's assistant. Apparently he has the correct container to carry out bones with as little disturbance to them as possible."

I sighed, feeling weary and hungry, but still committed to helping my best friend, not to mention Jeannie and her lost daughter. "You know I'll do anything I can," I said.

"Could you stop at Penelope's house?" Candace asked. "Maybe she wants to duck these big problems, but as the lead councilwoman, she should be here. I figure you'd know how to ask the woman to come and do her job in a polite way. I'm really running short on polite talk after my chat with Morris—who told me the high school kids he'd interviewed said Kay Ellen probably wanted to get away from her mother and claimed they hardly knew the girl, anyway. He confirmed his theory she was a runaway, which is not good police work, I'm sorry to say."

"I don't know Penelope all that well, Candace, and I'm not sure about how to ask her what she's been doing all day. I mean, what's the nice version of, 'Where have you been while all heck has been breaking out over at the mill'?"

"You'll think of something. She lives at 116 Grace Street. On the hill. Big house with gables. You can't miss it." She disconnected.

She was the second person to hang up on me in the last hour. I took a nice deep breath. Candace had a lot on her plate and she was my best friend. I would cut her all the slack she needed—because she would do the same for me.

You can do this, I told myself as I made a U-turn on the deserted highway leading to the mill. Back to town I went, practicing what I would say to Penelope Webber all the way. I finally settled on, *Ms. Webber, we're wondering if your phone isn't charged, because Chief Baca and Deputy Carson have been trying to reach you and the calls go straight to voice mail.* No need to mention Lucas Bartlett or Ward Stanley or the crowd of people still waiting outside that mill, I'd decided as I pulled into her driveway.

I opened my car door and hesitated. The two-story white house with its black shutters stood in unwelcoming silence in the gloom of this late-winter evening. The birds were all settled in for the night, so there were no happy chirps—and no lights on inside the house.

No sign anyone's home, I thought as I slid from behind the wheel. I wondered then about family. Did she have any? But perhaps she lived alone in this giant house. This inner dialogue only confirmed that I knew next to nothing about this person I was about to confront.

More questions ran through my mind as I walked toward the front door, but when I realized Boots was prancing ahead of me, her white-tipped tail curled in the air, I had to shake my head, bewildered at why this was happening to me. Was I destined to have a ghost cat follow me everywhere from now on? I climbed four steps up to etched glass double doors. Beside each door was a

Greek-style urn with green leafy plants that seemed to be thriving even in this chilly winter. I didn't recognize the leaves, but then, I'm no gardener. The doors were beautiful, surely custom made, but why would anyone have doors where you could practically see straight into the house?

I pressed the doorbell and heard the lovely chimes ring inside. As I waited, I stared down at Boots. I wanted to ask her why she was tagging along everywhere now, but of course not only was she a cat; she wasn't even . . . *real*.

I tried the bell one more time after about twenty seconds passed with no response. Nothing again.

The glass doors were too hard to resist. I mean, if I pressed an eye between some of the beautiful etched scrolls, I might be able to see inside. I remembered Tom's visit here yesterday. Had it been to improve security? He was supposed to work with her phone and add the apps so she could watch her house while she was away. That might have involved adding more cameras. I had noticed two, mounted above to my right and left. If I pressed my face against this door, would an alarm go off?

But would that be the worst thing in the world? I asked myself. Tom would be alerted immediately by an alarm and that might be exactly what I needed.

Go for it, Jillian.

I still felt guilty about peeking inside a relative stranger's home. I glanced behind me to make sure no neighbors were watching—though they'd need binoculars since the nearest house was half a block away.

I cupped my hands on either side of my eyes and peered through a space where the glass was clear.

And immediately stepped back, whispering, "Oh my goodness. Oh no."

A hallway light must have been on because, though the living room ahead of me was unlit, I could still see

feet—feet shod in expensive-looking gray heels. The
shoes looked like the pair Penelope was wearing earlier.
I pulled my phone from my pocket and dialed Mercy PD.
A 9-1-1 call would pull resources away from the mill—
and perhaps create chaos. For all I knew, the woman
could be a diabetic and passed out from low blood sugar.
B.J. answered my call immediately.

"B.J., this is Jillian," I said, sounding as if I'd just taken
speed or something. "I'm outside Penelope Webber's
front door and it looks like she's fallen, maybe hurt herself, could be unconscious—I don't know. Can you call
for paramedics?"

"Sure. The address?"

After I gave it to him, he said, "I'm dispatching to
them right now on the computer. Is there any sign of foul
play? Broken windows or locks or—never mind. I'll send
someone, but if the door's not open—you tried the door,
right?"

"No. Should I?" I truly didn't want to. I had a bad feeling about this and so did Boots. She was crouched where
the double doors met, seemingly sniffing the air coming
from inside the house for clues.

"Maybe you can help her," B.J. said. "Everyone is so
tied up with all that business at the mill. Just try the door.
I'll stay on the line."

Thinking how Candace would handle this, I said, "I'm
putting you on speaker." After I did, I set the phone on
the concrete porch, pulled my leather gloves from my
jacket pocket and put them on. If there was even a hint
of foul play, Candace would expect me to not leave my
fingerprints. I pressed down on the curving latch-style
handle and the door cracked open. "It's open, B.J. I'm
going in," I said as I picked up my phone.

"Paramedics are a few minutes out," he answered.
"Tell me what's wrong with her so I can relay any information to them on their computer."

Boots hurried in ahead of me and made a beeline for Penelope Webber. I took a more cautious approach, my heart thumping against my ribs.

"Ms. Webber," I called to the prone figure. Her upper body was blocked from view by a white leather sectional sofa. "Are you okay?"

Dumb question, I thought. Nothing was okay about any of this. Not her on the floor. Not me being inside her house. Not a ghost cat rushing to Penelope Webber's side.

"Jillian?" B.J.'s voice came out of my phone and startled me. "Can you tell what's wrong with her?"

I was staring down at Penelope Webber, lying in the murky room. Staring at the blood blossoming like a giant red poppy on her white blouse. Staring at the splatters of blood marring the white leather sofa. A large pool of almost-black blood beneath her neck had soaked into a white looped carpet.

"Everything's wrong, B.J.," I said in a shaky voice.

"What do you mean?"

"Her eyes are wide open. And there's blood. So much blood." My voice seemed as if it belonged to someone else. But the words were mine. This was indeed real and so horrible. "I can't help her. No one can."

The sound of a siren jarred me and at the same time brought a sense of relief. Even though this poor woman was dead, she would be taken care of by the paramedics and then by others trained to deal with violent death.

B.J. said, "Get out of the house, Jillian. Don't disturb anything."

"Yes. I'm leaving this instant," I said.

But before I left, I noticed a familiar object lying on that spattered carpet.

It was an old, and probably very sharp, heddle hook, the kind they would have used at the mill. And it was covered in blood.

Eighteen

When paramedics Marcy and Jake arrived, I quickly told them what I'd found and then they rushed inside the house. Unlike me, they flicked on lights and I stood on the now-illuminated porch for a few seconds. But I was so cold. So chilled, inside and out. I went to my van and got behind the wheel, started the engine and hoped the heater would warm up faster than it usually did.

I still had my gloves on but had to pull one off to tap the cat cam icon on my phone. I needed to see my friends at home. Needed to see peace and beauty and familiarity—and erase the images in my head of poor Penelope Webber. My cats still slept and I wanted to hold one, feel soft fur against my cheek. That was when I felt the pressure on my lap, the warmth I so needed right now. Boots was a mind reader, too, it would seem. Her presence was not as comforting as one of my own fur friends, but it was enough for now.

It took only another minute before Marcy and Jake came out of the house. They looked stoic and Jake was talking on the phone. As Marcy took her unneeded emergency bag to the ambulance parked behind my van, she passed my window and shook her head when our eyes met. We shared a look of despair. There was nothing to be done to help here. Nothing.

I waited for the interview I knew would come after the police arrived. And oh dear—after Lydia showed up. She wouldn't be shut out of *this* case.

Candace and Morris drove up fifteen minutes later. They didn't come with sirens blaring, but they did draw their weapons before entering the house. I'd not thought about a killer still hiding in the house or anywhere nearby. I had no clue why I hadn't considered this except that my mind didn't work like a cop's. I didn't believe danger lurked around every corner. Jake and Marcy hadn't come rushing out of the house, so maybe they'd checked for intruders.

Candace came out of the house after a few minutes and walked over to my van. I rolled down the window.

"Sorry we took so long getting here," she said. "Had to get help from the sheriff's department to take over guarding the mill. Given half a chance, I believe all those gawkers would have stormed that place for a look at what we were doing. You'd have thought we had King Tut hidden in there."

Her joke was meant to soothe me. Candace could read me well and probably knew I was hanging on to my composure like a baby clings to a precious piece of an old blanket. I forced a smile. "It's an awful scene in there."

She gave a curt nod. "Tell me everything, from the minute you arrived." She had her little notebook ready.

I explained what happened, about calling B.J. and walking inside, and then said, "But that heddle hook creeped me out. Do you think someone took that from the mill?"

"Heddle hook? Is that the funny-looking tool with the wooden handle next to the body?" she said.

"Yes," I said. "Weavers use them for threading or even to reach in and grab loose threads on the looms. That one I saw is a long version—for a large loom."

"I thought it was some kind of weird ice pick with a hook on the end," she said. "Thanks. You've just given us our first lead."

She went to her patrol car then and grabbed her evidence kit. She paused at the front door and put paper booties over her shoes and disappeared inside the house.

I couldn't leave. The ambulance had pulled out and was parked on the street, but now the Mercy PD patrol car blocked me in.

That realization—that I couldn't drive away—made panic take hold of me. *No. No. I have to get away from here.* I picked up my phone and called Tom.

"Please. Can you come and get me?" I said when he answered.

"Sure, but you sound like you can't catch your breath. What's wrong?"

I explained in a brief and halting dialogue what had happened and ended with, "I can't sit here thinking about what I just saw. *I can't.*"

"Take a deep breath. Take twelve of them. I'm on my way," he said.

He made it to Penelope Webber's house before Lydia arrived, thank goodness. As we drove away from the murder scene in Tom's Prius, we passed my stepdaughter, Kara, speeding toward the Webber house. This was the second time today we'd passed and exchanged brief waves. She'd obviously heard about the murder, which meant that perhaps the crowd at the mill would soon shift its focus to this once-quiet street.

I called Candace as we drove to my house and she answered with a tense, "Yes?"

I told her Tom had picked me up and if she had more questions, we'd be at my place.

She said, "Sorry I left you outside. I was still upset with B.J. for telling you to go into the house, but I can't blame him. He's still learning. He should know Marcy and Jake would have arrived within five minutes. There's just way too much going on in this little town with only a half dozen cops to handle everything. I'll be in touch."

As soon as I hung up, I thunked my head with the heel of my hand. "Turn around, Tom."

He looked over at me. "No way. I'm getting you away from that place. You look exhausted and should go home."

"I was supposed to take cat food to the mill. But it's all in my van and—"

"We'll stop and buy every bag of cat food they have at the Pig," he said.

The Pig was what the locals called the Piggly Wiggly.

I said, "But there's no one to let us inside the mill and Allison told me where I was supposed to put the food inside the feral shelters and—"

Tom rested his right hand on my knee. "It's all right, Jilly. Shawn is probably free now. I'll call him and take care of this once I get you home."

I wanted to protest—but then . . . I didn't, not really. I prided myself on being strong and independent, but right now it felt okay that Tom was taking care of what I'd forgotten to do. "Good idea," I said quietly. *Good idea, indeed.*

After we returned home, Tom phoned Shawn about the cat food problem and they worked out a solution. Then he called for a pizza delivery and I had to admit it was the best pizza I could remember eating in a long time. As soon as I'd finished my third piece, I felt my brain begin to clear. I couldn't recall the last time I'd eaten.

The cats sniffed around as we ate, but only Merlot decided to try a little bit of cheese. Chablis wanted to sleep and Syrah was, well, *preoccupied* with the invisible visitor.

As we sat on the couch enjoying the decaf Tom made,

he noticed Syrah acting as if he was stalking a bug or mouse and said, "Seen any rodents or spiders lately? Syrah sure does seem interested in that far corner."

"You know how he loves to chase anything that's invaded his territory—even creatures we can't see." And I *couldn't* see Boots right now. Odd how she seemed to appear only at certain times. But I was sure she was there, teasing Syrah. My relationship with a ghost cat, however, was a secret I still couldn't share with Tom.

Finally I felt ready to talk about finding Penelope, especially after remembering that Tom had been at her house last night on a security job.

I said, "When Penelope called you to work on changing her phone for more security options, did she seem worried?"

"I've been mulling over exactly that," he said. "She seemed . . . anxious, maybe? More like impatient than worried. Then she got a phone call and hurried me out of her house."

"Right," I said, nodding. "She showed up at the mill not long after."

He said, "I take it the system wasn't armed when you went inside? Because I would have gotten an alert—that is if I didn't screw up a connection when I was adjusting her cameras. Before she went racing off, I told her I'd be back to repair that camera. But the alarm would have still gone off had the system been armed."

"The door was open; no alarm went off. I've read enough crime novels to know that might mean she knew her attacker. And man, was that poor woman attacked."

"What exactly is this heddle hook tool that could be the murder weapon?" he said.

Rather than explain, I grabbed paper and pencil and drew a picture for Tom.

"They used these in the mills?" he said, holding the envelope I'd grabbed to draw on.

"Yes," I said. "Some weavers actually made their own. The one next to ... to Penelope was maybe seven or eight inches long. The little hook on the end can grab thread on a loom and pull it through an eye or even capture loose threads."

He stared at my crude drawing. "Looks like a thin blade. They're sharp?"

"They're usually made of galvanized steel. I just never considered that a tool used in a wonderful, peaceful craft like weaving could become a murder weapon." I shook my head, feeling renewed sadness over Penelope's death.

"Galvanized steel?" Tom said. "Wow. That'll do the job."

"I saw a couple reed hooks and heddle hooks on the floor in the mill yesterday," I said. "Maybe the killer picked it up in there."

"That could mean whoever did the murder had been inside the mill at one time or another," Tom said.

"Or the person's a weaver," I replied. "And who knows if there're tools and cones scattered on the surrounding property. Or if a former mill worker committed the murder. The mill culture and its demise left a lot of people without jobs—and a bitter taste in their mouths. Maybe Penelope's enthusiastic campaign to transform the mill stirred up bad feelings that had been lying dormant."

Tom nodded. "You might be onto something."

I checked the clock on the DVR and saw that it was closing in on ten p.m. I squeezed my eyes shut and said, "Oh no. I forgot all about Jeannie. She had her surgery today and I wanted to be there when she woke up. She's all alone, Tom. How could I have forgotten?"

"Because this has been a terrible day," he said, taking my hand. "Besides, she's probably full of pain medicine and wouldn't know you from Adam."

"I'll go first thing in the morning," I said.

"Get a good night's sleep if you can," Tom said as he rose.

I stood and he took me in his arms and kissed me good night. Then he said, "I'll pick you up at, say, eight tomorrow morning?"

"Pick me up?" I said, confused.

"You don't have a car, remember?" he answered.

"Oh. I *am* tired," I said. "Yes. Eight o'clock. And thanks for everything today."

We kissed again and he left.

Nineteen

If I thought Tom could simply drop me off at the Webber house and I'd pick up my van and be off to the hospital the next morning, I was sorely mistaken. First off, I woke after a fitful night feeling groggy. That feeling was replaced by guilt when all three of my cats refused to eat even one bite of food. They just sat and stared at me as I prepared a travel mug filled with strong coffee and rummaged in the pantry for a granola bar or two. I'd not given them the attention they deserved in the last few days and they were letting me know it.

When I heard Tom's car pull into the driveway, I hurried out the back door, but I did pause to blow the cats kisses. They didn't seem impressed. My lap and my love were needed at home and I vowed to offer both today.

We reached Penelope's house within five minutes, but my car was still blocked in by a Mercy PD patrol car—and the dent in the front confirmed it was the car Candace and Morris usually drove.

Crime scene tape sealed the elegant front doors. I recalled peering through those same doors last night and shuddered. As Tom and I got out of his car, I caught a glimpse of someone wearing a green uniform just disappearing around the back of the house.

"I think I saw Candace. She's out back," I said, hurrying up the driveway.

Tom called, "Wait. You might disturb footprints. All this crime scene tape is here for a reason."

I stopped and turned back to face him. "Sorry. I just want to get my van and leave. This place gives me the creeps."

"I understand." He yelled Candace's name through cupped hands and then smiled at me. "That ought to get her attention."

But it was Morris, not Candace, who appeared from behind the house. He marched toward us, his eyes trained on the ground.

"Hey, Morris," Tom said. "Long night?"

"Yup, and I'm betting it will be an even longer day." He stopped about four feet away, his gaze on me. "Suppose you came for your van?"

"I did. Sorry I left it here. I—I had to get away." I stared at the asphalt, the vapor from my rapid breathing like little clouds of doubt and fear visible to both these men.

"I get it," Morris said. "Didn't cause a problem."

The softness in his tone surprised me and I looked up, meeting his eyes. He seemed not just tired from what had probably been an all-night job here at this crime scene, but weary. Weary to his bones.

"Are you okay?" I asked.

"Been better," he said. "These haven't been my finest days. Chief's pissed at me, Candace is pissed and we got an old body and a fresh one. I'm thinkin' I'm gettin' too old for this."

"Mistakes were made, man," Tom said. "Cops make them sometimes."

"Our quota of mistakes should be lower than civilians' and you know it," Morris said. "At any rate, I'm gonna make this right before I retire. I let Jeannie Sloan and her daughter down with bad police work ten years ago. That ain't happenin' again. And havin' said that, I'll back my car out and let you go, Jillian."

He moved slowly, as if his joints hurt, and I wanted to tell him that I believed in him, grouchy old guy or not. But he was already behind the wheel of the patrol car. I gave Tom a quick kiss and went to my van. A few minutes later I was on my way to the county hospital.

I stopped and bought a vase of white roses in the gift shop before I made my way up to Jeannie's room. No sign of Boots this morning, so perhaps she'd decided her work was done. *I kind of miss her,* I thought as I entered Jeannie's room.

A woman in dark blue scrubs was checking Jeannie's blood pressure while another woman in turquoise scrubs stood beside her, stabbing the screen of a computer tablet.

Jeannie's eyes were closed.

"Is she all right?" I whispered.

The woman in turquoise turned to me. I read L. REED, RN on the picture ID hanging from a lanyard around her neck. "She's fine. She had her first time sitting up and it was tiring," she said. "Are you the Kay Ellen she keeps asking for?"

I walked across the room and set the roses down on the windowsill, saying, "No. I'm a friend."

The lady in dark blue—who had JODY and MEDICAL TECHNICIAN on her picture ID—smiled at me. "She'll be glad to see a friendly face. What's your name?"

"Jillian Hart. But I can come another time. She needs her rest and—"

"Please don't leave," the nurse said. "She'll heal faster with the support of friends." She then touched Jeannie's shoulder and said, "Miss Sloan, your friend Jillian has come to visit."

Slowly Jeannie's eyes opened. I saw her wince and glance down at her left side, but then she looked around and settled on me with a surprisingly bright look. "Ah. Where's Boots, then?"

The aide placed the call button close to Jeannie's hand. "Remember, Miss Sloan. You press this and one of us will come help you, okay?"

Jeannie nodded and the two women left.

"Did she come with you?" Jeannie asked, twisting to raise herself so she could see past me.

"Let me help you," I said. I showed her the controls on the bed rail and how she could raise her head up.

"This is some fancy bed, huh?" she said. "Clean sheets, too."

The idea that this woman's spirit would be buoyed by a hospital bed and clean sheets made my heart ache. "I brought you flowers. I hope you like roses." I pointed toward the window.

Jeannie smiled broadly at what she saw. "I do. And so does Boots. She might eat those petals if we let her stay on that windowsill. Thanks for bringing her."

Strange, but now I can't see the cat and Jeannie can. If Boots decided to stay here, I was sure it would help Jeannie recover more quickly. *Listen to yourself, Jillian. This ghost cat has you convinced she's real.*

"I heard you sat up," I said, dragging over a chair and placing it at her bedside.

"I did." She glanced up at her IV tubing. "The medicine they put in this here tube makes it not hurt. Okay, not hurt much."

"I'm amazed. You'll be walking before you know it," I said.

"Today, they said," she replied. "And I'll be needin' to walk if I want to get back home. That's a holy place, you know. It's my job to protect it."

"Protect what?" I asked.

"They was my Kay Ellen's bones, right?" Jeannie said. "I was sure she was there, been knowin' she went to a better place all these years. When they prove my spit matches her bones, I'll need to go back and watch over her spirit."

She'd recalled the visit from Candace and me—but she had no clue the bones would be moved. She would find out soon enough, and I wasn't about to upset her while she was fresh out of surgery, so I said, "We can figure that all out later. I was wondering about the night you fell. Do you remember what happened?"

"Them creepers again," she said. "Always sneakin' around. I used to shove the desk up against the door so they wouldn't come in where I stayed. They mean to do harm, them creepers."

"But you weren't in . . . the place you lived when we found you. You were out in the mill," I said.

She glanced at the window and smiled. "I was lookin' for silly Boots. Wasn't sure if one of the stray cats got hold of her or what. And then I heard them. The creepers. So I started to run back to my place and I fell."

"Have you ever seen the creepers?" I asked.

"Nope. Just hear 'em. They's always pulling up boards, tearing at plaster. At least that's what it sounds like they's doin'. Hard to see much of anything in that old place once they bricked up the windows."

"You remember them bricking the windows?" I said.

"I was just a kid. Mama and Daddy brought me to work with 'em and I ran errands and stuff for the workers. One day Mr. Ward Stanley himself comes and says they was gonna make the place better with nice cool air. But they took away the sunshine to do it." She shook her head. "I thought it was a sad day that we couldn't look out and see the sun and the trees."

"You worked in the mill from the time you were a

child, then?" I said, thinking she was speaking not about the Ward Stanley I'd met, but probably his father.

She nodded. "Stayed on, too. Worked there until they closed the place up. But I didn't want my Kay Ellen to be without the sunshine her whole life. She was gonna go to the kinda school they let you go after high school. She had dreams, my Kay Ellen. Big dreams."

A lump formed in my throat and I slid my fingers between the bed rails and took Jeannie's hand. "But you said you understand she's gone, right?"

"Like I said, I was knowin' that way back when, not that anyone would listen. So I had to protect her restin' place." She said this so matter-of-factly, it struck me then that this was a woman who followed a path she'd felt destined to follow, who had a child she needed to protect even in death.

No, I most certainly couldn't mention they had to move Kay Ellen's remains. Telling Jeannie about what was happening would have to wait. So I decided to get back to her life inside the mill.

"How long have you been living in that old office?" I said.

"Don't know. Long time. Once I figured out where Kay Ellen was goin' the night she disappeared, I went there. And then I knew I'd found her. Felt it—here." She tapped her chest with her free hand.

"How did you figure out where she went?" I asked.

"I found the boy. The one Kay Ellen fancied. He told me." Her lips tightened into a line and she nodded curtly. "Yup. Soon as I walked into Mr. Stanley's old office, I knew I'd found my girl."

"This boy? You didn't say anything about him to Deputy Ebeling, did you?" I asked.

"The policeman kept sayin' she ran off and I wasn't thinkin' about this boy. Besides, they wasn't about to do nothin'. I was from the village, see?"

"So you knew who this kid was?" I said, wondering why she'd never told anyone.

"When I remembered the name, I went to see him. He felt shame, that boy," Jeannie said. "Told me his mama and daddy would throw him out if they heard he liked my Kay Ellen. And he was afraid, too."

"Afraid of what?" I said.

"That Morris Ebeling would come after him. Blame it all on him," she said.

"Blame him for Kay Ellen's disappearance?" I said.

"I guess. I could see Morris Ebeling doin' that, too. He always wanted the easy answer." I heard bitterness in her voice for the first time.

"But maybe this boy *did* hurt her," I said gently.

She shook her head vehemently. "Nope. I could tell he never done nothin' to my girl. He was tore up. Broken-hearted. Just like me. I knew where my girl was. I went to the mill and was with her again. That was all I wanted."

"What's the boy's name?" I said.

She stared straight ahead. "I promised I'd never say. And I keep my word. Don't want to bring shame on the boy—and he would be shamed because one of his kind loved a mill girl."

Before I could press Jeannie further about this important piece of information, I heard cheerful hellos coming from the door. I turned and saw Pastor Mitch and Elizabeth come into the room.

Jeannie turned her face away from them, but at that instant, I saw Boots—yes, *saw her again*—jump on Jeannie's stomach. She was so surprised and so happy, the sulky attitude brought on by these new visitors disappeared. She let go of my hand and rested it on Boots's back.

The Trumans stood at the end of the bed, their smiles genuine and caring.

Jeannie looked at me. "You the one told 'em I was here?"

I nodded.

"Guess it's okay then." She lifted her eyes and took in the pastor and his wife. "We're over our troubles?"

"We are," the pastor said, his bald head gleaming under the fluorescent lights in the hospital room.

Elizabeth opened the tote bag slung over her left arm and pulled out a multicolored afghan. "Remember Cora? She made this, wants you to be comforted by her handwork."

Jeannie's eyes widened like a child at Christmas. "That's for me?"

Elizabeth spread it over Jeannie's feet. Immediately Boots scooted down to the end of the bed and curled up.

Jeannie glanced my way. "Did you see that?"

Before I even knew what I was doing, I smiled and nodded.

"See what?" Pastor Mitch said.

I could feel my cheeks burn with embarrassment. "Nothing. What else do you have there?" I said to Elizabeth, who was pulling a tin out of her bag now.

"My lemon cookies." Elizabeth walked over and set them on the small table beside the bed. "For when you're ready to eat." Then she came in close to the older woman and took Jeannie's face in her hands. "I missed you, Jeannie Sloan. The Lord has missed you in his house of prayer, too."

I stood. "I'll leave y'all to visit." I looked at Jeannie. "But I'll be back."

I left quickly after saying good-bye, a mix of emotions swelling in my chest—and thoughts about what she had told me swirling in my brain.

Who was this boy? We had to find out.

Twenty

Driving home, I received a call from Kara. She wanted me to meet her at Belle's Beans. Neither of us said anything about the events of the last two days, but I was sure that was what she wanted to talk about. I never passed on an opportunity to have coffee with Kara, and no matter what she wanted to talk about, today was no different.

When I walked into Belle's thirty minutes later and the smell of fresh-made coffee and baked goods hit me, I felt tension leave my body. Funny how the comfort of food and drink can reduce stress better than any drug. It worked almost as well as a cat on my lap.

Kara was sitting at a back corner table and when I started for the counter to order a latte, she gestured for me to come over. I saw then that she'd ordered for me. I waved at the "Belle of the Day" barista behind the counter and bypassed her. Belle Lowry, who owned the place, had every barista wear a BELLE nametag—no matter what the barista's gender. This was her special way of advertising.

After I kissed Kara on the cheek, I slid onto a stool opposite her and said, "Thanks for the coffee." I pulled off my gloves and stuffed them in my pocket. It was chilly in here—or I'd brought the chill with me—so I kept my jacket on.

"Vanilla latte for you," she said.

"Thanks. Just what I need." I gripped the tall paper cup with both hands and enjoyed the warmth.

"We've passed on the road twice in the last few days, so I thought we should sit down for a talk," she said. "This is not for publication in the *Messenger*. I'm just concerned about you. I heard you found Penelope Webber's body."

"I did. Pretty awful, I have to say." I picked up my latte and sipped the rich milk and vanilla-laced coffee. Belle used Madagascar vanilla and this made the drink a customer favorite.

"You okay after such a horrible discovery? You sure look tired," Kara said.

"Didn't sleep well after all the trouble last night," I said. "Plus I've already been to the hospital this morning."

"To the county hospital? Why?" she said.

"It's kind of a long story—one you might want to write about after the police are ready to release information. For now, it's just the two of us talking." I stared into her brown eyes—the ones so like her father's—and I saw her concern. She wouldn't print anything until she knew the time was right.

Kara glanced around the café. Since it was now late morning, the place wasn't too crowded. "Just keep your voice down while you tell me what's going on. There are plenty of ears in this town ready to share gossip with the first person they see."

"I know." I leaned on the table to get closer to her and, in a low voice, explained about Jeannie and the skeleton. I talked about everything that had gone on since the day before yesterday.

When I was finished, Kara sat back, her eyes wide. "Wow. I heard rumblings about bones in the mill. I was sure they'd find out it was some animal that died in there a long time ago. But this is the first I've heard about this Jeannie person."

"I'm glad her reappearance isn't part of the town gossip talk yet," I said. "I sure hope she's left alone once people do know."

"The murder of Penelope Webber has grabbed the spotlight," Kara said. "She was well-known, but finding any extended family has been difficult. I know because I tried so I could get a quote for the paper. I think that's sad."

"Her house is so big. I thought she at least had out-of-town family—maybe even children," I said.

"Word on the street is she never married and never had children," Kara said. "B.J. told me they're looking into a sister who might live on the West Coast but I sure couldn't find her. A stabbing is so personal—I mean you always hear that, right? The murderer in those kinds of cases is usually someone the victim knows well."

"Her door was unlocked—as though she'd let her killer in," I said. "That's another clue she knew who murdered her. Someone who was very angry, in my opinion."

"I've been covering this mill renovation story," she said, "and the two groups vying for the . . . let's call it the *prize,* don't seem to like each other too well."

"I noticed that when I met them yesterday," I said. "They sure seem to have different visions for the mill's future."

"I agree," she said. "Ward Stanley seems a little desperate—as if he wants vindication for the bankruptcy, for the loss of jobs and for the stain on the community that mill has become."

"But wouldn't you say it's more self-serving than altruistic?" I asked. "Seems to me he's trying to save face rather than save the town."

"Yup," she said. "I've been at every town council

meeting. I mean, how many jobs will a condo project create in the long run? Sure you'll have the renovators and contractors. And the bank will be happy if they can loan out mortgage money. But the urban village group will do the same and provide jobs for shop owners and museum keepers, and they plan to rent out a large common area for banquets and weddings."

I smiled. "I see which way you're leaning. But we don't get a vote. This is private money coming in. Either idea would work."

"Condos don't draw tourists," she said. "This town needs something new like the urban village, so yes, I'm hoping their investment group wins."

I took another long drink of my coffee. "Seems wrong to be talking about these projects when Penelope was the one leading the debate. Do you think her death might have been connected to these plans for Mercy's future?"

She cocked her head, her long dark hair blanketing her left shoulder. "I hadn't thought about it—hadn't had time to think about it. But there are people in this town who want everything to stay the same—that run-down mill included."

"Mill villagers or town people?" I asked.

"Hmm. Good question," Kara said. "I know next to nothing about the mill villagers and how they feel about living in the shadow of a decaying structure. If I lived there, I'd want it cleaned up. Wouldn't you?"

"I'd have to put myself in their shoes," I said. "Their neighborhood would change. More traffic, more strangers around no matter which project goes forward. Change isn't an easy thing for many folks and there would be plenty of change."

Kara rested her chin on her fist. "Would killing Penelope Webber stop the mill cleanup from going forward, though? I mean, the state's mill renovation legislation with tax breaks for places like Mercy makes it pretty darn sweet to clean up that mess across town."

I had a thought then. A dark thought. Lowering my voice to barely a whisper I said, "What if her murder is about kickbacks? What if Penelope favored one project over another? What if that made someone very, very angry?"

Kara nodded. "You know what? You could be right. My investigative journalism background could come in handy here. I sniffed out plenty of political backroom deals back when I was a reporter in Houston. I can do it again."

I felt my face drain of color. "How many of those investigations involved vicious murders? Now I wish I'd never even talked with you about this."

Kara reached across the table and gripped my forearm. "Don't worry. I can take care of myself."

"I'm betting Penelope Webber thought the same thing."

Unsettled by the determination I'd seen in Kara's eyes when we parted with a hug outside Belle's Beans, I left a message on my way home for Candace to call me. I wanted her to know about this conversation. Kara wouldn't print anything yet, but she did intend to dig a little deeper into the backgrounds of both Ward Stanley and Lucas Bartlett, something, she said, she should have done when the proposals for the mill came in anyway.

As I pulled into my driveway, I told myself Kara was compelled to investigate in her role as editor of the newspaper. That was just how she operated. But I couldn't quite convince myself her eagerness today wasn't my doing.

Three cats sat waiting for me when I walked in the back door, but I'd only managed to kneel and pet my friends before my phone rang. Not Candace. It was a number I didn't recognize.

"Hello?" I said after I connected.

"Mrs. Hart? This is Pastor Mitch. Do you have a moment?" he said.

"Sure." I tossed my empty Belle's Beans cup in the trash and walked into the living room. Chablis followed and the other two cats stayed back. Did that mean Boots had come inside with me? I so wished she would stay with Jeannie.

"Elizabeth and I talked to the doctor. We told him we're willing to take Jeannie to our home when she's ready to be released. If she agrees, this is what will happen. But the timing is much quicker than we realized. She can come home the day after tomorrow."

"But she had a big operation, didn't she? That seems so soon and—"

"I agree, but the doctor assured us in this time of high technology for a surgery like hers, three to five days is routine." His tone darkened when he said, "It would seem three days is more common when one has no insurance and no funds."

"I see. How can I help?" I stroked Chablis. She'd crawled into my lap the minute I sat down and was already purring like a diesel engine.

"Jeannie trusts you," he said. "She will need rehabilitation, although they were getting her up for a walk when we left the hospital. The doctor explained the rehab process, but perhaps you could be involved, maybe to simply hold her hand, motivate her a little. Is that possible?"

"Absolutely possible," I said.

We talked more about the rehab center where she would go a few days a week, the walker he'd learned Jeannie would need and how best to help her through what would probably be the biggest shock—that she could not return to the mill.

I had just hung up from my call when I heard the slamming of car doors in my driveway. Seconds later I was leading Lydia and Candace into my living room. The assistant coroner's arrival sent poor Chablis racing for my bedroom. Merlot and Syrah hadn't come around me since I'd come home. They were obviously preoccupied—and I feared I knew why.

Lydia wore a fringed purple suede jacket and dark pink jeans. At least today her hair was tamed by barrettes. I could tell by Candace's demeanor she was none too happy to be accompanying Lydia here.

"So *you* found the body, huh?" Lydia said as she plopped down on my sofa. "Let's chat about that discovery and exactly why you were over at Penelope Webber's house in the first place."

An exasperated Candace said, "I've told you twice already I sent her there. What is it about—"

Lydia held up a commanding hand. "My job as an assistant coroner in the state of South Carolina and Mercy County is to investigate suspicious deaths. Not with hearsay. With direct knowledge. You got that, Candace?"

Candace rolled her eyes. "Got it." She looked at me. "Tea, anyone?"

"Not for me. This is not a social call," Lydia said.

I'd never name any visit from Lydia a *social call*, but I wasn't about to say it aloud.

"I'm having tea. Jillian?" Candace raised her eyebrows at me.

"Not right now, but you go ahead," I said. As Candace walked into the kitchen, I sat on the chair opposite Lydia. "What do you need to know?"

"Time of day you found the body, how you got in that house and why in heaven's name you *did* go inside, for starters." She pulled her small tape recorder as well as a notebook from her oversize satchel-slash-purse—the one with a zebra print.

After she turned on the recorder, I again related the events of last night, trying to be as detailed as possible so Lydia would leave quickly.

When I was done talking, she said, "This murder weapon. Exactly how is it that you knew it was—" She flipped through notebook pages. "Ah, here it is. How did you know it was a heddle hook when no one else did?"

"Because my background is in fiber arts," I said.

"Who in the heck has a *background* in fiber arts?" she said. "And what does that mean, anyway?"

Candace came into the room, carrying a glass of sweet tea. "It means, unlike you, this woman has a master's degree in stuff you couldn't begin to understand. You do know what a master's degree is, right?"

I withheld the smile that almost betrayed how grateful I was for Candace's presence.

"You can be quiet, Deputy Carson," Lydia said. "This is my part of this murder investigation and I don't need any attitude from you."

Candace waved a hand. "Go on then. Ask what you came to ask."

Lydia refocused on me. "You said B. J. Henderson told you to walk into that house. Is that right?"

I nodded.

"Please say yes or no for the tape," she said curtly.

"Yes," I replied.

"Do you always do what an inexperienced dispatcher— who's not even a police officer—tells you to do?" she said.

"If Penelope needed help, like CPR, I felt I had to go inside. I made the ultimate decision, not B.J." Just then I caught sight of Syrah slinking around the side of the couch, Lydia in his sights.

"How sweet of you to protect Henderson," she said. "Both of you could have seriously compromised this investigation. You do realize that?"

"Maybe I shouldn't have gone in—but what if she'd still been alive?" I said.

I saw a look of triumph on Lydia's face then. "You admit you were wrong? That evidence could have been destroyed?"

"But it wasn't," Candace said. She had remained standing over by the picture window that allowed a breathtaking view of Mercy Lake. Candace may have been hoping the lake view would calm her, but from the sound of her voice, it hadn't worked.

"Lucky for both of you that Jillian didn't walk through blood or move anything," Lydia said. "Especially since you, Deputy Carson, were so consumed by some fancy professor and a pile of bones that it took you fifteen minutes to respond to the scene. That's going in my report, by the way."

Candace took a step toward Lydia, her fury showing in every tense muscle all the way up to her forehead. "That *pile of bones* happens to be the remains of a sixteen-year-old girl. Maybe I'll call up the coroner and tell him what you just called Kay Ellen Sloan."

Lydia smiled and wrote something in her notebook. "Ah, so that's the other victim's name. Thank you, Deputy Carson. I'll be leaving now."

She stood and walked toward the foyer, but not before Syrah managed to pounce on her boot and wrap himself around her lower leg. I hurried over to grab him before he bit her—which he was quite capable of doing.

"You've got to do something about that stupid cat," Lydia said before rushing out the door.

I set Syrah down and he bounded off in the direction of the kitchen.

Candace dropped into one of my easy chairs and threw her head back. "Why do I let her get to me?" She looked at me then as I took the spot Lydia had vacated.

"I gave her Kay Ellen's name and now she'll be all up in our business."

"Lydia gets to me, too. She would have found out eventually anyway," I said.

"You were cool as a cucumber, but then you didn't have her riding your bumper all the way over here," Candace said. "I swear she was ready to run me off the road. Didn't want me coming here while she interviewed you. But now I'm sure she's glad I came."

"Let it go. You'll be concerned about more important things after I tell you what Jeannie said." I related what had happened during my hospital visit and how Jeannie had confirmed there was a boyfriend—and that this boyfriend wasn't a mill villager. But this kid apparently knew Kay Ellen was headed for the mill the night she disappeared.

Candace set down her empty tea glass on the end table next to the chair. "This is important information, but several questions come to mind. Why didn't Jeannie tell anyone years ago? Why would that girl head out to a mill that had just been stripped of equipment and fenced up? And last of all, did Morris know anything about this?"

"You answer those questions and I'll bet your cold case heats right up," I said.

.

Twenty-one

Candace's blue eyes had been bright with excitement when she left my house. We'd decided to meet at the Main Street Diner for supper at about five o'clock. She had paperwork to finish because of last night's murder, plus more folks to interview in Penelope's neighborhood—though she said Morris had been busy as a beaver canvassing the area. He'd been *unusually* quiet, she'd said, but busy.

Needing distraction from the terrible events of the last few days, I decided Jeannie needed a quilt to welcome her back to the pastorium. Made with love and with focus, quilts healed those in need. I decided to pour myself into this project. The quilting would have to be all machine done, however, since she was being released from the hospital so quickly. I do prefer hand quilting, but I was certain Jeannie wouldn't mind.

Three cats followed me to my quilt room and soon, as I was choosing fabrics from my stash, I learned Boots was indeed here, too. She sat and watched as I picked out pastels—soft roses and pinks, pale greens and a tender brown. A log cabin seemed perfect since I could cut and piece that pattern in my sleep. I only stopped working for a quick lunch and soon all the blocks were ready to be sewn together. My three cats—or four if you counted the one who did *not* belong to me—slept through the afternoon, content that I was where they knew I belonged. Tomorrow I would hunt through my collection of larger yardage fabrics for a floral backing. I was sure I could have the quilt done by the time Jeannie was released.

I'd just finished sewing the twin-size quilt top together when I realized it was time to meet Candace at the restaurant. I quickly washed up and changed and was halfway to the Main Street Diner when Tom called.

"Sorry I didn't phone you earlier. Been tied up all day with new security system orders. A murder does make people scared for their lives," he said.

"What are you doing for supper?" I asked.

"I was about to ask you the same question," he replied.

I told him I was meeting Candace and he said he'd see us there in a few minutes.

The Main Street Diner is a 1950s-style place with wooden booths, a long chrome counter and red leather stools. Candace had already arrived and I was surprised to see that Morris was with her, sitting across from her in the last booth on the right.

The smell of grilled burgers, onions and French fries awakened my stomach. It seemed like ages since I'd gulped down cottage cheese and pineapple for lunch. I slid into the booth next to Morris, remembering the look on his face the last time I'd seen him. He'd needed a friend then, and it looked as if he and Candace might have mended fences. He actually offered me one of his begrudging and rare smiles.

"I invited Tom. He should be here—" I turned and saw he'd just come in the door. I waved to him.

When he joined us, he helped me take off my jacket and hung both our coats on an old-fashioned rack by the hall that led to the restrooms.

He and Morris shook hands and I reclaimed my spot

while Tom sat next to Candace. Tom immediately put his foot next to mine and I smiled at him.

Once we'd all ordered and had iced teas in front of us, Candace said, "Morris and I finally had a chance to sit and talk about the cold case as well as the fresh one."

"Mistakes were made ten years ago," Morris said. "Can't take 'em back, but I can work my darnedest to right the wrongs."

"I've learned today that Jeannie might have put up a roadblock herself," I said. I explained how Jeannie was protecting the name of her daughter's boyfriend.

I glanced at Morris and saw his shoulders slump. "A boyfriend? Jeez. I shoulda known those high school kids I talked to didn't tell me everything."

"My question is," Candace said when I'd finished talking, "how do we get her to give up the name?"

"She's pretty darn stubborn, that one," Morris said. "But I hear she's liking you, Miss Jillian. Think you could work on her?"

Morris, who had complained of my involvement in police investigations in the past, was actually asking for my help. Miracles never ceased. After a sip of my tea, I said, "I tried talking to Jeannie today—without any luck. I know the ring they found with the skeleton pretty much confirms the victim is Kay Ellen, but do you have the DNA results yet?"

"No. But we'll have them day after tomorrow," Candace said. "Still, I don't think there's much doubt."

"I'm still scratchin' my head wondering what that girl was doin' at the mill," Morris said. "Who knows? Maybe she died elsewhere and her body was hidden there by this mysterious boyfriend."

"Maybe you're right," Candace said. "We certainly don't have a way to know if the mill was the crime scene. And she sure as heck didn't die in that fireplace, so her body was moved at least once."

"Maybe we could ask Belle about Kay Ellen?" I said. I was thinking how Belle loved to gossip, and she'd been in town long enough to know the girl when she was growing up.

"Like right after we finish eating?" Tom said. "I already had thoughts of heading across the street for coffee when we're done."

"It's worth a try," Candace said as she and Morris nodded in unison.

"She'd just opened up right before the mill closed," Morris said. "And that woman has a memory like an elephant." His cheeks reddened and he pointed at Candace. "But don't you go tellin' her I mentioned her in the same sentence with elephants or I'm in for big trouble."

We all laughed and the sound warmed me. Deep down, Morris was a good man. Lazy at times, yes, but his heart was in the right place. Maybe this case that was now coming back to haunt him would make him a better cop in the long run. But the word *haunt* reminded me I had a secret, one I didn't want to think about right now. Thank goodness our food arrived and I could put thoughts of a ghost cat aside. I needed to concentrate on a Texas chili dog with sweet onions—the Main Street Diner's specialty.

When the four of us walked in, we found Belle's Beans humming with activity—and music. Belle had apparently added a "live mike" night. A young man with bicolor hair, wearing an NC State T-shirt and plenty of earrings, was playing acoustic guitar in the far corner.

I liked the idea, but Morris wasn't pleased.

He said, "Great. Belle moves out three tables for a hippie."

"Hippie?" Candace said. "There are no more hippies. Besides, sounds to me like the guy can play."

"Whatever," Morris grumbled.

Tom pointed to the left. "Jillian, you and Candace grab that table where those folks are just leaving. Morris and I will get the coffee and ask if Belle is around."

Low tables filled the center of the café, but the table Tom directed us to was one of the tall ones along the wall with barstool seats. Candace and I hung our jackets on the stool backs and settled in. A few seconds later, Belle Lowry appeared and put one arm around each of us.

"Glad to see y'all—including them." She nodded at the counter where Tom and Morris stood giving our order. "Heard you wanted to talk to me."

"I'm so glad you're around tonight," Candace said.

"First night for Wesley's gig and would you listen to this old woman using a word like *gig*? But that's what it is." She offered a smile made crooked by her coral lipstick. Belle obviously never looked in the mirror when she applied it since the color always ran below her lips, above her lips or too far past the end of her lips.

"He's good. Where'd you find him?" I asked.

"He's my nephew," she said. "The boy's takin' a break from school to see if he can make it doin' what he loves. I'm glad to help."

Tom came up behind Belle carrying a cardboard tray filled with steaming cups of coffee. She moved aside so he and Morris could sit down.

"My Belle of the Day says you got some questions," she said. "Think I'll drag a stool over and—"

Tom got up, saying, "I'll find one. You wait here."

Belle squeezed my arm. "He is such a kind man. You snagged a good one, Jillian."

When we were all seated again, Morris spoke first. "Belle, we was wonderin' if you recall that girl who went missin' from the mill village about ten years ago."

Belle's eyes widened and she tucked short strands of silver-white hair behind one ear. "Is she the skeleton in the mill?"

Nothing gets past you, Belle, I thought.

"Where'd you hear that?" Candace said, sounding exasperated.

"Does it matter? Everyone's speculating about all the activity over there and when that university professor came in here for coffee, I asked her why she was in town and what's her profession. She does love her bones." Belle smiled, a twinkle in her eye.

"Can you keep that under wraps?" Candace said. "We're still investigating."

She said, "Why, of course I'll keep my mouth zipped about the skeleton. Besides, most folks in here are talking more about Penelope Webber than the mill. Horrible thing to happen to that woman. Hard to get a feel for her and now it's too late."

Morris said, "For right now, we're wonderin' about Kay Ellen Sloan. Do you remember her?"

Belle shook her head. "Dropped the ball on that one, huh, Morris? Feeling a little guilty?"

Through tight lips he repeated, "Do you remember her?"

I shifted uncomfortably and Tom pressed his leg against mine and patted my knee. I could almost hear him say, *Relax, Jillian. This is Belle and Morris we're dealing with. They'll work it out.*

"I do remember the child, Morris. I remember her comin' in here a couple times. Didn't even know she was a mill child until after she disappeared and her mama started coming around asking questions. She loved that girl. I've wondered all these years if Jeannie Sloan went and took her own life out of pure grief and that's why we've not seen her in town for so very long."

She didn't know about Jeannie, I thought. I glanced at Candace and saw relief in her eyes.

"Kay Ellen came in here?" Candace said. "Was she alone?"

Belle's eyes narrowed. "You're taking me back in time here. Give me a minute."

We waited while Belle squinted as she glanced around the room. "I had smaller tables back when I first opened. They were cheaper than these." She rapped her knuckles on our table. "It got pretty dark in here late afternoon but ... I do recall Kay Ellen sitting over there, where Wesley is right now."

"Alone?" Morris asked.

"Hmm ... I don't think so." Her gaze swept over us and she smiled. "She was with a boy. Their knees touched under that table and I could tell they fancied each other."

"Do you know this boy's name?" I asked.

"Seems I did at the time," Belle said, squinting again, as if looking back in time. "Thought they were an odd couple. Mill girl and town boy. I just can't remember, maybe 'cause Kay Ellen grabbed all my attention. Sweet girl. Polite."

"How many times did you see them?" Morris asked.

"Twice at the most," she said. "They could have come in here when I wasn't around, though. But the Belles of the Day I had back then are all long gone, so it's no use looking to ask any of them."

"Great," Morris said. "I guess at least we've confirmed this boyfriend."

"Belle," Candace said, leaning toward her to ask a question Morris should have asked all those years ago. "Was it just the two of them?"

"Oh no," she said with a laugh. "A bunch of young folks from the high school have been coming in here ever since we first opened. I always wonder if their folks know they're trading their Pepsis and Cokes for lattes and iced sweet coffee."

"So these two were with a group?" Tom asked. He'd finished his coffee while the rest of us had been too caught up in the conversation to touch ours.

"Well, each table back then could only seat two. But I could tell they all seemed to know one another." She closed her eyes this time while she thought, and when they opened, she pointed at Morris. "The Franklin twins were here at the same time. Rachael Franklin got married and I believe she's living in Woodcrest. Talk to her. She's got a young mind and might actually remember something useful."

Twenty-two

Morris and Candace left Belle's Beans a few minutes after we were done talking to Belle. Morris said he had to be up early tomorrow to finish reports so he could then hunt down Rachael Franklin. Candace looked plain exhausted and wanted to get home to play with her cat, whom she felt she'd sorely neglected the last few days. I couldn't argue with that since I felt exactly the same way.

Tom bought us two more decaf lattes and we enjoyed the music. Belle's nephew seemed to be quite talented and sang a few original songs before taking a break. That was when we were joined by a surprise visitor—Lucas Bartlett.

"May I join you?" he asked as he stood by our table.

"Sure," Tom said, seeming a bit confused.

"This is Lucas Bartlett—one of the investors hoping to purchase the mill," I said.

"Tom Stewart." The two shook hands and Tom added, "I thought you looked familiar, but you're not from Mercy, are you?"

"No. I'm from New England." He slid onto the stool Morris had vacated. "Mrs. Hart here is the only truly familiar face I saw in here. The rest of the men working with me have left for their homes. Being interrogated by the police in a murder investigation has sent them looking for the comfort of their families while this whole situation is sorted out."

"Yet you stayed," I said.

"I live alone," he said quickly. "Besides, it's all very . . . *interesting*. And I do want to be here if we can move forward with the mill decision—no disrespect to Penelope intended. I understand the town may need to grieve the loss of its councilwoman first."

"What brought you to the South for a mill renovation?" Tom asked. "I mean, how did you even find out about it in the first place?"

"I'm familiar with mills," Lucas said. "Though my investments have never been real estate connected, I wanted to expand my horizons."

"The earlier textile mills in this country were located in New England," I said, "so I suppose you have seen your share."

"No renovations left to be done up North," Bartlett said. "At least with the money I pulled together. Real estate is more expensive up there. But here—well, it's a gold mine in North and South Carolina if you want to take on a big project—and I do."

"You sound pretty excited," Tom said, smiling. "Just so you know, neither Jillian nor I have any sway with the town council."

"Oh, I know," he said. "Mrs. Hart here—"

"Call me Jillian," I said.

"Good. First names all around," he said. "Anyway, I understand that you, Jillian, are a bit of an expert on textile mills. At least that's what your friend Deputy Carson tells me."

"I hope you're learning about more than just this one citizen." Tom put a protective arm around me. *My goodness, he might be jealous,* I thought. *Does he really think I'd be interested in this stranger?*

"I've learned way more than I want to about Ward

Stanley and his bunch," Lucas said. "Jillian here was the first truly friendly person I've talked to."

"Thanks." I smiled. "But you know, I detect a bit of a drawl—and I know they don't drawl in New England. Where are your roots, Lucas?"

"All over," he said. "I was an army brat. Unfortunately, my parents passed away not long after I finished college and I decided to stay right near the university I graduated from."

"Let me guess," Tom said. "Harvard?"

In the dim light of the café it was hard to tell for sure, but I believed Lucas Bartlett blushed. "Yes. Class of 1987."

"Smart one, here, Jillian," Tom said with a hint of admiration.

But getting to know Lucas Bartlett would have to wait because from the corner of my eye I saw Ward Stanley making a beeline for our table.

"They don't get a vote, Bartlett," Ward said.

"Hey, Ward, how are you?" Tom said.

Not taking his eyes off Lucas, Ward said, "Jillian. Tom. Evenin'."

"I'm merely making friends in town, Stanley," Lucas said. "Hustling votes is more *your* style."

"What's that supposed to mean?" Ward said.

The contrast between the two men couldn't have been more pronounced. Now that he'd told us about where he was from, I couldn't believe I hadn't noticed Lucas's Ivy League roots before—his smart haircut, tailored gray wool coat, articulate and confident manner. It was obvious to me—as obvious as the fact that Ward had come on hard times. His well-worn jacket with the missing button and what seemed like permanent worry lines on his forehead spoke volumes.

Lucas Bartlett's tone was cold when he said, "What it means is I think you're projecting your own behavior on to me, Ward. My proposal to the council will do the talking. I don't need to hang around council people and beg."

The pleasant evening had turned tense in an instant. Lucas must have read my discomfort because he stood. "I don't want to upset the lady. Do you even notice your poor manners have bothered her, Ward? No. You wouldn't." He turned to Tom and me and bowed slightly. "Hope to see you again."

He left, understandably not bothering to say goodbye to Ward.

"I apologize," Ward said. "I didn't intend to barge in and spoil your conversation."

"We appreciate your apology, Ward. Will you join us?" I said. The man did seem troubled.

"Things not going quite the way you planned?" Tom asked, apparently not agreeing that he was ready to accept Ward's apology.

"I sure didn't expect a murder to interrupt the town's business. Sad thing, that." He sat.

I noticed a small tear in his jacket to go with the missing button. He needed a new coat. But more than that, he needed that mill project and a fresh start. I'd heard his wife had left him—went to California with the children.

"Murder is bad business for everyone," Tom said.

"Word is you're the one who found her—Penelope," Ward said to me. "I'm sorry. Heard it was a terrible scene."

"Yes. Um, how's your mother doing?" I said, wanting to change the subject. "I used to see her in the quilt shop occasionally, but not lately."

"She went through chemo for breast cancer. But she's doing better now," he said, forcing a smile.

"I am so sorry. I had no idea. Can I call on her?" I said.

"That's kind of you," he said, "but she wouldn't want you to see her in her present circumstances. She's a proud woman and after we lost the house . . . well, big house to tiny place. It's been tough to handle."

I couldn't seem to offer anything to brighten the mood.

"The insurance business keeping you busy?" Tom asked. Obviously he wanted to find some area of small talk that didn't go down a sad or lonely road.

"Yes. Busy. Listen, I've got to be heading home. Sorry to have butted in." He took off, hurrying to the door.

I said, "Whew. Talk about awkward."

"That's what happens when family money is lost," Tom said. "But from what Ed told me, that's not the only problems with the Stanley family. It went way back."

"Tell me about it," I said. Between our two visitors, I'd hardly touched my second coffee and now took a long sip.

He said, "Ward's daddy, also Ward, was the one who closed the place. Thing was, he hung on as long as he could even after everyone was fired."

"Bet the upkeep was outrageously expensive. That place is mammoth," I said.

"Yup," he said. "The elder Mr. Stanley finally sold off the equipment to India and China and then came the tax foreclosure. He was in the middle of a messy divorce during all this and then he had a stroke. Died six months later, before the divorce was final. That left Ward and his mother with a worthless, giant piece of property that the whole town considered the Stanleys' problem—and their doing. The guy doesn't have many friends."

"How sad," I said. "But you know, even though my first impression was of a morose man, his anger is palpable. And as we saw with Bartlett, also at times quite visible."

"With his personality, I'm wondering how he got anyone to put up funds to buy back the mill." Tom drained his cup.

"I guess he must have a little salesman in him," I said. "When you're raised in a privileged way, you can still act as if you are privileged. And from what I know of the mill culture, the owners ruled liked kings at one time. Unions and legislation snatched some of their power, but reputations like the owners had last for generations."

He said, "From the way mill villagers avoid this town, I'd say you're right."

"Ready to head home?" I said.

"If you stop at my place, we might get a few minutes to visit with Finn. Want to follow me home?"

"Why, yes, I do," I said with a smile. Finn was one of my favorite people.

Tom's stepson, Finn, was indeed home and I swore he'd grown six inches since moving in with Tom. Nineteen and fresh-faced, he was happier than I'd ever seen him. It felt good to hug him and sit down to get caught up. Yoshi, Finn's rat terrier, jumped into my arms when we arrived and we snuggled a bit. The dog had stayed with me last fall and I adored him.

I learned Finn was applying to Duke, UNC and Clemson for the next fall semester. He hoped to major in pre-med and I had no doubt he'd be accepted by all three, considering how bright he was. Then the topic turned to the events in Mercy.

"People are even talking at the community college about the murder," Finn said. "You both knew this lady?"

Tom and I sat on the worn sofa opposite Finn. He'd brought a dining room chair into the small living room.

Tom said, "Jillian knew her better than I did. I assume you heard she found the body."

Finn's eyes grew wide. "Are you kidding me? How rough is that?"

"Pretty rough." I swallowed, reminded of Penelope's dead eyes staring up at nothing.

"Why'd she get killed?" Finn said.

Tom smiled. "Good question. Sure you don't want to go into law enforcement, Son?"

"No way," Finn answered. "But when someone dies like that, seems that's the first question, right? Why this person? Oh, and also, why *now*?"

I nodded slowly. "So much has happened lately, and happened so quickly, I never took time to think about why Penelope needed to die. But that's apparently the decision the murderer made. But we can't blame Penelope. That's wrong."

"I'm not saying that at all," Finn said, looking inquisitive and interested. "That would be buying into the crazy Just World theory—that people get what they deserve. It *is* wrong. But what about Ms. Webber's relationship to a . . . a *social group* like the town council. Did that contribute to her death?"

"Whoa," Tom said. "This is beginning to sound like a college lecture. As a former cop, I can tell you I always looked at the victim first—as the center of the problem. Whom did he or she know, what events happened prior to death, what was he or she planning that might have meant the person needed to be silenced? Was it an argument right then? Spontaneous, in other words? Or was there a buildup of emotion before the crime? Because I can say with certainty, murder involves intense emotion."

Finn said, "Unless you're dealing with a serial killer—a psychopath. I understand they lack emotion and—"

"Okay, genius," Tom said. "You do know that serial killers represent a tiny percentage of all murderers, right? Most of the time the killer is a regular person in a very irregular moment in his or her life."

Finn smiled. "Yes. That makes sense."

"What happened to Penelope that day?" I said. "I mean, right before it happened?" I'd been listening, thinking about what brought her to that awful moment when she found herself confronted by a killer.

"When we know that, we'll know who killed her," Tom said. "Candace can sometimes get caught up in the details, in the physical evidence. Don't get me wrong; I believe she's a great cop, but she adores you, Jillian. Maybe tomorrow you should ask the question we've been wondering about tonight. *What happened right before Penelope died?*"

Twenty-three

For the first time since I'd walked into the Lorraine Stanley Textile Mill several days ago, I slept well. All the cats joined me, taking their spots on the kitty quilts at the foot of my bed. Right before I nodded off, I thought I saw Boots sitting there, too—watching them. My three amigos might trade off on who slept on which quilt, but they would never share one with a ghost cat.

That was why, as I made my morning coffee, I had this harebrained idea that Boots needed a kitty quilt of her own. I could take it along to the pastorium with the quilt for Jeannie. She would be thrilled, of course. Boots would have a spot of her own. And I would have confirmed to myself and at least one other person that I believed in ghosts. Silly? Yes.

But I did it. I made the kitty quilt. It was after lunch when I finished the pink and green log cabin quilt for Jeannie—and the matching eighteen-inch square one for Boots. All explanations to anyone but Jeannie would have to be avoided. I would say I had extra fabric and made the quilt to encourage Jeannie to get a new cat.

During the time I'd spent sewing the bindings on by hand, I'd thought about our conversation with Finn last night. What we'd said about Penelope could also be applied to Kay Ellen's death. What took her to the mill that night? Who was this boyfriend and did he have reason to murder her? These questions probably haunted Morris now that he knew how wrong he'd been ten years ago and I felt renewed compassion for him.

Jeannie held the key. She had the boy's name and since I had formed a bond with her, I might be able to help her understand the importance of sharing this information. I knew there wasn't anyone in a better position to try. I could imagine what Candace would say to her. *Don't you want your daughter's killer brought to justice?* Knowing Jeannie, that would mean someone would have to explain to her about the murder—explain that someone choked the life out of her beloved daughter. I knew those details would only make Jeannie withdraw. Did she really need to hear about such a horrible thing? No. She *never* needed to hear them. There had to be another way. And if Candace would leave this to me, I believed I knew how to get Jeannie to give up that boy's name.

With the quilts finished, I put them in a box and wrapped them in flowery paper with a fancy ribbon. I wondered how many times Jeannie had received a gift wrapped up just for her. I knew she would be happy.

As if she could read my mind, Boots appeared and sat by the gift box on the dining room table and inspected it. She cocked her head, then pawed at the ribbon. But of course the ribbon didn't move. *Because this cat isn't real, Jillian.*

I was wondering if she'd ever be only Jeannie's imaginary cat again when I heard Candace's familiar knock on my back door.

I hurried to answer, glad a real presence would be joining me.

Once Candace came in, she made a beeline for the fridge. I'd made tea this morning, so there was a fresh pitcher in there. She sighed contentedly as she poured us both a glass and then sat at my counter bar that separated the kitchen from the dining room table.

"Pretty gift," she said, nodding back at the box.

I slid onto the stool beside her. "I made a quilt for Jeannie. Did I tell you she'll be staying with Pastor Mitch and his wife when she's released from the hospital tomorrow?"

"If you did, I've forgotten," she said. "Too wrapped up in the new case. But I did remember this." She took a picture out of her uniform shirt pocket and slid it to me.

"What is it?" I asked.

"I know Jeannie wants her stuff back—the items we took from that mill office. I mean, she obviously had made the place her home. We haven't had time to go through everything yet and have to hang on to most of it, but when I saw what was written on the back of this photo, I decided she needed to have this now."

The black-and-white photo had turned sepia with age and was wrinkled and worn. Three men ranging in ages from maybe thirty to fifty mugged for the camera, their arms draped over one another's shoulders. They were standing at the mill entrance and, from their clothing, I'd guess the picture was taken in the 1960s. They looked as if they worked in the mill. I turned the picture over. Written in a shaky, childish print was the word "Daddy."

"Don't know which one is Jeannie's dad, but I'm assuming one of these guys," Candace said. "The picture looks like it's been handled a lot. She might be missing this."

"You're right," I said, staring again at the men's faces. For some reason two of them looked familiar. One had Jeannie's eyes, so I was betting the man on the far right was her father, but the other familiar one . . . the guy in the middle. There was something about him.

Candace said, "Might need that in her hand when we tell her that the skeleton definitely belongs to her daughter. We just got the results. Lab did a rush on the DNA, thanks to the professor's influence."

"Yes," I said quietly. "She'll need this close, I think."

"You visiting her today?" she asked.

"No," I said. "I thought I'd be there at the pastorium tomorrow when Pastor Mitch arrives with her. He texted me from the hospital earlier that she'll be back in the mill village late morning, but that today was filled with rehab and instructions and learning how to use the walker she'll have for a few weeks."

"A *minister* texted you?" Candace said, smiling. "Seems weird, but I guess if you're in the people business like he is, you've got to keep up with the new toys."

"I use technology and I'm not that much younger than Pastor Mitch," I said.

Candace's fair skin went pink. "I know. I know. It's just that my mother thinks her cell phone is the most frustrating object ever thrust upon her. Guess everyone in her generation isn't technologically challenged."

"Glad you get we old people still know how to learn new tricks," I said with a laugh. But then I grew serious. "Listen, do you think Penelope's death is connected to the mill?"

"The timing would sure indicate that," Candace said. "Especially since Penelope Webber seems to have been one lonely woman. Her phone contact list included town council members, the investors, Dustin with the puppy dog eyes, her hairdresser and a few take-out restaurants."

"Must be hard to get to know a victim with so little to work with," I said.

"You're telling me?" Candace said. "We're checking the GPS in her car to see where she might have been aside from the mill and city hall in the last few days. She did have an address book, but all the people in there are out-of-towners. We tracked down her sister and I talked to her this morning after the chief relayed the news. They were estranged, hadn't spoken in years. We don't know if she's even going to show up and claim the body once the autopsy is complete."

"Sounds like you're trying to get to know Penelope as the person she was before she was a victim," I said.

"Have to, because all I saw was a pushy lady who seemed to have a lot of money—which she didn't by the way," Candace said once she'd drained her tea glass. "She was living on credit. She'd had several jobs in the past, her last being that small boutique that went belly-up last year. I'm still hoping to learn more about her, but it's hard finding anyone who knew much about the woman."

I smiled inwardly. Maybe Tom had more to learn about how good a cop Candace really was. I said, "I kind of wish I'd tried harder to get past Penelope's tough façade. She always seemed so in control, and so . . . cold."

"People like that are in protection mode," Candace said. "Something bad happened to that lady long before we ever knew her. You don't push people away like she did unless you feel as if you have to."

I nodded my agreement. "Controlling people *are* defensive. Who knows what Penelope Webber's story was? But I have every confidence that you'll find out."

I fixed Candace a sandwich when I heard her stomach grumble. Apparently she'd been so wrapped up in trying to solve two murders, she'd failed to eat. I'm no cook, but I can slap turkey, lettuce and mayo between two slices of bread. She took off, sandwich in hand.

I put the photo in a small envelope to protect it and then began cleaning up the quilt room. I was just about finished when the doorbell rang. Lydia was the only person I knew who usually called at the front door, so my stomach tightened as I went to answer. Three cats and a ghost followed on my heels.

I was surprised to see Dustin Gray standing on my

front stoop. I welcomed him in, hung his jacket in the hall closet and offered him coffee or sweet tea.

"I would love a hot drink. It's cold out there today—almost New York cold, which I didn't expect in South Carolina." He had his computer tablet with him and clung to it with both hands. "Hope I'm not bothering you, but I'm in limbo, waiting to be allowed back in the mill."

While I made a fresh pot, he petted each cat—except the one he couldn't see, of course—and I watched how tender he was with them. He was a gentle young man. Why couldn't Candace fall for someone like him? I mean, Billy Cranor, the volunteer fireman she pined after, was still dating girls fresh out of high school. Didn't she want a more mature guy like this one?

We sat in the living room with our coffee—he liked lots of sugar—and he commented again on the beautiful lake view and how he'd like to live in a place like Mercy one day.

"Bet you wouldn't find much work here, though," I said.

"Greenville is booming, so I'm in the right spot," he said. "But it wouldn't be such a horrible commute if I lived here."

"Especially if a certain young woman were waiting for you to come home," I said.

His cheeks went fire red. "Do you think I have a chance?"

"I have no idea," I said. "You need to know Candace is extremely dedicated to her job. She works long hours and once she has a case—and right now she has two—she hardly sleeps."

"I like that about her. She's so focused, but she also . . . has those *eyes*. So blue. And she's smart."

I smiled. "You stick with it, Dustin. You know where she lives and works." I looked at the small silver tablet on the sofa next to him and nodded at it. "Did you want to show me something?"

"I've been holed up here—they don't have another job for me at the firm since I'm new—so I decided to take what I'd learned about the mill and create images of the two proposals." He cleared his throat. "I'd love to have your input since you know so much about old mills. I didn't want to lose the flavor, you know. The history shouldn't be lost."

I moved close to his side. "Show me."

The renderings he'd done were amazing. I didn't own a tablet like this myself—I had enough trouble with my smartphone—but as I looked at the images he'd created, I immediately wondered if I could design quilts on one of these.

"These first plans are examples of what condos would look like. I call it the 'Lofts at the Mill' project." He started sweeping his finger on the screen.

I saw page after page of loft-style apartments with exposed brick, beamed ceilings contrasted by furniture he'd put into the apartments that was sleek and modern. The pictures he'd created were so detailed I could see myself standing in one of the condos, knowing I was still in the mill but in the *new* mill.

Astonished by his talent, I said, "Is this part of your job?"

He said, "Not really—but I hope it will be one day. Combining my knowledge of structure with design. My boss knows what I want to do and that's why he chose me for this project."

"This is exciting stuff, Dustin," I said. "You are so talented."

"Um, thanks." He refocused on the screen. "The other proposal I call the 'Heritage Project.'"

This creation took my breath away. I could imagine

the bare bones of that first floor of the mill, but Dustin had transformed it into a museum with glass cases down the center and shops with eclectic facades to the right and left.

I said, "You'd have displays of pictures and tools in these cases, right?"

"Yes," he said. "There's room in the offices for more ways to show off some of the old machinery, perhaps give a timeline of the creation of the mills and then their demise—so people will know what happened across the South. How these behemoth buildings grew and then decayed into giant rubble piles."

"Wow," I said, sweeping my finger along the tablet surface to look at all the images and pictures he'd used. "Being inside that mill seems to have inspired you. It kind of did that for me, too. I made a quilt for Jeannie in the last few days—just got so busy after realizing how creating with our hands is what we were meant to do. Even if we tear down what we've built, we need to honor what was there. Your designs do that."

"That's the nicest thing anyone's ever said to me." He looked at me for the first time since he'd shown me what he'd created. "You think this will make a good presentation?"

"Absolutely," I said. "Trouble is, you may have made a tough decision even tougher for the town council. How will they choose?"

"I have some ideas about that," he answered. "But I think I'll work on my presentation more before I say anything. I know Ms. Webber was leaning toward the condo project, but—"

"She was?" I said, surprised. "How do you know?"

"Well, maybe I shouldn't say," he said haltingly. "I mean, she is dead and someone else will take her place. I'm not sure it matters."

"It might matter to Candace," I said. "She's scrambling right now to figure out why someone wanted Penelope dead."

"Oh. I never thought about that," he said. "Here's the deal."

He went on to tell me and the minute he finished, I said, "You need to talk to Candace. Come on. I'll take you to the police station."

Twenty-four

I called Candace to make sure she was at the station before we left my house. Dustin followed me into the center of town.

As we walked up the steps of the courthouse, he said, "This is a cool old building. I've wanted to see inside this place."

The courthouse lobby was indeed beautiful and Dustin stopped to take in the mosaic tile floor, the beautiful oak-paneled walls and the domed ceiling.

"This is so amazing," he said. "The structure will last forever. Very sound. There were some great architects back then."

I could tell Dustin might stand here in the lobby for hours, so I tugged his elbow. "Come on."

The police offices were situated at the back of the courthouse. Dustin's expression changed from awe to surprise when we made the turn down the corridor and headed to where Candace worked.

"Um, this corridor could use a renovation," he said. "I mean, the lobby is beautiful, that one courtroom I peeked into had all the oak and walnut well preserved, but this? This is awful. And it smells bad."

We'd reached the benches where people waited to talk to an officer or folks arrived to make bail for a

friend or loved one spending time in the basement jail.
A few of Mercy's less-than-finest citizens slouched on
the seats along the wall.

"Not quite Mayberry in this part of the building," I
said.

"Huh?" he replied.

The reference to the *Andy Griffith Show* was lost on
him. Too young. I pushed open the scarred door with
frosted glass and MERCY POLICE DEPARTMENT stenciled on
in green paint.

B.J. sat at his desk to our left. "Hey, Mrs. Hart," he
said. "She's waiting for you in the break room."

After I introduced Dustin and B.J., I pushed open
the gate separating the waiting area from the corridor
that led to the interview rooms and police offices. Dustin
followed me to the end of the hallway and we found
Candace sitting at the round table in the center of the
room. Candace scrambled to her feet when we came in
and she wiped cheese cracker crumbs from her mouth
with a paper towel. She tossed the cracker cellophane
and paper towel into the trash, saying, "Hey, Jillian.
Dustin. Chief Baca's not here, so we can use his office.
I need a comfortable chair about now. Besides, my
cubbyhole around the corner isn't big enough for three
people."

She was right. When I visited Candace here, we either
talked in the break room or in the chief's office.

After we went across the hall, Candace eased into
Mike's leather desk chair with a sigh. We took the two
armchairs across from her, Mike's big shiny desk separating us.

"What's all this about Penelope Webber?" she said,
staring at Dustin.

His return gaze was accompanied by a rather slack-
jawed, awestruck look. "It's nothing really. Just some
things she said."

"For context," I said, "I think you should see what Dustin has done on his tablet for his presentation to the town council. What he thinks can be done with the mill."

"Okay," Candace said, sounding skeptical.

But after she looked at what I had seen in the last hour, I saw a new respect for Dustin Gray in her eyes. "This is really something. I mean, you think this could happen in our town?"

"Certainly," he said. "I mean, the investors will have their own architects and designers, but I took the existing space, saw what I thought it could structurally support and came up with these ideas."

Candace was staring at the pictures, swiping through them for a third time. "They're *great* ideas." She looked at him. "I'm impressed."

"Tell her about Penelope—about some of the things she said when you shared your ideas with her," I said.

Dustin leaned back, eyes narrowed in thought. "I want to be as accurate as I can. See, I met with her in Greenville when I was first assigned the project last month."

"Oh," I said. "You didn't mention that part."

"I remembered on the drive over here. I guess it's an accumulation of what she said that I was thinking about when I talked to you, Jillian." He looked at Candace. "But in your job, I'll bet you want everything to be very specific. Which is sort of like my job, too." He smiled.

"You met with her in Greenville last month," Candace said. "What happened?"

"She had drawings, the old blueprints of the mill, pages and pages compiled by the investors for their very different proposals," he said. "She kept saying this had to be all very *above board*. I thought at the time, well, yeah, it does. Why wouldn't it be?"

"That was a strange thing for her to say. Go on," Candace said.

"That was the first time she mentioned she was a Realtor," he said.

"What?" Candace said. "No, she's not. Or rather, she wasn't."

Dustin blushed. "Maybe she wasn't, then. Maybe she wasn't telling me the truth."

Candace shook her head and said, "Sorry. I didn't mean to cut you off. It's just that I haven't finished looking into her background. But as far as I know, she was never a Realtor in Mercy."

"Oh," Dustin said. "She seemed pretty proud of it, so I thought she was a Realtor currently. Anyway, when I came here to Mercy and we talked, she started telling me how much the economy needed a boost through residential real estate. This was a conversation we had when I thought we were just making small talk. Not about the mill. Then she said it again later. I *still* didn't put it together. Not until I told Jillian."

Candace leaned back hard, her eyes on the ceiling, "Oh my goodness. I missed something somewhere. Seriously missed something."

"What are you talking about?" I said.

"You can't just decide to become a Realtor one day. Either it's in your past or you're working on it. If she was involved in real estate investment of any kind—even if she wasn't a certified Realtor—that would be a serious conflict of interest. She was the head councilwoman. She could influence others to vote the way she wanted them to. For the *condo* project, if residential real estate was her interest." Candace looked at us, her gaze steely.

I said, "That's what I thought. Choosing the condos would put money in her pocket down the road. But she could have been lying to Dustin."

"What do you mean?" Dustin said, sounding upset by the suggestion.

"What if she wasn't ever involved in real estate before?" I said. "What if she got big ideas when the proposals came in and how they could benefit her? Luxury apartments could mean big commissions, whereas a museum and urban village wouldn't exactly help someone trying to cash in right away. From what I understand, the commercial shops of the museum project would only come down the road—well after the museum was set up."

"You're right," Candace said, pointing at me. "As far as Ms. Webber becoming a simple real estate agent, rather than, say, a Realtor, you can learn that stuff online—how to buy and sell property. Eventually maybe learn enough to actually do it or find out what classes to take and where. If she was looking into a new career, I need the forensics report on her computer *yesterday*." She grabbed the phone on the chief's desk but then set it down. "Sorry. I'm getting ahead of myself." She reached behind her and grabbed paper from Mike Baca's computer printer, then took a pencil from the penholder to her right.

"Dustin, I want you to tell me every word Penelope Webber ever said to you."

After Candace finished writing down Dustin's conversations with Penelope, she made the call to the county crime lab asking them to get her any information they'd uncovered on the woman's computer as quickly as possible. She thanked Dustin and gave him her card with her cell number, telling him to call her if he remembered anything else.

Dustin and I walked out together into what was turning out to be a surprisingly sunny, warm day and I swear he couldn't have stopped smiling if he'd tried. When we reached our cars, he told me he had to make a trip to the office in Greenville, but he would be back. He still had work to do inside the mill. What he'd shown Candace and me on his tablet was just the beginning.

Before I left, I decided to check my cat cam. I saw Chablis asleep on the sofa in her favorite spot. But I'd tuned in just in time to watch a major cat chase. Since Syrah never chased Merlot, I knew Boots was involved. What could I do about this ghost cat in my life? And why did she need to stay around me?

I'd set the phone down on the front passenger seat and was about to put the van in reverse when a face appeared in my side window. Startled, I blinked, but then I let out a sigh and pressed my hand to still my heart. I rolled the window down. "Hi, Morris. You scared me."

Puffy pillows of fatigue under both eyes told me the man was exhausted.

"Hey, there," he said. "What are you up to?"

I told him about Dustin's information concerning Penelope.

He paused, looking thoughtful. "We should be taking a sharp look at those museum investors, then. Can't find out much about one Mr. Lucas Bartlett, that's for sure. But I did find Rachael Franklin. Married name is Pickens. Anyway, she didn't want me comin' to her house. Said she'd come to me."

"This is the young woman who might know the name of Kay Ellen's boyfriend?" I said. "She's meeting you here?"

"Not exactly," he said. "Thought I'd take a page out of Candace's book. She can get folks to talk by makin' them feel comfortable. As you may know, I have no friends—human or otherwise—because I'm not good at that stuff. Ask my ex-wife. She'll tell you."

Morris had been married once? Who would have thought? "How do you plan to make her feel comfortable?" I said.

"I hadn't quite thought it through, but she is meeting me at Belle's. Guess I'll buy her coffee," he said. "Take it from there."

Why was he telling me this? And why was he lingering? Then I understood. "Do you need help, Morris?"

His features relaxed and he almost smiled. "I do. I screwed up Kay Ellen's case and I want to make it right, but I'm beginning to see what others see—a cranky, impatient old man. But you could give me a few pointers, seein' as how you're the nicest person I know."

The Grinch's heart really can grow a few sizes, I thought. "When's this meeting?"

"In twenty minutes," he said. "Thought I'd change into street clothes. Less intimidating, don't you think?"

I smiled. "Good idea. You sure you want me to go with you?"

His shoulders slumped with relief. "Would you? I've seen you help Candace with interviews before. I mean, it's not like this is some criminal I'm dealin' with. But I do need help getting her to remember stuff from ten years ago."

I grinned. "I'll meet you over there—and I cannot wait to see you in street clothes. That will be a first." He ambled off in the direction of the courthouse, his pace more labored than I'd noticed before. Change was a difficult thing—and for a curmudgeon like Morris, probably especially difficult.

But this wasn't just about him. I glanced at my phone, the screen still lit, and suddenly had the answer to the questions I'd asked myself a few minutes earlier. This cat spirit, this charming little cat, wanted to make sure I attended to Jeannie's business and that I followed every clue to bring peace to the poor woman. Maybe running into Morris in this parking lot had nothing to do with chance at all. If I hadn't stopped to check the cats, and paused to watch them chase Boots, I would have left before Morris arrived. I would have missed him.

Belle's Beans was just a few blocks down Main Street and I found a parking spot right in front. I checked the time on my phone—fifteen minutes to four—and as I walked into Belle's and paid for a decaf skim latte, I glanced again at my cat cam. I shivered when I saw little Boots staring straight at the camera on top of the entertainment center.

"Decaf skim latte," called the Belle of the Day, whose real name was Joanne.

"Thanks, Jo," I said, sliding the phone into my pocket.

The café had only a few customers and I sat at one of the center back tables with four chairs. One of Colbie Caillat's cheerful songs played through the overhead speakers and the music, coupled with late-afternoon sun shining in through the big window, gave me a sense of calm and purpose.

I removed my jacket and hung it over the back of the lacquered chair. I was taking the first sip of my latte when a young woman walked in and glanced around. I'd never seen her before, so I assumed she'd moved to Woodcrest before I came to Mercy several years ago.

I got up, hurried over to her and said, "Are you Rachael?"

She seemed surprised and more than a little wary. "Who are you?"

"I'm Morris Ebeling's friend," I said with a smile. "He's on his way, but I came to make sure to buy you a coffee."

"No coffee," she said, laying a hand on the baby bump I hadn't noticed.

"They have wonderful green tea here—or hot chocolate," I said.

She glanced at Joanne, who was waiting patiently at the cash register. "Um, green tea, no sugar," she finally said.

I pointed to the table where my coffee sat. "Have a seat and I'll bring your drink."

When I joined her and placed her tea in front of her

a minute later, she seemed more nervous than wary. "He said he'd be here."

"He will. I'm Jillian, by the way. When's your baby due?"

"Four months." She smiled and laid her hand on her belly again.

"Your first?" I asked after I'd taken a sip of coffee.

She nodded. "Only the doctor knows if it's a boy or a girl. We want to be surprised."

"You used to live in Mercy, I understand." *Might as well jump right in,* I thought.

"Yes," she said. "This is about that girl who disappeared. I tried to tell the policeman I didn't know any girls from the mill village and didn't want any police coming around my house. But Deputy Ebeling wouldn't take no for an answer. When he said we could meet here . . . well . . . it brought back memories." She glanced around. "The place is so different now. Mrs. Lowry's kept up with the times."

"She has plenty of energy," I said. "But . . . did you say you didn't know any girls from the village?"

Rachael rested her hand on her throat and averted her eyes. "Doesn't mean I didn't see the girl in the hall at the high school. But I don't remember her except what people said afterward. That she ran away."

I was so focused on Rachael's body language and so convinced she was lying, I didn't see Morris until he was standing right behind Rachael.

He slid a wallet-size picture in front of her. "Got this from the Mercy High School yearbook. Recognize her now?"

The young woman hardly looked at the picture. She pushed it away as Morris took the chair next to her. "I was just telling Jillian I knew *of* her. I take it you're the policeman?"

Morris had tried his best to look less intimidating. He

wore a plaid wool shirt and had slicked his gray hair back. But even so, his whole demeanor screamed "cop."

"Yes, ma'am," he said. "Thanks for meeting us here, Mrs. Pickens."

"I couldn't have you come to the house." She turned to me. "See, I live next door to my mother-in-law. She'd ask questions, believe I was in trouble, dream up a dozen ways to Sunday to imply to Rick that I'd done something wrong."

"Rick is your husband?" I said.

"Yes," she replied. "He's a banker. His reputation in Woodcrest has to remain pristine. You do understand?" She glanced back and forth between Morris and me.

Morris nodded, trying to smile. It just wasn't working. He didn't like pretentious people and Rachael had shown her hand.

"I most certainly understand," I said quickly, knowing I needed to intervene—especially since I'd already caught Rachael in one lie Morris hadn't been around to hear. She knew Kay Ellen. Belle said the group of teenagers had been together the day she saw them here. I tried to sound understanding when I said, "Hanging around with a mill village girl wouldn't have been too cool back then—and I don't mean that as a criticism. It's just how things were, right?"

She smiled, and seemed relieved. "It's not like we were snobs. Kay Ellen was a nice person and—" She flushed from her neck to her forehead. "I mean, I *heard* she was a nice person."

Morris rolled his eyes. "What else did you *hear*?"

"Nothing. Absolutely nothing." She stared at the teacup clutched between both hands.

I reached out and laid my hand on her wrist. In a soft voice I said, "You didn't do anything wrong, Rachael. No one has to know you had a friend from the mill village. But Kay Ellen has been missing for ten years. Her mother deserves to know what happened to her girl. If your child, heaven forbid, ever went missing, you'd want to know."

She seemed to be thinking about this. Finally her eyes met mine and she whispered, "Her boyfriend's name was Earl Whitehouse. His parents never knew about Kay Ellen. You can't tell him I was the one who told. Please?"

"Judge Whitehouse's kid?" Morris said, not bothering to keep *his* voice down.

"Quiet," Rachael said harshly, glancing around, apparently to see if any heads had turned at the mention of the judge's name.

I could tell by the set of his jaw Morris couldn't care less who'd heard. "No one at the high school ever mentioned Kay Ellen Sloan hung around with the likes of you or the judge's son when I did interviews there."

Still keeping her voice low, Rachael said, "You only talked to a few kids and the principal and the counselor. How would they know anything? Kay Ellen was fun, she was pretty—but she was still from the village. We couldn't have our parents know we included her in things. What would they say?"

What indeed? I thought. Before Morris could chastise Rachael and make her shut down—and I could tell by the look on his face he was in chastise mode—I said, "This young man, Earl. Do you keep in touch?"

"No way," she said. "But he didn't do anything wrong. He was crying when she didn't turn up. Crying real tears."

Real tears? I had the feeling Rachael Pickens was familiar with tears of the unreal variety—and that made me sad for her and for her unborn child.

She went on, saying, "I left Mercy when I went to college and never came back. My parents retired and moved to Arizona. But since Rick and I were in love and he had a great offer at the bank in Woodcrest, we moved. He's very successful—and that's why you can't say anything about this to him. I can't be involved with the police." She looked at her watch. "He'll be home soon. I have to leave."

"Wait," I said as she stood, grabbed her purse and started for the door.

But Morris said, "Let her go. It's Earl Whitehouse I need to talk to. And I'll be wearing my uniform this time."

Twenty-five

Morris thanked me profusely before I took off for home. The gloom-and-doom face he'd been wearing of late disappeared. I almost kissed him on the cheek, but I feared it would have been too much for him. He now had a lead on a cold case he believed he'd botched. I felt lucky I'd been able to help, but not lucky I'd met Rachael Franklin Pickens. People like her I could do without, although I did have to give her credit for showing up at Belle's and giving up Earl Whitehouse's name.

As I pulled into my driveway, I wondered if this young man—a man who must be in his late twenties now—had murdered Kay Ellen. Perhaps his *real tears* when news of Kay Ellen's disappearance spread through the high school, not to mention the tears he shed when he'd talked to Jeannie, were *guilty* tears. Maybe a spat between young lovers had turned ugly. I hoped Morris now had the key to unearthing the truth.

It was already dark and my motion sensor lights at the back door welcomed me home as did my cats. We'd spent the day quilting and I guessed they wanted me back at the sewing machine where they could keep track of me. Cats do like to keep track of the people they own, after all. But it was not to be. No sooner had I finished my Stouffer's microwave dinner than Tom called. He said we needed to pay someone a visit and felt I could be his sidekick on this job. Could I be ready in five minutes?

"Ready for what?" I said. "I'm in my usual blue jeans and a sweatshirt."

"You're ready. I'll pick you up," he said and hung up.

He liked a little intrigue and he'd for sure pulled me right in. It wasn't until I was sitting next to him in his Prius that he told me what had been going on in *his* life today. He'd been very busy.

"What's this about?" I said.

"We're headed to the mill village," he said. "See, I had a call from Mike Baca this morning. With two big cases and not enough officers, he offered me contract PI work. This is an identity check. I *love* this kind of case. Only took me about six hours to figure it out and I'll get a nice paycheck from the town of Mercy. I told Mike I'd take money only if I discovered things important to the investigation about this person's background."

The dash lights revealed his smile and I could tell he was pleased. Tom not only installed security systems; he'd been doing investigative work ever since he'd left the police force in North Carolina. Most of the time in his current job, he followed people and took pictures for divorce cases. Pretty boring, he always told me. But this case, whatever it was, couldn't possibly be boring. Not with the way he was grinning.

"So what's the deal?" I said.

"You'll see. And you'll be surprised—if I'm right, that is."

A few of the mill village brick bungalows showed signs of life inside. Bright yellow seeped around closed blinds, porch lights were on, but many of the houses were dark. Were they empty? Foreclosed on? It made me sad to see this place at night, a once-vibrant community so desolate.

The house we parked in front of did have an amber

bug light casting a faint glow on the driveway and carport, and though the curtains were drawn on the two small front windows, lights shined inside. Someone lived here.

"Come on, Tom. Tell me what you're up to," I said.

"Nope," he said. "There's a slim chance I'm wrong and in front of the woman I love, well, I'll want to save face."

As we walked to the front door, I noticed a car in the carport—a Lexus SUV. A *Lexus*? Unfortunately, a vehicle like that seemed out of place in this neighborhood. I said, "You don't have to save face with me, Tom. Come on. Tell me who lives here."

"A woman named Wanda Burgess. There. Is it all clear now?" he said with a sly smile.

"You know it's clear as mud." We'd reached the door and I punched his arm playfully. "Tom, tell me."

"You'll understand in a minute." He knocked on the door. A nice knock, a polite knock.

The door cracked almost at once and a woman who looked to be in her late sixties peered at us through thick glasses. "Can I help you?"

"You can, Mrs. Burgess. We want to talk to your son," Tom said. "I believe he's staying here while he's in town."

"You must be mistaken," the woman said unconvincingly.

A male voice came from inside, saying, "Don't lie for me, Mom. Let him in."

She turned away from us. "Are you sure?"

"He knows. I've been waiting for someone to figure it out," the man said.

She opened the door and we stepped inside.

Lucas Bartlett stood in his mother's tiny living room.

Twenty-six

After Lucas Bartlett introduced us to his mother, Mrs. Burgess offered us coffee and I readily accepted. She hurried into the kitchen just off the living room. We'd walked into her home under strange circumstances and I knew she felt uncomfortable. If it were me, I'd want to make coffee, bake a cake, work on a quilt—anything besides talk.

"Have a seat," Bartlett said to Tom. He waved a hand at a red chintz love seat that had seen better days, while he sat in an old swivel rocker circa 1970.

The arms of the love seat were threadbare, but I had to say, it was a surprisingly comfy sofa.

Bartlett said, "Not the quality of furniture you're used to, I'm sure. She won't let me change anything in this house. Or buy her a new home in town. My mom believes she belongs here, where she's spent all her life."

"I think this is a lovely home, so I don't blame her," I said, glancing around the living room. The furnishings may have been old, but the tidy room felt welcoming. One wall was filled with photographs and I was drawn to a larger version of the picture Candace had given me to return to Jeannie. I pointed at it. "Who's that in the picture?"

Bartlett turned to look. "My father and two of his friends. Why do you ask?"

Ah. That's why the man standing next to the person I believed to be Jeannie's father had looked familiar. Lucas Bartlett had his dad's jaw, the same-shaped face. But since Jeannie's story hadn't made its way into the grapevine yet, I couldn't share what I knew, so I said, "Just wondering. It's a great picture."

Bartlett's jaw tightened. "One of the few my mother has of my dad."

"That's why you want to buy the mill, right?" Tom said. "Because of your father?"

Bartlett folded his arms. "How'd you find out about me?" he said, avoiding the question.

"The police have me on contract," Tom said. "I sometimes do investigative work for them—especially when Mercy's small force is struggling with two tough cases. It wasn't difficult to figure out you had two identities. You've been planning this for a while, from what I could tell."

"You said *two* cases," Bartlett said. "You mean Penelope's murder and those old bones they found?"

"Yes," Tom said. "But I came here about you. You have a score to settle, I get that, but why—"

"Wait a minute," I said. "What score?"

Just then, Mrs. Burgess came into the room carrying a tray with coffee cups, sugar and cream. She set it on the maple coffee table in front of Tom and me. "He's thinkin' he has to finish old business. Mill business," she said. "I hope y'all like the darker beans. That's what we drink."

I smiled at her. "My favorite." I took one of the pretty porcelain cups—probably her best china—and carefully added sugar and cream.

Tom did the same, the little cup looking fragile in his large hand.

I glanced between Bartlett and his mother. "What old business?"

"You didn't tell her?" Bartlett said to Tom.

"Haven't even told the cops yet," Tom said. "Thought I should give you the chance to come clean on your own. They won't be happy you came here using a fake name — but the rest of it? The success you've had, the fortune you've earned? That's all true and you should be proud."

"Who'd have thought a kid from the mill village would ever go to an Ivy League school?" he said with a sardonic laugh. "And I'm sure you've learned, I went to Yale, not Harvard, as I told Jillian."

Tom nodded. "You made a name for yourself there — one you couldn't cover up. What I want to know before I talk to the police is why you had to create this fake identity. Why *not* be proud of your accomplishments?"

Lucas Bartlett's laser stare and his angry downturned lips made my stomach clench. Wanting to ease the tension, I said, "Is Lucas your real name? Or should we be calling you something else?"

Mrs. Burgess said, "He's Landon. Landon Burgess — just like his daddy." She'd dragged in a kitchen chair and was sitting next to her son. She turned to him and said, "I want the same answers Mr. Stewart does. I'm proud of you, Son. I just don't get why you're not proud of yourself."

Lucas — or rather *Landon* — sighed heavily. "It'll all come out now. I could have pulled it off, convinced the council to accept my proposal, but now everyone is under a microscope. The fact that you've uncovered the truth before I could seal the mill deal will ruin everything."

"You're the stranger in town," Tom said. "Or at least they thought so. They hired me to do routine background checks on the strangers. If it makes you feel any better, I looked into the other man new in town, Dustin Gray. He's young and doesn't lie, so his life is an open book. You were the tough one to figure out. You set up this Lucas Bartlett guise five years ago, but you couldn't hide all your business dealings as Landon Burgess. And Landon Burgess's roots led right to Mercy. You've been planning this a long time, man."

Landon said, "As soon as South Carolina passed the mill renovation legislation, I knew what I needed to do. But I couldn't do it as Landon Burgess."

"Why not?" I asked.

He decided to take the coffee left on the tray, but I noted the cup rattled a little in his hands.

After he sat back down, he said, "I'm from the mill village—born in this very house. Do you think for one minute any proposal I offered would be accepted?"

"Why not?" Tom said. "Your money is just as green as the next person's."

"You don't get it," he said tersely.

"I get it," I said softly. "And you could be right. I don't claim to know all the council members. The few I do know wouldn't care about where you came from, but the others? Their prejudices might not allow them to ever vote for your proposal."

Tom looked surprised. "It's that bad, huh?"

"I've discovered that town people and village folks do not socialize much in Mercy," I said. "The mill culture was paternalistic, and that way of life creates prejudice that lasts for generations."

"She's right." Landon gestured as if tipping a hat. "Kudos to you for your knowledge and understanding."

His words still held a bite. His anger was deep, but I sensed there was more to this story. I said, "So did you work in the mill as a child beside your father? I know the labor laws weren't supposed to allow it, but children still went into the mills, didn't they?"

"My dad wouldn't allow it, even when I asked to go with him. He said it wasn't safe for kids. And he was right. It wasn't safe for anyone." He picked up his coffee cup, his hand still shaking, his gaze averted. "Lung disease from inhaling cotton fibers, toxic dyes seeping into the water. Why do you think all these mills are in ruin across the South? It costs megabucks to clean them up, to transform them into useful properties again."

Mrs. Burgess cleared her throat. "My son wouldn't want me to talk about this, but my husband died in the mill. Fell off a scaffold."

"Fell off a scaffold as the piece of junk was *collapsing*," Landon said. He closed his eyes, then turned toward the window to his right to avoid my surprised look.

"I am so sorry," I said to Landon and to his mother. "That's terrible."

"Changing lightbulbs, he was. Such a simple thing," Mrs. Burgess said. "Coulda happened to anyone."

"If I'd been there, it *wouldn't* have happened. I wouldn't have let him climb up there." Landon's anger was palpable—almost as if another person were with us in the room.

"You blamed yourself," Tom said. "But you were how old? Five?"

"You know everything about me, don't you, Mr. Private Investigator?" Landon said. "Yeah. I was five."

Tom said, "And you were sent away to live with a cousin, then?" I could tell Tom felt uncomfortable and wanted to move past the emotional pain of these two people.

"Got a chance to send him up North, but I sure missed him somethin' awful," Mrs. Burgess said, shaking her head. I saw tears glistening in her eyes despite the strong lenses she wore.

"Did you send him to this cousin because there was no money? I mean, the mill didn't give you a settlement or anything?" I asked.

"They gave me five thousand dollars," she said.

"That's all?" I was unable to hide my shock.

"Seemed like a lotta money at the time," she said.

"They paid off my mortgage, too. But see, my cousin was smart—smarter than me. I knew he could make that money work for my son—so Landon could go to good schools, get away from this here place."

"While *you* stayed," Tom said. "To care for your parents, I understand. They were mill workers, too?"

"They was. But my daddy had the shakes—that Parkinson thing." She turned to Landon. "They needed me bad, Son."

His features softened. "I've told you a million times not to feel guilty. You did what you had to do after the mill killed Dad. It's not your fault."

Tom said, "One of us—you or me—has to give the police this information. I don't know if it will alter their investigation, but dishonesty won't go over well with the cops. I was a cop once, so I know."

"I'm a liar, so I'm probably guilty of murder. Is that it?" The edgy tone was back.

"You're not giving Mercy PD much credit. They won't jump to conclusions that you're a killer without evidence," Tom said.

But I was thinking about what I'd learned. Had Landon Burgess discovered what I knew and what Candace knew as well? That Penelope wanted the condo proposal to win the vote? I wondered if Tom or I could be there when Landon told Candace and Mike Baca about the fake identity—because it would indeed be best if he was the one to reveal the secret.

I guessed I wanted to be in on the interview because I was worried how that conversation would go. Beneath Landon's seething façade, I saw hurt in this man's eyes, the hurt of a deeply wounded soul. He would probably be as defensive and as angry as he was tonight. I wanted to protect him—protect him from himself. I understood him.

Landon's anger—the anger he couldn't hide—might

make Mike and Candace believe this man stabbed Penelope Webber to death. I didn't want him to land in prison because his plans for the mill, his plans to right what he felt was a grievous wrong, made him seem like a man willing to kill to get what he wanted.

But then, perhaps that was exactly what had happened.

Twenty-seven

The next morning, Syrah watched as I hurriedly vacu-
umed. He felt the vacuum cleaner was a beast to be
observed and perhaps eventually conquered, whereas
Merlot and Chablis retreated under beds or hid behind
bookshelves. They wanted nothing to do with the horrible machine. But Boots joined Syrah in the vacuum
watch and it seemed these two had come to accept each
other.

I fervently hoped that Boots would join Jeannie at the
pastorium when she was released from the hospital
today—but how did I catch a ghost cat and force her into
a carrier? Containing a living, breathing feline in a carrier was difficult enough.

*That won't be happening, Jillian. This little kitty has the
run of the world. She goes where she wants, when she
wants.*

As I pushed the vacuum around with vigor, I thought
about last night. Landon Burgess had asked Tom for
time this morning to first tell his investor group the truth.
Apparently they didn't know who he really was, either.
He then promised he would go to Mercy PD and talk to
Candace. Tom offered to go with him and Landon had
accepted. This surprised me, but then, Landon Burgess
was full of surprises.

After I put the vacuum away, Syrah sat outside the closed closet door, his tail swishing with irritation. Another lost chance to attack the beast. Merlot and Chablis cautiously reappeared in the living room, glancing around, ready to hide again if need be. My jaw dropped when I saw Chablis walk right through Boots to get to her favorite spot on the sofa. I closed my eyes, wishing Boots would be gone when I opened them, but she was still sitting in the same spot on the Oriental carpet and now she and Merlot were nose to nose.

Time for me to get out of here, I decided. This ghost cat business, though fascinating and at times comforting, certainly did unnerve me. Besides, Elizabeth Truman told me to come to the pastorium around eleven to greet Jeannie when the pastor brought her there—and the time had come.

Soon, with a travel mug of sweet tea in the cup holder, and the gift I'd made for Jeannie on the seat beside me, I was on my way. I decided to drive by the mill and was relieved to see the place appeared deserted except for a lone patrol car parked near the high fence. I surmised hunting for evidence in such a large building took several days and an officer was inside still searching for anything old enough to be tied to Kay Ellen's murder.

I drove around the corner and parked on the street. Elizabeth greeted me outside. She'd been pulling weeds that had sprouted beneath the shrubs that lined the path leading to the pastorium. Apparently weeds didn't mind the winter weather.

She smiled warmly and said, "Good to see you, Jillian. Now I can give up this task and we can have a nice cup of coffee while we wait for Jeannie's arrival. Come on, then."

She walked ahead of me but turned back and said, "What do you have there?"

"Just something I made for Jeannie," I answered. *And for her cat,* I added to myself.

"What a nice way to welcome her here," she said as we walked into the pastorium. "I made a coconut cake. Jeannie always loved sweets and I imagine she has not had anything homemade, aside from those cookies I took to the hospital, in a long time."

"That's for sure," I said.

Elizabeth led me into the pastorium living room and gestured at the gray striped sofa and matching chairs with their half dozen complementary pillows in gray, red and white. The Victorian style suited the room with its arched windows and old but beautifully restored fireplace.

She stoked the fire and it came to life. After returning the poker to the tool stand, she said, "I have coffee, hot chocolate, tea. Whatever you'd like."

I'd moved a few pillows and sat down on the sofa but started to rise, saying, "Coffee would be great, but let me help you."

"No, no. Please sit," she said as she walked toward the hallway that must lead to the kitchen. "I do enjoy fixing for company. Sugar, cream?"

"Both," I said.

As I waited, I set the gift on the floor next to me and took in the room more fully. From what I'd seen in the study the other day and now in this room, Elizabeth Truman apparently had the decorator gene. Everything seemed as if it could be photographed for a magazine. I thought about Jeannie living here. She'd been holed up with no comforts except her ghost cat for a decade. This place would probably seem like a palace.

The smell of coffee brewing wafted into the room. I loved that smell and settled back. *Lovely sofa,* I thought, *but not half as comfortable as the love seat in the Burgess house*. What would Candace and Mike think when they learned about Landon? I grew somber then. He could be a murderer. He certainly had a strong motive—and the thought was disheartening. But though Penelope Webber may have been deceitful and greedy, she didn't deserve to die. My sympathy lay with her, not with her killer.

Just then, Boots appeared, walked across to a lovely accent chair—upholstered in red damask—and began to sharpen her claws on the wooden leg. I almost got up to scold her before I came to my senses. *She's a ghost. She can scratch anything she wants.*

I felt relieved she'd decided to come here to be with Jeannie, though. But how did she know to accompany me? It wasn't as if I'd told her. The real question was, however, how do ghosts know how to do anything? I wasn't about to voice that question aloud to anyone.

Elizabeth appeared, carrying two matching floral mugs, and handed me one. But I'd managed only two sips when we heard the front door open and the pastor's deep voice call, "Our guest has arrived."

I set my mug on a coaster on the oval coffee table and both Elizabeth and I went to see if we could help the pastor with Jeannie.

He was behind her as she pushed toward us using a walker.

Elizabeth smiled broadly and clapped her approval while I said, "You're amazing, Jeannie."

Jeannie returned our smiles and said, "Got a brand-new hip and I can tell you it works better than the old one."

I laughed and said, "Guess this hospital visit wasn't so bad after all."

"Nope. But I'm glad to be outta there. Lotta noise at night. You'da thought the creepers followed me all the way there."

We backed up so she could come into the living room.

Elizabeth said, "Oh my. There is far too much furniture in this room for a person needing a walker." She looked at the pastor. "Mitchell, could you move the coffee table out of the way?"

"Certainly can," he said, removing his coat.

Elizabeth took it from him and after I picked up my coffee, he easily slid the table off to the side using the needlepoint rug beneath it as a pull. Jeannie now had a clear path to walk slowly to the red chair.

She was wearing a pink velour jacket and matching track pants with zippers low on the sides of the legs. Probably a gift from Elizabeth and easy to get on and off. Her hair had been parted and combed and was held back by rhinestoned combs on each side. She probably felt like a princess, thanks to the pastor and Elizabeth.

She made it to the chair and sat with Pastor Mitch's help. She glanced around and said, "This place is different than I remember. Fancy." And then, I knew she spied Boots, because she was looking at the floor and tears shimmered in her eyes. She whispered, "She's here."

Elizabeth said, "Who's here, Jeannie?"

"Boots. Boots came to be with me." She pushed her walker to the side and patted her lap. "Come here, Bootsie."

"Are you talking about Kay Ellen's cat?" Pastor Mitch said, looking confused.

"Yes," she said. "And I know you can't see her. Only me and Miss Jillian can."

I felt my face heat up and shook my head slightly when Elizabeth gave me a quizzical look. A small lie, one I felt guilty for offering. Thank goodness Jeannie was concentrating on the ghost cat now sitting in her lap and didn't see my tiny, false denial.

"Are you hungry, Jeannie?" Elizabeth said. "I've prepared that chicken salad you used to like so much."

She continued to smile down at the cat curled in her lap. "Yes. Hungry. I stay hungry."

"We'll have to fix that," the pastor said. "Let me help you in the kitchen, Elizabeth."

They disappeared, probably anxious to discuss how to handle Jeannie's seeing cats that didn't exist. I couldn't blame them.

I sipped my coffee. It was rich, with real cream and plenty of sugar. So, so good. Then I said, "I cannot believe how well you look, how easily you walked in here. You are one strong woman, Jeannie."

"I am," she said. "Soon I'll be back at the mill. Gotta protect my girl."

The truth—that her daughter's remains had been removed—would be difficult to explain. I decided I might need the pastor's help. But perhaps Jeannie knew more about her daughter's disappearance aside from Earl Whitehouse's name—things she didn't even realize were important to finding Kay Ellen's killer.

"Why do you think your daughter went to the mill the night she died?" I asked.

She stroked the cat. "I was thinking she mighta gone after Boots and run into trouble."

"I never thought of that. Had Boots ever done that before—gone into the mill?" I asked.

She nodded. "Lots of cats was findin' their way in there—to be safe from the cold. Animals need shelter just like us folks, you know."

"They do," I said. "Had Kay Ellen ever gone in there to rescue her cat before that night?"

"I'm thinkin' she said something about it—how Boots wandered in and she went after her," she said. "But even with Kay Ellen bein' so little, I don't know how she got into the place."

"But *you* managed to get in there," I said.

"Made a hole in the fence for me and Boots. She led me there, to the place where my Kay Ellen was," she said.

"Boots did that?"

Jeannie nodded. "Yup. Once we got to the building, I had to work at the window to find a way inside. Dug out the stuff between the bricks with my old reed hook. Then I had a big hole to climb in."

A reed hook was a small weaving tool and an old, sturdy one like Jeannie probably had would have done the trick. "I see. And then you stayed in the mill after that," I said softly.

"Had to be with my girl," she said.

Her downcast eyes told me she was beginning to shut down. This was a tough topic and I understood it was time to stop asking questions. "I'm glad you're doing well and glad they repaired your hip and you came back to the mill village on your own two feet."

She looked up. "Me, too."

Elizabeth came into the room then and said, "Think you can make it to the kitchen, Jeannie?"

She nodded and soon the four of us enjoyed a wonderful lunch. After we'd all enjoyed the meal and the luscious cake, she opened her gift and seemed happy about the quilt. I didn't have to tell her that the small one was for Boots. I could tell she knew.

Elizabeth had turned the hearth room off the kitchen into a bedroom so Jeannie didn't have to climb stairs and she was ready to nap with her new quilt when I left. But I told her I'd be back to help her in the days to come. We could walk around the neighborhood together.

On my way out, I saw a car pull up behind my van and a woman climb out of the Corolla. Her hair had been dyed a dark auburn, but her features and gait told me gray was probably her real hair color. She halted, then glanced nervously at the pastorium and then at me.

"Is Jeannie Sloan inside that house?" she said in a meek tone. "I heard she was coming here today."

"Hi. I'm Jillian," I said, deflecting her question. I had no idea who this person was, and I smiled at her expectantly in the hopes she'd tell me.

"Beatrice Stanley," she said absently, her focus on the house. "I need to talk to her—to Jeannie Sloan."

"Are you related to Ward Stanley?" I asked.

"He's my son." She looked at me then, penciled-in eyebrows raised and all her timidity gone. "Is she in there?"

"She is," I said. "But she's resting. Maybe you could call Pastor Mitch and ask when would be a good time to visit."

"I *need* to talk to her," she said, starting for the walkway leading to the pastorium.

"Maybe I can help," I said. "I've gotten to know Jeannie pretty well in the last week."

She faced me. "I didn't come here to talk to you, young woman."

Young woman? I hadn't been called that in maybe twenty years. "She's just been released from the hospital. I'm sure you can talk to her at a better time."

"No better time than now," she said, her gaze focused on the pastorium.

I blocked her way on the path and I took my phone from my jacket pocket. "I'll call the pastor then, but I'm sure he'll ask you to come another time. Jeannie's *not* ready for visitors." *Especially unfriendly ones like this woman.*

She pointed a finger at my chest. "You're pretty full of yourself. Seem to believe you're in charge. Who are you to deny me what I've waited years to find out?"

I shook my head, confused. "What have you waited years for, Mrs. Stanley?"

"I'm not telling *you* anything," she said vehemently.

"But know this, young woman: I'll talk to that squatter and I'll find out what she knows sooner or later. You can't stop me."

She turned on her heel and marched to her car as I watched. The encounter, I then realized, had left me trembling.

What did Jeannie know that this woman was so anxious to learn? Could it be the same information that made Kay Ellen a victim? I didn't know, but I got in my van and headed straight to Mercy PD.

Twenty-eight

Candace, Morris and Tom were busy talking to none other than Landon Burgess when I arrived at the police station. I knew this because B.J. told me—and because I could hear Landon shouting through the walls of the interview room about ten feet away.

Fortunately, Mike Baca walked out of his office right then. I waved to him and asked if he had a minute.

"I have more than a minute for you, Jillian," he said.

I joined him in his office and he let me ramble on about Jeannie, her arrival at the pastorium, Beatrice Stanley's appearance and my tense interaction with her. I said, "Why would she need to talk to Jeannie? I mean, the woman seemed desperate."

"I have no idea. My question is, how did she even know where to find her?" Mike said.

"I don't know," I said. "I think you guys have done a good job of keeping the cold case under wraps."

"Of course she works at the discount store where everybody and his brother shops." He rocked back in his big leather chair. "It was only a matter of time until word about the skeleton and Jeannie Sloan got out."

"But what would make Beatrice Stanley so determined to talk to Jeannie?" I asked. I'd taken off my jacket but now took off my wool cardigan, too. Morris always turned the thermostat way up when they questioned a suspect and apparently the Landon Burgess interview was no different.

"What were her exact words again?" Mike asked.

"Let me get this right." I thought for a second and said, " 'Who are you to deny me what I've waited years to find out?' "

"Hmm. The situation for the Stanleys since the mill went under has gone from bad to worse, so I can understand her being a little intense," he said. "But what would Jeannie know about any of that?"

"She wouldn't. She's been hiding out for years. Exactly how badly did the mill foreclosure affect the Stanleys?" I said. "Because I'm beginning to think there's a connection between their empty mill and the person who'd been living inside there for years."

"Beatrice is a cashier at a discount store, Jillian. Doesn't that tell you how bad it's gotten? She was once a woman who went to charity events wearing diamonds and now she works as a *cashier*."

"She *is* bitter. That much I know," I said. "So if they're broke, how did Ward Stanley pull enough money together to make a bid on the mill?"

"You really should think about working for me," he said with a smile. "I asked myself the same question and did some digging. Ward's got this investor group, old-money folks who knew his dad for the most part. But when we started looking at the paperwork presented to the town council, we learned there's a shadow member— an unnamed financier. I'm hoping Tom will help me find out who it is, because background investigations are what he does best."

"But if he or she is unnamed . . . ," I said.

"Ward says another man in the investor group brought in this unnamed person," Mike said. "And he's telling me that since it's got nothing to do with Penelope Webber's murder, he doesn't need to tell me. Candace did his interview and says he left in a huff yesterday, saying she'd questioned his integrity. But it could well have everything to do with Penelope's death."

"Guess Beatrice isn't the only Stanley with an attitude," I said.

"You weren't here when they ran this town, Jillian. They've fallen hard, but they're full of pride. If we give the man time and space, maybe he'll come around. But in the meantime, I'm putting Tom on this. I mean, it only took him a couple hours to discover everything about Landon Burgess."

I smiled. "Tom's good. You should be asking *him* to join the force."

Mike said, "I couldn't pay him half of what he was earning as a homicide detective in North Carolina. Not that it was megabucks, but all we have are puny bucks here. His business is doing well and he's only doing these background checks as a favor to me—oh, and a little extra cash."

"But aside from this shadow investor, you have information about everyone else in Ward Stanley's group?" I asked.

"We do. They're clean as rain," Mike said.

"Okay," I said. "I won't keep you much longer, but maybe you can help me understand Beatrice Stanley better—because I know she'll be coming back to bother Jeannie. The Stanleys lost their business, but wasn't there money from the sale of all that equipment inside the mill? What happened to it?"

"Bad investments, is my guess," Mike said. "Maybe spending beyond their means? And then there were the medical bills. Ward Stanley's father had a stroke about ten years ago, but he lingered. Spent weeks and weeks in ICU. Maybe the bills ate up their fortune."

I nodded. "But you'd have thought they had good insurance. That mill was a hundred years old and they surely created a hefty nest egg. And what about life insurance when old Mr. Stanley died?"

"From what little I know about Beatrice Stanley, she did have extravagant taste. She could have blown through a lot of money, Jillian."

"You think she was the one to do the spending and not her son?" I asked.

He shook his head. "I don't know. We're trying to solve two murders and now that we have Landon Burgess, an admitted liar, right here in my interrogation room, I believe we'll have answers soon—ones that point right in his direction."

"He is one angry guy." I stood and put my sweater back on. Mike came around and helped me with my coat. "But don't forget about Beatrice," I said. "Jeannie shouldn't be harassed by that woman—not when she's trying to recover."

As he walked down the hall, he said, "You're protective of that old lady. But why should that surprise me?"

I smiled. "That I am. Oh—and one more thing. What about the feral cats? Shawn and I will need to get in and check on them, put out more food. I did promise to help him and you know how impatient he gets."

"We're finishing up in there today," Mike said. "You can tell him that he can have access to the mill again tomorrow. I'm sure Dustin Gray wants to finish up his job for the town council as well. As far as I'm concerned, my people have done a thorough job in the mill. There's not much evidence from ten years ago. The place is in bad shape. A few walls in the offices were torn up, floorboards pried out and then hammered back in. But I can't see how that has anything to do with Kay Ellen Sloan's murder. I suspect vandals."

"Jeannie keeps talking about *creepers*, as she calls them. In fact, she said she was being chased when she fell. My question is, how were they entering the building? She was climbing in and out through a window at night."

"Teenage boys these days try to replicate video games," he said. "And they're like monkeys. I mean, they can scale walls. They were probably getting in the same way Jeannie was—except on the upper floors. We found loose bricks on several windows. Unfortunately, we found no evidence we can connect to Kay Ellen's murder. My guess is she was killed elsewhere and taken there because, well, it was a good place to hide a body."

I left the police station, realizing as I drove off that Mike's priority was solving Penelope Webber's murder. Jeannie and her daughter were not at the top of the list—and I understood why. Penelope, a prominent citizen, died in a horrific way, and any leads in her far more recent murder had to be followed up on immediately. Still, I was bothered that my small town had so few resources that they couldn't work both cases simultaneously. But by the time I returned home, I had an idea on how to get Kay Ellen's murder more attention and at the same time find out what Beatrice Stanley wanted from Jeannie and why.

Before I could call Kara to help me out with my plan, my three cats needed attention. Both Merlot and Syrah seemed to be waiting for Boots to come through the door after me, but apparently that didn't happen. They gobbled up their treats as quickly as Chablis did, so I was hopeful the little ghost cat had stayed to keep Jeannie company.

After the big lunch and delicious coconut cake I'd eaten at the pastorium, I wondered if I'd even be hungry by suppertime. But I called Kara and invited her over anyway, asking if she'd like to share a pizza. She happily agreed and said she'd arrive around six once she'd put the newspaper to bed.

I had a couple hours to myself, but instead of checking to see if I had any new quilt orders, I found myself with Chablis on my lap watching afternoon talk shows. I must have dozed off because I awoke to find Kara smiling down at me.

"You'll get a crick in your neck sleeping like that," she said with a smile. "You didn't hear me knock, did you?"

"No." I sat up, rubbing my eyes. Chablis seemed unhappy that I'd disturbed her and climbed off my lap. "I didn't leave the door unlocked, did I?"

She slipped off her navy peacoat. "Nope. You're getting better at watching out for yourself. I used my key when you didn't answer. I was worried you might be in trouble."

"Why would I be in trouble?" I stood and stretched, realizing I'd needed that nap after nearly a week of restless nights.

"I'm worried because we've got not one, but two murders to be concerned about in this town. And you've got your fingers in both of them." She cocked her head. "Did you read my piece about Penelope Webber?"

"Sorry, no. Did it run today?" I asked.

"This morning. Not much to report, unfortunately," she said. "The victim's sister wouldn't give me the time of day when I finally tracked her down and called her for a quote. Apparently there's no one else to give Penelope a proper burial."

"How sad," I said. "Maybe the town council can do something. At least give her a memorial service."

"Already in the works," she said. "It's being organized by the next in line to the town council throne, Robert Andrews. But now it's time for pizza. I'm starving."

After I ordered a large veggie—my second pizza order this week—Kara pulled off her calf-high leather boots and uttered a grateful "Ah" as she tucked her feet beneath her on the sofa. "I'm not a fan of those boots—

and they cost me a pretty penny. Maybe I can sell them to pay for groceries. Being a homeowner is more expensive than I thought it would be."

Kara had just moved into a custom house she'd built on the outskirts of town. She'd used the money John had left her to buy both the house and the newspaper.

"Do you need money?" I asked. "I can help out." I had a nice little nest egg thanks to her father. John had been so good at saving. But his passing away during his first year of retirement hadn't been part of his plan. And it hadn't been part of mine. Gosh, how I missed him.

"I was kidding about selling my boots," Kara said, pulling her dark brunette hair back and fastening it with a black elastic band she'd had around her wrist. "I didn't spend all Daddy's money and, believe it or not, I am making enough at the newspaper to pay my bills."

"But if you ever need help—"

She held up her hand. "Same goes for you. We're family and we'll always help each other."

"You've offered a fitting segue," I said. "I could use your help—but not with money issues. It concerns this cold case, the one you agreed not to write about yet. At least I think it's about the cold case. I'm not sure."

Kara turned a little more in my direction after grabbing a lap quilt from the shelf under the coffee table. She spread it over her knees. "Oh, good. Tell me." Her brown eyes sparkled with interest.

By the time the pizza arrived, I'd pretty much caught her up to speed on everything that had happened in the last few days. I was hungrier than I thought and when we were both full, only two pieces of pizza remained. Merlot, as usual, ate a bit of cheese, but the other two cats seemed quite disappointed in our supper choice. Chablis would have definitely preferred ice cream.

I wrapped up the remaining pizza slices and put them

in the fridge while Kara made coffee. Usually this time of day I go for decaf, but my stepdaughter never did. She always said, "Go for the real thing—in every aspect of life."

We settled back into the living room with our mugs of Kona and the cats in their usual spots—Syrah on the top of the sofa behind me, Chablis in my lap and Merlot stretched out between the two of us.

I said, "As I was telling you, Beatrice Stanley wants something from Jeannie—seems desperate to talk to her. Whatever it's about, I have this gut feeling it has to do with Kay Ellen. I was wondering if you could visit Beatrice and tell her you wanted to do a story about the Stanley legacy now that the mill is making news again."

Kara considered this, her hands clutching her mug chest high. "You know, that might be a compelling human interest piece. But you have to remember, this is a family that feels humiliated by its circumstances. If I upset her even the tiniest bit, hint that the family would be shown as downtrodden in this article, I'd lose her cooperation."

"What if I go along and offer to be there while she talks to Jeannie? Do you think that would work?" I said.

"Dangle Jeannie like a carrot, you mean?" Kara said, her surprise evident.

"No, nothing like that," I said. "See, this woman is determined. I could read it in her eyes. One way or another, she'll get to Jeannie. I'm thinking it would be far better if we try to control the meeting by making sure I'm present when it happens."

"I see." Kara gnawed on a cuticle, obviously thinking about all this. "Okay, but there's something I want out of this if I give the cold case lots of front-page exposure—which is what you want, right?"

I nodded.

"If I do the Beatrice interview, this boyfriend you mentioned—Earl Whitehouse—has to be part of our deal. I want to talk to him, Jillian. I want to talk to him more than I want to talk to Beatrice Stanley. Whatever his role is in all this, it will sell more papers than anything about the Stanleys because, let's face it, they're old news in this town."

I closed my eyes. Kara was smart and even though we loved each other, business was business. I said, "But I don't even know if Morris had a chance to interview him yet. We can't go to him before he gets his shot."

Kara pulled her phone out of her jeans pocket. "I'll ask Candace."

"No," I said, wanting to snatch the phone from her hand. "She won't be happy I've been talking about this."

"She's been unhappy before," Kara said. "It's not like everyone in town isn't discussing why one of the Franklin twins returned to Mercy and was seen talking to the police inside Belle's Beans."

I sighed. This wasn't going as planned and yet I couldn't blame Kara. At least she'd agreed that finding Kay Ellen's killer was worthy enough to use her ink and newsprint.

She made the call and I had to get up and walk into the kitchen where I couldn't hear any strident notes from Candace coming from Kara's phone. Maybe I'd regret spilling everything I knew to her.

But when Kara was finished talking, she said, "You're safe, Jillian."

I walked back into the room, Chablis on my heels and sat back down. "What did she say?"

"She's cool with me interviewing Whitehouse," Kara said. "Said Morris got absolutely nowhere with him. The guy stonewalled, said he never knew Kay Ellen Sloan. So now Morris is having to hunt up more kids—now adults, of course—from that high school class and press them for information. She's thinking that maybe a visit from the local press will make him reconsider his earlier statement."

"Ah. So Candace thinks publicity might force Whitehouse to come clean?" I said.

Kara smiled. "Exactly."

Twenty-nine

I don't know how Kara convinced me it was a good idea to visit Beatrice Stanley right away. I guess I told myself that my stepdaughter was correct in her assumption that since the woman showed up at the pastorium today, she probably had the day off. Plus, Kara wanted to do a little research on Earl Whitehouse before she talked to him. "If Mrs. Stanley happens to be working the evening shift tonight, no problem. We'll catch her tomorrow," Kara had said while pulling her boots back on.

With help from a little Internet sleuthing, we found her address, and we also discovered her old address in the process. Kara decided to get some perspective for her story—old versus new—by first swinging by the old Stanley mansion not that far from where Penelope Webber had lived and died. We couldn't get close enough to see the place because not only was it pitch-dark outside, but the mansion's driveway was fronted by an arching wrought-iron locked gate. The neighborhood was about as upscale as Mercy had to offer. This gave us *both* plenty of perspective when we arrived in front of Mrs. Stanley's aging duplex, which was literally across the railroad tracks. How many people had lost everything and ended up downsizing to this degree after the economic mess this country had been in? The contrast between where the Stanleys once lived and this place gave me a clear picture of what they'd lost, that was for sure.

A porch light led us up the walkway to the aging duplex's "B" unit. Kara knocked with authority.

The door opened almost at once, but it wasn't Beatrice standing before us, but rather her son, Ward. He wore a flannel shirt with frayed cuffs and looked surprised. But if he'd shown up on my doorstep, I'd have been surprised, too.

"Um, hello, Mrs. Hart," he said. "And it's Kara, right? I've seen you at several council meetings covering the mill issues for the *Mercy Messenger*. What can I do for you?"

"We came to talk to your mother," I said. "Is she home?"

He grew wary at the mention of his mother. "My *mother*? What do you want to talk to her about?"

"Is she here?" Kara asked.

"She's gone to bed. She has to be up by five tomorrow morning for her job." The muscles in his jaw tightened.

"When does her shift end tomorrow?" Kara asked.

"What's this about?" he said tersely. "I mean, you're a reporter. What would a reporter want with my mother?"

"Maybe *you* can help us understand something," I said with a smile. His features had darkened and I hadn't come here to upset anyone. "A little publicity for your mill proposal wouldn't do any harm, right?"

He seemed to ponder this and finally opened the door wider and let us in. "Please keep your voices down."

The duplex seemed to match Ward Stanley's appearance: worn out, run-down and shrouded in gloom. A TV in the corner was tuned to a basketball game, the sound muted. He picked up a remote from an end table by the reclining sofa and turned the set off.

Besides the sofa, there was only one other seat—a tapestry wing chair that seemed to be the only pristine item of furniture in sight. I wondered if it had been rescued from their foreclosure.

Ward said, "Okay, tell me what this is about."

I sat on one end of the sofa, Ward on the other, leaving the wing chair for Kara. I didn't bother to take off my jacket, hoping Kara would take this as a cue that we weren't staying long. I didn't like the man's vibe and besides, we hadn't come here to talk to him.

He spoke to Kara before either of us could ask the question we'd come to ask Beatrice. "Did I hear right?" he said. "Did you indicate you might give the condo proposal a nice boost with a little publicity?"

"Not exactly Jillian's words," Kara said. "Do you think the proposal *needs* a boost?"

He laughed. "Can't hurt. I'm a desperate man."

I wanted to ask if he was desperate because he'd lost Penelope's support when she died, but I couldn't. That question was police business.

"*Desperate* is a strong word, Mr. Stanley," Kara said. "Why is the mill so important to you?"

"Because we created it. Owned it for generations. It belongs to us," he said.

"I believe Mercy owns that mill now," she said. "But tell me more about your interest in reviving it—and why you think residential real estate is the way to go."

This isn't why we came here, Kara, I thought. But she was making our visit seem about a topic he had a keen interest in. Probably a good idea before we asked about Beatrice. And for all I knew, maybe this was exactly the kind of story she wanted to run: MILL ROOTS RUN DEEP FOR STANLEY FAMILY.

"The answer is simple," he said. "Real estate is coming back. Textile production will *never* come back. But go ahead. Ask anything you want. It's my favorite subject."

He grinned and I realized he'd completely forgotten

we'd come here expecting to talk to his mother. This was all about him and he liked it.

"How do you think Penelope Webber's murder will affect the town council's decision on which proposal will win approval?" Kara said.

He leaned back, considering the question. "Terrible thing, her dying. But from what the police are telling me, Penelope must have had a past that involved discord. The woman had no friends and not one person has come to town to mourn her death. I believe her murder had nothing to do with the mill and will not affect any future outcome."

He made it sound like the woman was a stranger to him—which I knew to be untrue. And he also seemed smug, as if he were already running a multimillion-dollar business. But was it all bravado? Penelope had been helping him get his wish and now she was gone. That had to hurt. *Yes,* I decided. *This attitude is all for show. Bet he's worried sick about what the town council will decide.*

Kara asked him more questions about his plans for the upscale condos, asking if he'd developed any floor plans—she got very specific.

He seemed happy, excited, but grew guarded when she started asking about his investor group. He said, "They want to stay in the background. I handle all the questions about financing. We *have* the money."

And one person wants to stay so far in the background, we don't even have a name—yet, I thought. I glanced at the hallway where Beatrice lay sound asleep in her bedroom—or so her son said. We came to talk to *her* and my eyes were starting to glaze over now that the interview had turned to a discussion about architectural firms interested in joining the project. Finally, Kara glanced my way and gave me a tiny nod as if indicating now was the time to ask about Ward's mother.

"How does your mother feel about your plans?" I

glanced around. "By the way, we had no idea you lived here, too." But from the men's running shoes on the floor and the collection of baseball caps I could see in the open closet hall door, he *did* live here.

"This is only temporary," he said quickly. "Once the council votes my project through, I'll be getting a place of my own. So, what *do* you want with my mother?"

"I ran into her today outside the pastorium in the mill village. She wanted to talk to Jeannie Sloan and—"

"Jeannie Sloan? She doesn't even live here anymore." He'd paled. "Does she?"

Oh boy. I hadn't anticipated I'd be giving out information he knew nothing about. No going back now. "Your mother seemed to think she was in town." *Knew* she was. And I'd confirmed as much to Beatrice. She'd tell her son what I'd said sooner or later.

Kara came to my rescue. "If Jeannie is back, why would your mother want to talk to her? Your family and hers didn't exactly run in the same circles ten years ago."

"Good question. I don't know," he said absently. He glanced at the hallway leading to the bedrooms. "Maybe I do need to wake her up."

I stood. "No. Please don't. Maybe it's just something she heard in town. Maybe—"

"Sit down, Mrs. Hart," he said coldly. "I want to know what you're holding back. See, I know my mother would never have gone to the mill village—not in a million years—if she didn't have a good reason, not to mention good information."

I sighed heavily and sat back down. Since Beatrice Stanley knew about Jeannie's whereabouts, about her story, then the word was out around town. It was only a matter of time until Ward found out.

I said, "Jeannie Sloan has been living in the mill, hiding out there, since not long after her daughter disappeared."

"Really?" he said. I wasn't sure what the look in his eyes meant. Realization? Surprise? Anger? Maybe a combination of emotions. He went on, saying, "She was there because she was homeless? Like we once were? Is that it?"

I'd forgotten to add bitter to the previous list of emotions. "Yes," I said softly. "Homeless." I wasn't about to add a word about Kay Ellen's skeleton. Beatrice hadn't mentioned it, so maybe that particular discovery remained a secret to the general public.

He blinked, looked at his hands and seemed to be thinking about this information so long that I grew even more uncomfortable. But Kara was studying the man, fascinated.

Finally he said, "Did my mother give you any idea what she wanted with that woman?"

"Not really," Kara answered for me. She knew I couldn't lie, but she'd been a tough investigative reporter once, used to getting answers any way she could. "Do you know what your mother might want with her? Because that's *why* we came here."

This time, Ward Stanley stood. "No, I don't. But when she's awake, I'll ask her. And now, I'd like you to leave before all your talking wakes her up."

We were herded out the door and as we walked toward Kara's SUV, I said, "He changed his mind. He doesn't want us to speak to her."

I wondered why.

Thirty

As I finished my breakfast of yogurt, granola and blue-
berries the following morning, I was focused on Beatrice
Stanley. The woman's mysterious appearance at the pastorium had me tossing and turning all night. But would
a meeting between her and Jeannie—with Beatrice's in-
tensity so obvious—upset Jeannie too much? Or would
a face-to-face not be such a bad thing after all? Jeannie
trusted me and I would be there for her. I had an idea
about how to set it all up without Ward Stanley finding
out, but I still worried whether it was the right thing
to do.

Then there's the Earl Whitehouse issue, I thought as I
sat on the living room floor for a little playtime with my
cats. I waved a feather on a string and had all three of
them interested. Syrah could jump circles around the
other two cats, but if I ran the feathers along the floor,
Chablis and Merlot had the edge. I tried to alternate, but
soon Chablis was ready for a nap and Merlot lost interest. Only Syrah wanted to keep jumping and chasing the
toy.

As I offered a few more feather passes and he leapt
high in the air gracefully, I thought about Kara. She'd
dropped me off last night, eager to find out where Earl
Whitehouse lived and worked. She had a plan of her

own to get him to talk and invited me to be an observer. She feared the publicity threat wouldn't work and that we'd end up with nothing. But she said she wasn't beyond using a fake name and her good looks to get him talking.

As a journalist in Houston, she hadn't had the luxury of deception, but since this encounter she was planning with Earl Whitehouse was more about helping the police than writing a story, I'd read more than a little excitement in her baby browns last night. But I worried about her and told her as much. What if he and Kay Ellen had had a spat and he killed her? He could be dangerous.

I didn't think Beatrice was dangerous, however. I sensed she was heartbroken beneath her angry facade. I glanced at the clock on the DVR. Time to visit Discount Mart, where she worked. Maybe get to her when she was due for a break.

I called Candace on my way there, but her phone went to voice mail, so I left a message telling her where I was going and why. Not that anything could happen in a busy store, but I always felt better when I told someone I knew what I was up to at times like this. After all, there was a remote chance that Beatrice Stanley killed Kay Ellen. But why would she murder a teenager she probably didn't even know? I had no idea. I only knew Beatrice Stanley was a dispirited, embittered woman who was aware of Jeannie Sloan's reappearance. She believed Jeannie held important information—and I wanted to know what this was all about.

The Discount Mart wasn't in Mercy, but halfway to Greenville. The thirty-minute drive didn't involve any freeways like the ones I'd always had to navigate when I lived in Houston. Trees on either side of the nearly deserted two-lane road I traveled reminded me of dark skeletal hands reaching skyward from the grave. It was rather spooky in the gloomy morning and I was glad Boots hadn't shown up in my car to make it even more eerie.

I spied Beatrice right away wearing the navy blue apron and red name badge all the employees wore. I waited patiently in line behind a mother with two children begging for candy at Beatrice's checkout stand. I watched her do her job, her face impassive. I guessed that when you did this kind of work, with loudspeaker announcements, screaming babies, ringing phones and customers unhappy about waiting in line, you learned to tune out a lot of stuff. I felt lucky that I could work in the peace and quiet of my home. Very lucky indeed.

Beatrice handed the young mother her receipt and immediately glanced at the conveyer for my items. Only when she saw nothing there did she look up and see me. Eyes half closed, mouth downturned, she said, "What do you want?"

"Are you due for a break soon?" I said.

"You have a lot of nerve coming here," she said. "I have nothing to say to you. I want to talk to Jeannie Sloan, not some do-gooder."

"I didn't come here to upset you," I said, realizing by her surprise at seeing me here that Ward probably hadn't told his mother about our visit last night. "What if I could get you a meeting with Jeannie?"

She glanced beyond me, checking for customers waiting or perhaps for a supervisor who might not like her conversing and not working. "Why the change of heart? You treated me like some monster ready to harm her yesterday."

"I'm protective, that's all," I said softly. "What about that break? Can I meet you at the McDonald's here in the store so we can talk?"

Beatrice checked her watch. I noticed her nails were manicured and her hands looked well cared for. I was glad she pampered herself in small ways. It meant she hadn't given up. Not yet.

She said, "I've still got twenty minutes until my time off. I'll meet you then."

A customer started piling items on the conveyor, saying, "Your light's on. Guess you're open."

I stepped away, wandered around the store for a while and then bought a yogurt smoothie at McDonald's. I was getting in my probiotics for today, that was for sure. The booth I chose was around the corner from the ordering area and I had to wet a napkin and clean off the sticky table. Beatrice slid into the booth and faced me exactly twenty minutes from the time she'd said she would.

"Can I buy you coffee? A smoothie?" I asked.

"I don't need you to buy me anything," she said. "Just tell me what I have to do to talk to that woman."

"Explain why you want to see her, that's all," I said, looking straight into her drained eyes.

She pondered this and I could see reluctance in her expression. She didn't trust me—and yet she wanted to talk to Jeannie in the worst way.

She rested her forearms on the table and leaned toward me. "What do you know about us? About the Stanleys?"

"I know you once had a lot of money—and that you don't anymore," I said. "I know your pride has suffered and that you could use a friend."

She pulled her lips in, eyes downcast. I don't think she had anticipated the last thing I'd said. When she looked at me again, I could see she was fighting tears. But her tone was insolent when she said, "That's not even half of what I could use. But maybe pride is part of that."

I said, "All you have to do is tell me what you want from Jeannie and I'll take you to meet her. I just have one other condition: that I remain in the room with the two of you."

Beatrice lifted her chin. "I want to know what she found in that mill. Because I know it's there."

"What's there?" I said. "What do you think she found?" *Does Beatrice know about the skeleton? Is that what she's talking about?*

"You have conditions?" she said defiantly. "Well, so do I. You take me to her and you'll see. Because that woman *knows*."

"How about this afternoon?" I said, keeping my tone even. She was beginning to frighten me a tad.

"I get off at three. I'll be at that preacher's house by three thirty." She stood and started to walk away.

"But what if I can't arrange it for today? Can I have your phone number or—"

She whirled and pointed a finger at me. "You wanted it your way. Make it happen."

As she left, I felt a pulse throbbing in my throat. *Maybe this wasn't such a great idea, Jillian.*

Tom called me as I drove back to Mercy and, perceptive as always, he said, "Something's wrong. What happened?"

I told him about last night's visit with Ward Stanley and this morning's meeting with his mother. "She's so . . . *angry*, Tom. They both are. I guess I should have done more research about the family. I thought I knew their story, but I'm beginning to believe there's a lot more. But I need to know how Jeannie fits into all this. I just don't get that part."

"I've talked to Kara, so I know what the two of you did, but you should have asked me for help yesterday," he said. "Since you aren't seeing Beatrice until this afternoon, we've got enough time to tap a certain source. His name is Ed and I'll meet you at his shop."

"Sounds perfect. But aren't you working on Earl Whitehouse's background check?" I said.

"Why do you think Kara called me?" he said.

"Because she works for you?" I stated this as a question, knowing there was more to this.

"True," he said. "She does, though not as much as I'd like. But now that your lovely stepdaughter has learned about Earl Whitehouse, she wants to do the background check on him. I told her to go for it. She's sometimes better than I am at hunting up dirt."

"Especially when she's sniffing out a good story," I said.

"Exactly," he said. "See you soon."

I arrived at Ed's Swap Shop first and found him eating a turkey sandwich in the kitchen section of his workplace.

"Well, lookee here," he said, standing to greet me. "One of my favorite people back to visit again in less than a week. I'm thinkin' this has something to do with all this trouble in town. Plenty of trouble, too."

I took a seat and he sat back down across from me. I said, "You have your finger on Mercy's pulse. Where else could I get information?"

"I heard they found bones in that mill," he said, picking up the rest of his sandwich off the paper plate in front of him. He took a large bite and ended up with mayonnaise on the corner of his mouth.

I tapped my mouth to show him and he wiped his face with a napkin.

"Who told you about the bones?" I asked.

He grinned. "I have connections with that lady, Laura, the one who runs the Pink House. She comes in here all the time lookin' for old linens, lace doilies, stuff like that. Uses them to create the right . . . What was her word? *Atmosphere*. Anyways, I guess she has this smart kid from Greenville stayin' with her and he's goin' a little wacky wantin' to get back to work inside the mill. Did some talkin' about what was found in the fireplace."

"Oh boy. More and more information is leaking out all over town," I said, wondering if Candace ever told Dustin to keep his mouth shut.

"That's how things go in Mercy, Jillian. You know that."

I heard the bell tinkle in the front of the store and soon Tom joined us. After he and Ed shook hands, Tom sat beside me and took my hand. His was cold and I put my other hand around his to warm it.

He said, "We need more on the Stanleys than you told us before, Ed. Do you know anything else?"

Ed rubbed his chin. "The Stanleys. Never thought I'd see the day they'd be ruined. Gotta know they ran through lots of money."

"You sound surprised," I said.

"Most folks I talk to think the medical bills did them in," Ed said. "Old man lingered on for months in that hospital with the wife and kid hoverin' like vultures. They got a rude surprise when he finally died. Judge Whitehouse—he does probate sometimes—anyways, he came in here one day lookin' for tools. He's a real collector. He was tellin' me he couldn't understand why there was nothin' left except the house. Course that meant Beatrice and Ward had no money to run the place. Big old mansion like that owes a big tax bill every year and about as big electric costs every month."

"Did you say Judge Whitehouse?" I said. "Earl Whitehouse's father?"

"Yup. Why?" Ed said.

"Because his son's name has come up in the last couple days," I said. "I was told he was dating Kay Ellen Sloan."

Ed's bushy gray eyebrows rose in surprise. "First I heard of that. Him bein' a judge's son and her being a mill girl, well, I'm bettin' that didn't go over too well at young Earl's house."

"Did the judge say how much money they'd run through by the time Mr. Stanley died?" Tom asked.

"Nope, and I couldn't venture a guess," Ed said. "Money's just paper to me. Recyclable just like everything else."

I said, "What did the Stanleys do when they lost their house?"

"They got relatives everywhere in town, but they kept gettin' kicked out," Ed said. "Those two aren't easy to live with, is my guess. Ward hadn't even applied to college after he got his high school diploma. Ended up takin' real estate courses at the community college. Even then he couldn't make it, but that probably wasn't all his fault with the economy the way it was. Bad time to be takin' up real estate. He works at the insurance company now. Too much of a sourpuss to be much of a salesman, though."

I nodded my agreement.

"They live over in them duplexes by the railroad tracks," he went on. "The man is still livin' with his mama, if you can believe it." Ed sighed. "Those folks used to be all dressed up and struttin' around Mercy like they owned the place. And come to think of it, they *did* own the place."

"Could Ward's father have run through a lot of money before he had that stroke?" Tom asked. "I mean, was he a gambler? Speculator? Anything like that?"

Ed considered this for several seconds. "I don't think so. He ran that mill all his life. That was all he knew. Maybe he got bamboozled by the foreigners that come in and bought up the equipment."

"You mean he never got paid for the looms and threaders and other machinery he sold them?" I said.

"I'm just guessin', Jillian. I don't recall any talk about what happened to all their money, except one day it was gone."

"What about Beatrice Stanley?" I said. "Does she ever come in here?"

"She's been in," Ed said with a nod. "Anyone who's fallin' on hard times has been in here. Sold her lamps one time, an old coffee table another. But you know what the Good Book says. Pride goeth before destruction and a haughty spirit before a fall. To my way of thinkin', haughty comes *after* the fall, too."

I smiled. "Yes. Haughty. Perfect word for her. How would you go about getting her to open up and drop her 'I'm better than you are' act?"

Ed cocked his head and squinted. "Tough question. She likes pretty things—always eyeing my jewelry under the glass counter out front. Woman still thinks the world owes her everything. I'd say, if you was to meet up with her, you shower her with compliments. Find anything you can about her that you can pat her on the back for."

I smiled. "Perfect. Thank you, Ed."

Thirty-one

Tom and I lunched together and when he headed back to his office, I went to the pastorium. I wanted to get there before Beatrice Sloan showed up so I could fill everyone in on who would be arriving soon and why.

When Pastor Mitch led me through the hallway to the pastorium's kitchen, he said, "Elizabeth is doing charity work in Greenville for a few hours. Jeannie seems quite well today and I know she'll be glad to see you."

As Jeannie emerged from the room off the kitchen, her walker leading the way, I could tell from her expression that she was indeed happy to see me.

"Wow," I said with a smile. "You're moving faster than yesterday."

"This hip don't hurt nothin' like when I fell," she said. "Never told you how glad I was you showed up with my Boots that night. I might still be lyin' on that cold floor."

I glanced at Pastor Mitch, but he kindly ignored the reference to Boots. He clearly was getting used to Jeannie's ways and taking them in stride.

"I'm happy I could help," I said. "Maybe we should all sit for a minute? I have something to tell you two."

The pastor helped Jeannie ease into a ladder-back chair at the large table in the center of the room. He offered tea or coffee, but I refused, anxious to get on with my confession that I'd invited Beatrice Stanley here.

Jeannie said, "Miss Jillian is bustin' at the seams to tell us something. Ain't that right?"

"Um, yes," I said, distracted by the appearance of Boots. She'd jumped right on the table and sat close to Jeannie—and stared at me, her little mouth curved into her Cheshire cat smile.

Jeannie said, "Is it a present like that quilt? I'm lovin' that quilt and Boots loves hers."

"I've gone and done something perhaps I shouldn't have—in hopes of getting a clue to help find out what happened to Kay Ellen. Thing is, I don't know if this will lead anywhere, but—"

In his soothing baritone, Pastor Mitch said, "We trust whatever you've 'gone and done' is the right thing. Just tell us."

Quickly I said, "I invited Beatrice Stanley here. She wants to talk to Jeannie."

Jeannie looked at me, puzzled. "Who's that?"

"She was married to Mr. Stanley. You remember him, right?" Pastor Mitch said.

"The boss's wife?" She seemed frightened now and I wondered why.

"She's not the boss's wife anymore," Pastor Mitch reminded her, and then turned to me. "Why does she want to talk to Jeannie?"

I said, "She wouldn't say, but I intercepted her outside this house yesterday. Word is out in town that Jeannie is back. Well, not that she ever really left, but—"

"Mrs. Stanley never came to the mill village when the family owned the mill," Pastor Mitch said, "but she would write the church a generous check every year at Christmas. She's welcome here. Her generosity is not forgotten."

But Jeannie's face had paled. "I've done somethin'

wrong. She's mad at me, right? For sneakin' into the mill?"

"That's not her business to be mad about anymore," I said. "The mill no longer belongs to the Stanleys and Mr. Stanley died almost ten years ago."

Jeannie gasped. "*Died?* That's terrible. He wasn't a nice man, plain mean most days, but he'd let me bring Kay Ellen to work when she was sick. And in summer when school was out. He did that for all us workers."

And made Kay Ellen work, no doubt, I thought. "I told Mrs. Stanley I have to be in the room when she talks to you. She's agreed."

Jeannie laid a hand on her chest and I saw how bruised it was from the IVs she'd had in the hospital. "That's good. I like you bein' around."

"I wish I could be here, too, but I have a sermon to prepare," Pastor Mitch said. "If you need me, I'll be in the church office." He pointed to the back door. "You can get to the church right through there and just follow the path. Jeannie knows the way."

She nodded. "I do. But Mrs. Stanley will be wantin' tea and—"

"I can handle making tea," I said.

Pastor Mitch left after pointing to a sealed glass jar on the counter near the double porcelain sink. It was filled with tea bags.

I smiled at Jeannie. "Let me help you into the living room—or would you rather talk to her in here?"

"This is where I stayed most days back when me and Kay Ellen was here," she said.

She seemed to be getting nervous again and I said, "Then I'll bring her back and we can all talk. I'll be right beside you."

"You was sayin' something about how it was that Kay Ellen passed," Jeannie said. "What's that mean, Miss Jillian?"

But the loud rapping on the front door interrupted us—and I was relieved. Jeannie knew her daughter died, but she didn't know how. That conversation might have to come soon, but not right now.

I glanced at Boots and her presence relaxed me. At my house, at least two cats would want to greet whoever had come knocking, but Boots hunkered closer to Jeannie, her paws tucked under her. Jeannie stroked her and her expression calmed. That little ghost cat could work magic at times.

I hurried down the hall and let Beatrice Stanley in. Immediately she said, "Where is she?"

Remembering what Ed had advised, I said, "I'm so glad you agreed to allow me to be with Jeannie during this chat. I think that was gracious of you." I hoped my words convinced Beatrice that she was in control—as she used to be once upon a time. "She's in the kitchen waiting for you."

"The kitchen?" she said with disdain as we passed through the lovely parlor. She glanced around as if she deserved to own everything in the room.

I had a sinking feeling that this would *not* be a pleasant meeting. Nothing about Beatrice Stanley was the least bit pleasant and I feared no matter how much I complimented her, it wouldn't matter. She might have lost material goods, but she hadn't lost the notion that she was entitled to them.

Jeannie was still stroking Boots when we entered the kitchen, but of course Beatrice couldn't see the cat. I was sure Jeannie's arcing hand rhythm in the air seemed odd at the very least.

Never taking her eyes off Jeannie, Beatrice slipped out of her camel hair coat. I should have commented on that coat when she'd arrived because it was a classic, probably an item from her former life—an example of the expensive clothes she had probably once worn all the time. She folded the coat neatly and placed it on the chair next to her.

Jeannie, meanwhile, had not made eye contact with Beatrice, and this conversation, like those before in the mill, would probably go through me. I offered to make tea, but Beatrice refused and Jeannie didn't even respond.

I sat down and said, "Mrs. Stanley, I believe you have a few questions for Jeannie?" I was breathing too fast and told myself to calm down. This was just three women in a room. No reason to be nervous.

"You've been living in my mill for ten years? Is that right?" Beatrice's tone was imperious and not a great way to start this dialogue.

Jeannie didn't answer. She put her arms around Boots and pulled her close.

Again, this must have seemed odd to Beatrice. She looked at me and said, "What's wrong with her? Does she have mental health issues I should know about?"

"Nothing's wrong with her," I said. "She's been through a trauma, that's all. Maybe if you ask me what you want to know, I can help her tell you."

"This is ridiculous," she said. "Look at me, Jeannie Sloan."

But Jeannie's focus remained on the cat invisible to Beatrice.

In as even a tone as I could muster, I said, "Please have compassion for her situation, Mrs. Stanley. She's been homeless a long time and isn't used to being around people. Ask *me* your questions and I promise I'll help you."

"Where's the compassion for *me*?" Beatrice shot back. But she took a ragged breath and said, "Oh, all right. Have it your way. I know that conniving, deceitful husband of mine hid assets so I wouldn't get them in the divorce. They're in that mill. I just know it."

"You mean money?" I said, taken completely by surprise.

"Cash, my jewelry that went missing, anything he could grab without leaving a paper trail once he'd divorced me. To his great regret, I'm sure, he never got the chance to actually spend any of it." She pointed at Jeannie. "And that woman has been inside the mill. She's probably been helping herself to my money all these years. In fact, I'm certain she has."

Unbelievable, I thought. Jeannie had been scrounging through a Dumpster at night looking for food while she'd lived in the mill. She didn't have this woman's money. But denying it, I now knew from my experience with Beatrice, wouldn't work. So I said, "From what I understand, you did still live in the family home while your husband was hospitalized. Wouldn't such a big place be a more likely location to hide these assets? He would have easy access to—"

"Don't you think my son and I tore that place apart before we were tossed to the curb?" she said. "No, that bastard stashed it in the mill. I'm sure of it."

Jeannie whispered, "She said a bad word. That's not right."

I wanted to agree with her, but instead addressed Beatrice. "Okay, what if your husband set up offshore accounts or—"

"What *don't* you understand about what I'm saying, Mrs. Hart?" Beatrice said through clenched teeth. "I know how my husband operated. What he took, what belongs to me, is hidden in that mill and this woman—" She pointed dramatically at Jeannie. "This woman knows where it is or she's stolen it."

"Stealin' is wrong," Jeannie mumbled.

"Yes, it is," Beatrice said. "So cleanse your conscience. Tell me what you've been doing in my mill all these years. How did you survive if you didn't take my money?"

Her mill. Her money. The woman was living in the past. And with her condescending attitude, I was finding it difficult to remain patient. But I had to. For Jeannie's sake. I turned and said, "Jeannie, Mrs. Stanley believes you took something that belonged to her. I don't believe that, but I will ask you. Do you know anything about any money or jewelry in the mill?"

"Don't know nothin'. You should ask the creepers. Maybe they know," Jeannie said.

The creepers. I'd thought Jeannie, because she'd lived alone for so many years, might have been having hallucinations, that these creepers were figments of her imagination. But what if they weren't? Had someone been sneaking into the mill and looking for what Beatrice Stanley so desperately wanted?

"Creepers?" Beatrice said. "What in heaven is the woman talking about? She *is* mentally ill."

Trying to explain to this woman anything about Jeannie's experience for the last decade was futile. I said, "Did you ever enter the mill after it was closed up, Mrs. Stanley? Look for this money you say your husband hid from you? Because perhaps Jeannie heard you and—"

She laughed derisively. "Are you implying *I'm* one of these *creepers*? How ridiculous. I wouldn't think of breaking into the building, not like *she* did, even though it's rightfully mine. Ask her again. She may act simple, but she knows exactly what I'm talking about."

I sighed. This was going nowhere. But I again turned to Jeannie. "Do you know anything at all about money or jewels? Know of any hiding places?"

Still gazing at the table, her ghost cat close to her breast, she didn't speak, just slowly shook her head no.

I wanted to question Jeannie further about these creepers I'd thought were imaginary, but I wasn't about to do so in front of this unsympathetic, hateful woman. I looked at Beatrice and said, "Who else knew your theory about hidden assets besides your son?"

"My *theory*? You think I'm making this up?" she said.

"I'm trying to *help* you." My patience was spent. "Why would the money be inside the mill?"

"Because Ward—my husband, not my son—practically lived in that mill. From what I heard, that one over there—" She waved a hand at Jeannie. "That one was living in my husband's old office, not to mention hanging around a dead body. Now she's lying about what she did to me. She ruined my life."

Jeannie lifted her head and emphatically said, "I don't lie. Not never."

It was the first time they'd made eye contact and I thought I saw Beatrice shrink back a little. "You can't make me believe that." She stood and grabbed her coat. "When the truth comes out, when they start tearing up that mill, they'll find evidence—a ring, a bracelet, a stack of hundred-dollar bills—and you'll be put in jail because most of my fortune is probably gone now. You know you'll end up in jail, don't you?"

Jeannie looked over at me, panic in her eyes. "Am I goin' to jail?"

"No, Jeannie, because you didn't steal anything." I stared up at Beatrice Stanley and I couldn't keep the ice out of my tone when I said, "You know the way out."

Thirty-two

Boots followed on Beatrice Stanley's heels as she marched down the hallway as if to herd her out of the house.

Big fat tears were streaming down Jeannie's face; I pulled my chair close to hers and put an arm around her shoulder.

"You won't go to jail," I said. "She's just an angry person who likes to take it out on other people."

Jeannie wiped her cheeks with the back of her hand. "I never took no money. Why did she say that?"

"I guess because you were living in the mill and she thinks someone hid her money there. It's her way of asking if you know anything." *And she could be right about there being money hidden there,* I thought to myself. "Tell me more about these creepers. Did you ever see them?"

"Nope," Jeannie said, shaking her head. "But they was pulling up boards and one time they came into the office while I was out gettin' food."

"How did you know if you weren't there?" I said.

"'Cause my stuff was all thrown around. And they pulled up the floorboards and then hammered 'em back down. But not the right way. They didn't go near where my Kay Ellen lay, though."

"And how could you tell?" I said.

"The hearth was dusty—hadn't gotten to clean it that week yet. It was still dusty when I come back that night. I cleaned it then." She swallowed and her eyes filled again. "It's a holy place."

I was reminded again that telling her Kay Ellen had been moved would be a very difficult conversation. "You keep saying *they* when you talk about the creepers. There was more than one?"

"Coulda been one. Still sounded like a shift change to me with all the noise they was makin'."

"Shift change?" I said.

"Like when we left and the new workers came in to run the looms. They'd come stompin' in."

"Ah. I get it," I said. "You think you heard more than one set of boots on the floor?"

"All I know is I'd hear the stompin', the hammerin'. Scared me somethin' fierce. I took to movin' the desk to block my door sometimes."

These creepers must not have cared about Jeannie's presence. All they cared about was searching the mill. I wouldn't put it past Beatrice to have been in on it—or Beatrice and her son.

My question was, how were they getting in? I'd have to tell Candace about all this and ask her if any of the loose bricks on other windows that Mike had mentioned could have been a way for these intruders to get inside. Because I believed Jeannie one hundred percent. She hadn't been hallucinating at all.

"Have you been walking much today?" I asked Jeannie. Bless her heart, the poor soul could use a nice peaceful walk in her old neighborhood.

"They told me to walk. Guess I should." She started to rise and I helped her to her feet.

I pulled the walker over. She grabbed hold and

straightened herself, taking the deliberate care she'd probably been taught at the hospital.

"Why don't we go outside? You could show me where you used to live," I said.

Her mouth cracked into a crooked smile. "Yes, and Boots would like that." Then her face fell. "I ain't got no coat."

She was wearing a blue tracksuit today, but she was right. It was chilly. I said, "Wear my jacket. I've got a sweater on underneath."

She shook her head. "No. I might get it dirty and you'd be mad."

"Nonsense. You need it more than I do," I said.

We took the path out the back door and when we hit the Y section where one walkway led to the church and the other to the street, we headed for the street. I walked slowly beside Jeannie, who, to my surprise, was hardly even limping. I texted the pastor that we were out for a walk and would be back shortly.

The old neighborhood seemed deserted, the silence interrupted only by the songs of cardinals or the chatter of squirrels in the trees that lined the street.

"Where did you live, Jeannie?" I asked.

"Way over there. Kinda a long way to go," she said.

"Maybe we can see your house another day, then," I said, not wanting to wear her out. "Why don't we walk up and down this block?"

"You can see the mill from down there." She pointed straight ahead. "Boots is already halfway there."

She probably thought of the mill as her home—and it really had been for ten years. I said, "Want to go have a look?"

She nodded. "Can't let Bootsie get too far. Don't want to lose her."

As we got closer, I saw that Boots had stopped. She

was sitting on the sidewalk, staring at a small boy and girl playing in a front yard. The ghost cat looked at us and back at the children as if beckoning us.

Jeannie picked up her pace. "Boots is wantin' us to talk to them."

"What?" I said. "Those are just little kids, Jeannie. Maybe Boots wants to play with them."

"Nope." Jeannie plowed ahead, her rolling walker bumping along the sidewalk.

When we reached the house where the children were playing, an older woman came out of the front door immediately. She seemed to be in protection mode, but then she smiled broadly. "Why, if it ain't Jeannie Sloan as I live and breathe."

Jeannie looked at the ground, but she said, "Hey there, Deborah."

"What you doin' with that walker?"

"Busted my hip," Jeannie said.

Deborah walked down to greet us. "Who's your friend?"

"This here is Jillian. She helps me," Jeannie said.

"Nice to meet you, Jillian. I seen you over at the mill when all heck broke out." Deborah looked to be about Jeannie's age, her hair thin and graying. I wondered if these two women had once worked together.

The two children, obviously curious, came running over and grabbed onto Deborah's housedress. She only wore a thin sweater on top of her dress, but she didn't seem bothered by the forty-degree chill.

"What's wrong with her, Granny?" the little boy said, pointing at Jeannie's walker.

"She hurt herself. Now you two go back to playin' and let the grown folks talk," Deborah said.

The children complied and ran back down the driveway where two tricycles sat.

"I heard tell you was livin' in that mill. Is it true?" Deborah said.

Jeannie looked up then. "Yup. Had to watch over Kay Ellen."

Deborah seemed confused. "Kay Ellen was there, too? I didn't hear nothin' about that."

I gave a little shake of my head, hoping to warn Deborah off this topic and she seemed to understand.

She said, "I'm glad to see you, Jeannie. And we'll all be happy when they fix up that old place we used to work in. Been an eyesore for years. And I'm tired of seein' folks sneakin' in and out of there." She realized her mistake quickly and said, "Never saw you, though."

"You saw people sneaking into the mill?" I asked.

But before Deborah could answer, Jeannie said, "Fix up the mill? What you talkin' about?"

I touched Jeannie's arm. "It's okay. It's nothing." I looked at Deborah. "Where did you see these people going in and out? Because Jeannie was telling me about trespassers, too."

"Maybe not people—just one person at a time is all I see. Probably a teenager. At the old kitchen entrance," Deborah said. "Thought they had it all locked up, but kids these days? Where's their parents, anyways?"

"I know what you mean," I said. "You can see the kitchen entrance from here?"

"I can when the moon's full and there's no clouds. My daughter's husband made me a nice room in the attic. He's good with his hands. I get a pretty view of the stars and the night sky through the little window." Deborah smiled proudly.

"You talkin' about Charlene? She okay?" Jeannie said.

Deborah nodded. "I watch her children while they work. I never did get to tell you how sorry I was about Kay Ellen goin' missin'. Sad thing, that."

"She ain't missin'. She's in a holy place." Jeannie tossed her head in the direction of the mill.

Deborah tried to hide her skepticism, but it wasn't lost on me. Just then, one of the children cried out and I saw the two of them were arguing over a tricycle.

"There they go again," Deborah said. "Got to settle this. Nice seein' you, Jeannie." She looked at me. "And nice meetin' you." She turned and walked up the driveway.

Jeannie looked tired and a tiny bit sad as she watched the woman retreat.

I said, "You've had enough exercise for today. Let's go back."

As we returned to the pastorium, Jeannie mumbled, "Charlene's okay. Charlene's okay."

It was as if Jeannie had been worrying that other teenage girls had gone missing along with her own—that the world at some point simply took your loved ones away. Yes, Jeannie saw things differently than most of us, but I was beginning to understand her.

Unfortunately, she then noticed that Boots had disappeared. She stopped and looked back, then called, "Bootsie, come on," several times. Then she looked at me. "Do you see my Boots?"

I didn't. "No, Jeannie. But she'll come back. She always does."

Jeannie hung her head. "I guess."

We walked back in silence. This hadn't quite been the pleasant walk I'd hoped she'd enjoy.

Elizabeth had returned home when we came in through the back door. She took one look at Jeannie and said, "Time for you to rest."

I said good-bye, but I didn't go straight to my van. I walked back down the block, crossed the street and went to the mill fence. I looked back at Deborah's house and spotted the attic window she'd talked about. My gaze swept back and forth between the window and the mill so I could determine exactly where this kitchen entrance was. I had to walk about fifty feet to my right where the fence turned. I saw an old driveway leading up to the mill, weeds sprouting through cracks in the asphalt. There looked to be a loading dock there and a big door. But without binoculars, I couldn't see much more than that.

I needed to talk to Candace or Morris as soon as possible.

Thirty-three

Before leaving the mill village, I checked my cat cam. If Boots had somehow transported herself to my house, I didn't see her napping with my three.

I got a text from Kara while I was watching and learned I needed to get home and change my clothes. She was meeting Earl Whitehouse for dinner and had reserved the table right next to theirs so I could listen in on the conversation. The place was about as fancy as Mercy got—but even then, all I needed to wear were dressier pants, a pretty shirt and my coat rather than my jacket.

My three cats were not happy when I came and left the house in such a hurry. As I drove to the police station to fill Candace in on today's events, I nearly hit the car stopped at a light in front of me because Boots had suddenly appeared on the passenger's seat. I couldn't take dealing with a ghost cat for the rest of my life and surely hoped that if I found out who killed Kay Ellen, Boots could go back to comforting Jeannie full-time. Her popping up like this unnerved me.

I was lucky enough to find both Morris and Candace at the police station before they'd left for the day. But since they were eating takeout in the break room, I had the feeling they weren't leaving any time soon.

I sat down at the table and explained what I'd learned

from Jeannie and from the neighbor. I then asked about the kitchen entrance to the mill.

Around a mouthful of sweet-and-sour chicken from China Palace, Candace said, "We checked that door. It's got a dead bolt inside and I didn't see any tool marks on the outside. But since you have confirmation from someone besides Jeannie that a person, or more than one person, was coming in and out of the mill, Morris can follow up. Don't get me wrong; I like Jeannie. She just isn't the most reliable witness."

"Did the neighbor say how long this has been happenin'?" Morris said.

"No. She didn't go into much detail," I said. "From what I gathered standing next to her house, I doubt this woman could have distinguished much more than that it was a person coming and going—not their age, race or gender."

Candace looked at Morris. "Sounds like you definitely need to interview this woman." She turned to me. "I can't follow up because I'm running phone records on all those big-money players vying for the mill. I swear from looking at these pages and pages of calls, that these guys talk on their mobiles more than a bunch of teenage girls. We also got this shadow investor to figure out. Tom's helping with that. I want to know how the town council allowed paperwork to be filed on the proposals without everyone's name on it. Doesn't seem legal."

Morris said, "They don't give a crap. They want to unload that elephant and they wouldn't care if a bunch of bomb-making idiots bought it."

Candace grinned. "You're probably right."

"Did Tom tell you that Kara is helping with the Earl Whitehouse lead in Kay Ellen's case?" I said.

"Glad it's her and not me," Morris said. "He's a judge's son and you want to know where the power lies in this town, you walk into any courtroom. You'll find the power sitting higher than everyone else."

"She won't splash this all over the front page of the *Messenger*, I hope," Candace said.

"She just wants to be ready with her story once the truth comes out," I said. "Tom believes she has the best chance of getting Earl Whitehouse to talk about Kay Ellen."

"Tom is one smart guy to use a pretty thing like her to get information," Morris said. "I couldn't get the time of day outta that boy. He was about ready to get his daddy on the phone when I decided to leave."

"She's meeting with him at the Finest Catch for dinner," I said. "Chatted him up at the post office after following him there."

"Bet his fiancée would like to know about that," Morris said. "He's got one of those, I hear."

"As long as the fiancée isn't anything like Lydia, it should be okay. I'm sure Kara will make sure Earl gets the cold shoulder after today—that is, if she learns anything. It will be interesting to see if he stonewalls her like he did you."

"I hope she gets him talkin'," Morris said. "'Specially if he killed Kay Ellen. And the way he's lied already, he's lookin' pretty good for her murder."

"Which is why I'm relieved Kara's meeting him in a public place." I glanced at the clock above the fridge. "Got to go. Don't want to miss anything."

I left my van parked in the courthouse lot and walked the few blocks to the Finest Catch. The hostess who greeted me whispered, "Kara told me right where to seat you, Mrs. Hart. She's already here."

My table was directly behind hers. She was alone, sipping on a glass of white wine. We didn't make eye contact—it was hard for me to walk right past her—and I sat so her back was to me and I would be facing Earl Whitehouse when he arrived. I sure hoped he didn't stand her up.

I ordered white wine, too, thinking of my cats when I did so. They had to be upset with me for rushing in and out after being gone all afternoon. On cue, as my thoughts turned to cats, Boots appeared. She seemed to know when I needed reassurance and when I was missing my own friends. As much as she sometimes unsettled me, I had to admit she was a nice little ghost, one who had led us right to Deborah, the neighbor, today. I had the feeling that was no accident.

Just as my wine arrived, a man in his mid-twenties with a patch of dark beard in the cleft of his chin and his head shaved bald sat opposite Kara. My heart sped up. Would she get him to talk? I had Mercy PD on speed dial if needed, though I doubted he'd make some terrible confession right here. I set my phone on the white tablecloth, right by Boots's front paws. There was a window by my table that looked out to Main Street. The green awnings on the shops had tiny lights on them and they made the street look so pretty in the evening. Boots gazed out the window, watching people walk past. She was always so calm despite the serious happenings she'd been a part of during the last few days.

The waiter took my order, a sea bass that sounded delicious, and I then turned my attention to the conversation at the next table.

Kara was saying she never usually asked guys out on dates, but Earl had just captured her attention.

He smiled and I had to admit he was a good-looking guy.

"You caught my eye, too," Earl said.

Kara went on to ask him several questions and we learned he worked part of the time in Greenville and part of the time here in town in some kind of techie job. I didn't catch the name of the company. He'd lived in Mercy all his life, but he had never seen her in town before. She told him she was new to the area. He called her

Roberta once and I assumed that was the fake name she'd given him. Then she asked about his family.

"My father is Judge Whitehouse. You don't ever want to go before him. Hard-ass is the only way to describe him."

Kara laughed. "I hope I'm never in enough trouble to end up in a courtroom. What kind of judging does he do? Is that the right term? Judging?"

I knew she was probably batting her eyelashes at him about now. She was sipping her wine, but Earl was on his second martini. Pretty soon, he'd be ripe for the tougher questions.

My salad had come and gone and my sea bass was in front of me when that time came.

"I grew up in Houston," she said. "It's so big you can get lost. But this is such a cute, small town, I'll bet you still know every single person you graduated from high school with."

He nodded, a forkful of salad in the air. "I do."

"Do they stay here to live as you have—or do some of them want to run as far from here as possible?" Kara said.

I saw his expression change. He seemed almost sad. "They almost all stay. Most all of us have deep family roots. As far as leaving, one of my good friends died from leukemia not long after we graduated and then there was this girl who disappeared. She'd had a rough life, so she probably *wanted* to get away."

"Disappeared? How interesting," Kara said. "I love the true crime shows and there's one program I watch dedicated to people who've disappeared. The endings are always so unhappy because most of the time, they don't know what happened to the person they're doing the show about."

"Well, they should come here and do a story about

Kay Ellen Sloan," he said. "The police were asking me about her just yesterday. Said they had some stupid lead that I was her boyfriend. Can you believe that?"

"Wow." Kara rested her elbows on the table and leaned toward Earl. "How exciting. Could you help the police?"

Her reaction apparently surprised him because he seemed to think about this for a few seconds. Realizing he was suddenly even more interesting to her, he said, "I didn't know her. I knew *about* her."

But I noticed him avert his eyes for the first time. He was lying to Kara now, just as he'd lied to Morris. What was he hiding?

"Were you nervous talking to the police?" she said. "I know I'd be, but then, I've never even been close to any kind of mystery."

"Why should I be nervous?" he said. "I couldn't tell the cop anything he didn't already know. The girl vanished. Besides, she was from the mill village. We didn't, um, *mess* with those types of people."

I wouldn't have been able to keep my mouth shut if he'd said something like that to my face. But Kara remained on point and on an even keel. "Oh, I see. There's more to the story. She was from the wrong side of the tracks?"

His cheeks had blotched. His neck, too. He understood he'd exposed his prejudice, perhaps with the help of what was now his third martini. "I guess you could say that. The people who live there are . . . different. Entrenched in their culture."

Kara said, "I'll bet there was plenty of talk in the high school, though. Crazy theories about what happened to her, right?"

Unfortunately before he could answer, their food arrived. Meanwhile, I'd been so wrapped up in listening to their conversation, my dinner was getting cold. I decided I didn't want to pay for a ruined meal and began to eat. *Delicious and still warm, thank goodness,* I thought.

Boots had taken a great interest in the sea bass, sniffing at my plate, looking at me, then taking another sniff. It was all I could do to keep from offering a ghost cat a tiny bite. *Right, Jillian.* And then they'd call for the guys with the straitjackets.

After both Kara and Earl commented on how good their dinners were, Kara started in again, saying, "I'm truly intrigued by this mystery." She really was amazingly good at this play-acting. "Nothing more exciting than the homecoming king barfing on the football field ever happened at my high school," Kara said. "The guy had sneaked one too many beers before the ceremony. But you had something truly interesting happen—and in this little town."

"Not *that* interesting." Perhaps Earl had sobered up a little, because he now seemed to want to move on from this topic.

"Oh, but it is," she said. "Do you think she was harmed or just walked away?"

"This happened ten years ago. I don't remember much about it, to be honest." He studied his food.

Yup, he was shutting down. *Change the subject for a while, Kara.*

She must have read my mind because that was exactly what she did. But the fact that alcohol had loosened his tongue wasn't lost on her.

She said, "While I was waiting for you, I saw a wine on the list that I've been dying to try. Want to give it a go?"

"Sure," he said, raising a hand to summon the waiter.

As they ate and kept drinking wine, Kara asked him about his job again, where he went to college and pretty much kept him talking nonstop. She'd obviously picked up on the fact that he loved to talk about himself.

I ate slowly, with the waiter hovering and glancing my way every now and then to see when I finished. I asked for the dessert menu when he finally came over to take my empty plate, telling him I'd heard they had wonderful pies and cheesecakes. While I read over the options, I kept my ear tuned to the conversation at the next table.

I heard Kara say, "Since I'm new in town, I don't know what's happening with that old mill. But something sure is going on. When I stopped at that darling little coffee place a few days ago, I overheard someone talking about how they had to stop working on the restoration because something strange happened."

"There's no renovation yet," Earl said with derision. "Just politics so far. I was in Greenville the first part of the week, so I'm not sure what's going on. If you're such a crime buff, what's more fascinating is that we've had a *murder*. My father was telling me about it. One of the council members was stabbed to death."

"I *did* hear about that," she said. "I've been making sure my deadbolt and my regular lock are fastened at night. Could it be a serial killer?"

He laughed. "In Mercy? No way. My father thinks her death has something to do with the mill. The woman who died was pretty involved in all that business."

"I guess that makes sense," Kara said. "Judges would know about such things. You never did say what your father does exactly—or maybe I just know nothing about how judges do their jobs."

"The judges rotate the dockets. Dad does everything from probate to traffic court to criminal trials," he said.

"So he's probably heard things about the murder," Kara said. "Inside things. And maybe even knows about the police investigation concerning that girl from your high school who disappeared. I'll bet you hear everything from him."

"I don't live with my father anymore, so I hear his war stories only when we get together," he said with a laugh.

"But I'm sure you did hear things when that girl disappeared. What'd he tell you about *her* case?" Kara said.

"He and everyone else knew she was a runaway," Earl said. "Nothing to hang around for if you lived in that mill village."

My dessert arrived—a chocolate mocha cake with caramel drizzled all over it. *Concentrating on anything but this piece of heaven will be difficult,* I thought after the first bite. Boots had taken to people-watching again, but I felt she'd come here as a little guardian angel.

Kara was saying, "Is it that bad living in . . . What did you call it?"

"The mill village—where all the mill workers used to live when the place was operational. Kay Ellen couldn't possibly have been happy living there. I mean, her mother was—let me be nice—a little *slow*. Kay Ellen had to do everything for her and—" Earl, who had been pushing food around his plate, looked up at Kara. He lowered his voice and I had to strain to hear him. "Okay, maybe I did know her."

"It's okay," Kara said gently. "I kind of had that feeling. You really think she ran away?"

Earl drained his wineglass and Kara obligingly refilled it. He said, "She never told me she was leaving—but that had to be what happened."

"You two never talked about her running away—or even running away together?" Kara asked.

"I could never run away with *her*," he said. He was beginning to slur his words now. "But you know, she was a nice girl. A pretty girl. I liked her even if my dad thought she was white trash."

"Were you upset when she just left like that?" Kara said.

"You bet I was. I even cried when her mother came to

ask me about her. But the two of us had no future, so it was best she left town." He picked up his fork again and began eating.

"You ever get any ideas about what might have happened to her if in fact she *didn't* run away?" Kara pressed.

Cocking his head, he seemed to be thinking. "Maybe she was in the wrong place at the wrong time. The day before she left, she was talking about how they'd fenced up the mill, but people were still getting in there. She said it was wrong. Said if she caught them again, she'd make sure they knew she saw what they were doing. Kay Ellen was like that." He smiled sadly. "A really good person. So mature. I was an ass to pretend I didn't know her. But I had to. My dad would have been so pissed at me."

"Would he still be pissed at you today?" Kara asked.

Earl hesitated before he spoke. "Maybe not." He straightened in his chair. "He doesn't tell me what to do anymore." He pointed at Kara. "You know what? I'm calling up that cop tomorrow. Tell him I knew Kay Ellen. Let him ask me anything he wants. It's the least I can do."

"That sounds like the right thing to do," Kara said softly. "Because it seems you might have been one of the last people to talk to her."

"I was, wasn't I?" he said.

The guy was definitely drunk. I doubted if he'd even remember this conversation tomorrow or recover his conscience without help from a bottle. But Kara had done a great job and I couldn't help but smile as I enjoyed my mocha, chocolate, caramel bliss.

Thirty-four

As I was paying my bill for the absolutely wonderful dinner I'd enjoyed—and the absolutely wonderful performance by my brilliant stepdaughter—my phone rang. I was surprised when Dustin said hello.

I started walking the few blocks to my van, Boots leading the way. Dustin was almost stammering with excitement. "We need to get back in that mill tomorrow."

I said, "The police believe it will be clear to go in then. You can finish your job and—"

"It's not just my job," he said. "Okay, maybe it is. But I've been going over the original blueprints and comparing them to the photos I've taken. I have this app where I can overlay my pictures onto the drawings."

"Sounds complicated," I said, "but very cool."

"It's easy," he said. "Anyway, the office where we found the homeless woman? The photos indicate a new wall went up at some point. The room lost three feet in that section."

"But how old are the blueprints?" I asked, clicking my remote to unlock the van.

"Original, so I get what you're trying to say," he replied. "This room alteration could have been done years and years ago. It's not a load-bearing section of the office and it would have been easy to slap up drywall and paint it. My question is, why do it? I mean, I didn't see any closet there."

I slid behind the wheel and saw Boots suddenly appear on the seat next to me. How did she do that? *Oh. That's right. She's a ghost. She can do whatever she wants.*

"Jillian . . . you still there?" Dustin said.

"I am. And I believe you've raised an interesting point." Then it dawned on me. Someone had been going in and out of that mill—and not just recently, but as far back as when Kay Ellen Sloan died. Was Beatrice right? Did Ward Stanley hide his fortune in that mill to keep his wife from getting her hands on his money? Hide it away between the walls?

Dustin said, "I know it's getting late and I wasn't sure if I should call Deputy Carson. But I'd like to get inside that mill tomorrow. It's not just this wall; I have more work to do. I can tell that you and Candace are good friends. You could get her to help me out."

"And I'm happy to do just that. I'll phone her and get back to you, okay?" I said.

"Would you? I am going nuts over here. I want to finish this project—and don't repeat this, but I don't think condos will work with the amount of money that particular investment group has put together. But I'll know better once I complete my assessment. I sure hope I won't upset too many people, but I have to do the job I was hired for—and do it right."

"I agree," I said.

He said good-bye and I drove home. Syrah and Merlot seemed thrilled Boots had come with me and they sped off for a game of chase. The groggy feeling from having wine, a big dinner and lots of sugar had worn off the moment I'd realized what Dustin might have discovered. I was as excited as he had sounded.

With Chablis purring on my lap and with the kitty

chaos I could hear happening in the hallway, I called Candace.

Before I even said hello, she started talking. "Did Kara get the judge's jerk of a son to tell the truth?"

"She did. But I don't think he's our killer," I said. "He's just a small person too embarrassed to admit he was hanging around with a mill village girl."

"Oh," she said, sounding completely deflated.

"But he did tell Kara that Kay Ellen knew someone was entering the mill at night," I said. "Sounds like she was a spunky girl who knew this person was trespassing."

"And she could have confronted whoever it was and gotten herself killed for her trouble," Candace said, her interest level suddenly rising again.

"But that's not the only reason I called you. I just talked to Dustin Gray." I went on to explain what he'd told me and her response was just as I expected.

"We've got to get in there," she said. "If there's money hidden between those walls, that could explain plenty— at least about the cold case. That girl could have seen something she shouldn't. I'm calling Dustin right now."

I told her I needed to be there in the morning, too, to feed the feral cats.

"Cats, huh?" she said. "I'm not buying it. You're as curious as I am and I don't blame you. Of course you can be there."

I hung up and was about ready to go to bed, maybe read a little, when my phone rang.

"Did Dustin come over there?" Candace said.

"No. You couldn't reach him?" I said.

"His phone goes to voice mail and when I called the Pink House, Laura said he left in a rush."

"Uh-oh. He's gone to the mill. He couldn't wait," I said.

"Yup, and he still has keys. I'm heading over there right now," she said.

"You shouldn't go alone," I said. "We don't know who's been in there—who these people are Jeannie's been telling us about."

"Jillian, when you have a gun and you know how to use it, you're never alone. I'll let you know what I find over there. Who knows? Maybe the guy just went out for a drink."

"In Mercy? On a weeknight?" I said. "We both know he's over there."

"And I'm on my way." She disconnected.

But gun or no gun, she shouldn't go to that creepy place in the dark alone. I tried Morris's number. No answer. I thought about calling Mike Baca, but he might be upset with Candace for rushing out to the mill, so I called the most reliable person I knew—Tom.

After I told him the problem, he said, "I'm driving back right now from a job across the lake. Shouldn't take me long to get there."

"It's not like she'll be truly alone if Dustin is where we think he is," I said. "I just worry."

"I know," he said. I could almost picture his smile.

"Sit tight and I'll let you know what I find out," he said.

But I wasn't about to sit tight. I couldn't. I went to my bedroom and changed into jeans and a sweatshirt—and out of the uncomfortable dress shoes. I was on my way to the mill within five minutes of my call to Tom.

I assumed Boots decided to stay and play at my house, because she didn't appear in the van. When I arrived at the mill, I realized it seemed even more mysterious and eerie at night. Of course, not until I got to the locked gate did I realize I couldn't get in. Candace's RAV4 was parked here and so was Dustin's Volkswagen, so the two of them were inside.

I started to call Candace's cell and then realized there was no reception in there. I remembered the kitchen entrance and how the neighbor Deborah had seen intruders using that door. I got back in the van and drove around the corner—it would have been quite a walk otherwise—and parked on that side street. Good thing I had my flashlight in the van; there were no streetlights on this side of the mill.

The area was fenced and no one had bothered to put a gate where the old driveway that led to the kitchen entrance began. *So how are trespassers getting beyond this barrier?*

I trained the flashlight along the fence and it didn't take long to find a place where the fence had been cut— or should I say newly *recut*. I noted a piece of fencing on the ground. Obviously the police had found this spot at some point and repaired it, but someone had come along after them and made sure they could get inside. *Not good.*

At that point I decided I'd been foolish to even show up here and started walking back to my van. I wasn't about to pull apart an opening in the fence and crawl through the space, only to find a locked kitchen entrance. Besides, this place gave me the creeps.

I turned to leave when I saw someone clad in black. The person was standing near a large tree and had attempted to hide when I'd turned around.

My heart in my throat, I decided to pretend I hadn't seen anyone. I had to get to my van and warn my friends inside that mill somehow.

I tried to act casual, walking, not running, as fast as I could to my van. As I did so, I pulled my phone from my pocket, but before I could press the number for Mercy PD, a gloved hand belonging to someone behind me covered my mouth. I felt a gun barrel press against my spine.

"If you stay quiet, I won't kill you right here. You understand?" the man said.

I nodded.

He whirled me around and I stared into Ward Stanley's eyes—just his eyes, because he wore a ski mask. But I recognized him immediately.

"Drop the flashlight and give me your phone." He held out his free hand, keeping the gun aimed at my stomach.

I did as he told me. Handing my phone to him felt like letting go of a lifeline—but then I remembered that Tom was coming. He'd be here soon. And in the meantime, I had to make this man believe I didn't recognize him.

"I don't have any money with me," I said, "but you can have the phone."

"Do you think I'm stupid, Jillian?" He pocketed my phone and pulled off his mask. "You know damn well who you're talking to."

So much for plan A. I sure hope plan B gets here soon. My hands had begun to shake—in fact I was trembling all over. "I—I don't know what you want from me, but—"

"I want you to come with me." He turned me back around and I felt the gun's pressure again. "Walk right back to where you came from."

I did as I was told, stumbling along the sidewalk in the dark. When I didn't go fast enough, he shoved my shoulder.

"Hurry up," he whispered harshly.

When we reached the spot in the fence where he'd cut the links, he peeled the aging fence back and told me to crawl through. If I'd had anything I could use as a weapon, even the flashlight he'd made me drop, I might have been able to smash him over the head when he came through the fence. But I had nothing—and I probably wouldn't have succeeded in knocking him out anyway.

He'd probably been coming in and out of this mill for

years, looking for the money he and his mother believed was hidden inside. Thank goodness he didn't know that I had friends in the building this very minute, not to mention a friend on the way. I clung to that thought. I had to.

When we reached the padlocked kitchen entrance, he pulled a key from his pocket. He made me stand to the left and kept the gun trained on me as he unlocked the door.

"Y-you have a key?" I blurted.

"Of course. All I had to do when the bank threw us out was change their padlock one night. Stupid suits thought a little lock would keep me out of my own mill? How dumb was that?" Once the door was open, he shoved me into a dark, frigid hallway.

From behind me, a beam of light came on and I realized he had a flashlight. I heard what I thought was the click of a deadbolt. He pointed his light straight ahead and said, "Walk. Now."

I'd never made it to this part of the building when I was here before, but Shawn told me he'd placed one of the feral cat shelters in the kitchen and I would have to find it to fill the food bowls—in fact he'd tried to put one shelter in each room on the ground floor and several in the big area where the looms once stood. I wondered where the shelter was and if I'd run right into it. I could hardly see two feet in front of me.

"We're going straight through this hallway, out the door and then to my father's old office," he said. "So keep going. Don't try turning into the kitchen where you think you can hide."

"But I can't see anything." I almost smiled, though. We were headed for Candace and Dustin—headed for safety.

I breathed a little easier as we made our way in the dark, our shoes thudding loudly on the wood floor. He obviously had arrived here after Candace and Dustin, parked on a street in the village and then must have sneaked through the neighborhood to get to the back entrance. He hadn't seen their cars.

"How did you know about the fence? About the back entrance?" he said as we walked.

"People in the neighborhood realize there have been trespassers and Jeannie and one of her neighbors—"

He shoved me—hard. "I'm no *trespasser*. Don't you and the rest of this town get that?"

I'd made this already ticking time bomb of a man even angrier. I had to handle this situation better if I wanted to get to Candace and Dustin. "I-I'm sorry. You're absolutely right. What happened to you and your mother was wrong. I know things have been difficult."

"What do you know?" he said. "Bet you never watched your mother scrounge for pennies to get her nails done. Bet you never had to give up your Porsche and the only home you'd ever known because the government decided what was yours was now theirs."

"And your reputation as a community leader as well," I said over my shoulder. "I cannot imagine what you've been through."

"Do you think I give a damn about Mercy? But you're right. You can't imagine what it's like to live how my mother and I have to live now." He didn't sound less hostile despite the sympathetic tone I'd tried to offer. But then, he'd had more than a decade for his resentment to fester.

"If it means anything, I'm really sorry," I said.

"Yeah, I'll bet you are." His voice was laced with sarcasm. "The door is about ten feet ahead of you. Put your hands out or you'll run right into it."

I did this and soon felt the nails and the splintered wood on the heavy old door beneath my fingers.

He said, "Find the bolt and slide it open. It's rusty, so

put some strength behind it." He pushed the gun harder against my backbone. "And don't even think about running."

I worked the lock open, saying, "The police bolted this room back up after they finished their search?"

"No, I did," he said. "And they didn't search hard enough, because if they'd found our assets, I would have heard about it. I'll find our money, and my mother and I will be long gone before they ever find you."

Find me? A fresh fluttering in my stomach began. What if Candace and Dustin had left already? And what if Tom saw them come out and then called my house and figured I'd gone to bed? I closed my eyes and took a deep breath. I couldn't focus on the worst outcome. I had to stay positive if I wanted to get out of this alive.

The door squeaked after he ordered me to open it and I was relieved at being inches closer to safety.

But when I saw lights from the halogens casting a faint glow in the hallway up ahead, I wanted to run toward it—because I knew Stanley had seen it, too.

"The police must have forgotten to turn out the lights when they left," I said.

But then we both heard a scraping sound echo down the hall. Dustin or Candace had probably moved that desk to get to the false wall. My stomach clenched.

Stanley grabbed my arm and yanked me back into the kitchen.

"Lock the door," he said, his voice strained with frustration and anger. *"Now."*

Thirty-five

My only hope now was that I'd closed the door loudly enough that Candace heard. After all, the sound of what *they* were doing in the office had traveled down the hall, so the reverse should be true. They must have heard the door. They *had* to have heard the door.

Meanwhile, Stanley was coming unglued. Now that my eyes were used to the dark, I watched as he paced back and forth in front of me, his flashlight moving like a candle in front of him. He'd placed his hand with the gun on top of his head.

"Got to think, got to think," he said.

Then I heard a sound I loved—footsteps coming down the hallway beyond the door. Candace called, "Who's in there?"

Stanley grabbed me then. "Out the way we came. And you'd better move fast or I'll shoot you right here and now."

But just as we reached the back door, someone knocked loudly on *that* door.

"Jillian? Are you in there?" Tom shouted.

He'd seen my car.

I cried out, "Yes. I'm here. Stanley has a gun."

Ward Stanley's forearm made contact with my cheek and knocked me to the floor. He pointed the flashlight at me and said, "You shut up. You're a hostage now and you'd better be a smart one."

I nodded, tasting blood in my mouth.

"Get up. We're moving away from these doors so I can think." He motioned with the gun toward the kitchen that I'd seen off the hallway we were in.

I got on my knees, my head still ringing from the blow to my jaw. I'd never been hit by a grown man, a strong, desperate man on a mission. I stood slowly, feeling dizzy, but turned around and walked into the kitchen. I paused at the entrance, squinting into the darkness.

Then he focused his small light on the room. I could make out tables in the center, long counters lining every wall. I saw the sinks and the spot where appliances had probably stood. But now the space was occupied by what looked like the cat shelter.

He started mumbling as he swept his light around the room, saying, "Got to tie her up somehow. Got to find string—something."

He ordered me to the farthest corner and started opening cabinets. Meanwhile, I could hear Tom's voice—it was so faint and seemed so far away. He was calling my name. Pounding on the door. I could also hear Candace—it had to be her—trying to get the other door open.

A frazzled Stanley stopped what he was doing and said, "You tell them all to shut up or I'll blow your head off."

He marched me to the door that led to the rest of the mill first. "Tell them I have you and that I have demands before I'll let you go."

"Candace," I called, "is that you?"

"Jillian? What are you doing in there?" she shouted back.

"You have to back off. Ward Stanley has a gun on me," I said, finding it difficult with such a shaky voice to make sure she could hear me.

"Who?" she answered. Unlike mine, her voice was like steel.

"Don't say my name again," Stanley whispered. "Get over to the other door."

I repeated the scenario with Tom, but unlike Candace, who sounded calm and collected, Tom was furious. He shouted, "You hurt her and I'll kill you, Stanley. That's a promise."

I was then shoved back to the corner and I could hear cats stirring in their shelter. I was surprised they hadn't panicked and come out. But then, perhaps these shelters made them feel safer than they ever had before. What would happen to them? Would this maniac kill them, too?

Stanley didn't resume looking for something to tie me up. He paced in front of me, gun hand again on top of his head. Trapped like an animal, he was trying to figure out how to use me to get out of here.

I took a deep breath and decided I had nothing but words to use as my weapon. "It's over, Ward. Let Candace in. Come clean about your trips inside the mill all these years and it will go better for you."

"I'll never get my mill back now. Never," he said, as if talking to himself.

"You've been looking for the things you and your mother believe your father hid in here, right?" I said.

"Duh, yes," he said. "And I knew I'd find the stash one day, especially once the mill was back in my hands. But *you* had to show up."

"What if I could tell you where it is?" I said. "You might spend a little jail time, but that wouldn't keep your mother from getting what belongs to the two of you."

He shined the light directly on my face. "What are you talking about?"

"The engineer found a false wall," I said. "That's why he and Candace are here tonight—to see what's behind it. Your father might have hidden money or jewels or whatever he was trying to keep from your mother right in his office."

"Next to the body?" he said, incredulous.

His words scared me more than the gun, more than the blow to my face, more than the hatred this man had revealed tonight. How did he know where the skeleton had been hidden?

Unless he'd put it there.

There was no use pretending I didn't hear what he'd said. "You knew about the body because you killed Kay Ellen Sloan when she followed you in here one night, right?" Trying not to sound accusatory, I hoped to make it seem that I was stating facts I already knew.

Meanwhile, I could hear Tom shouting, but I couldn't make out his words.

"You've got it all wrong," he said. "I didn't kill her. My father did." He began pacing again. "Oh, I helped him wrap her up and put her in the fireplace, all right. Did as I was told. Didn't ask questions. And how does he repay me? By denying me my legacy. Denying me what was mine."

"He was sneaking in here, too, then?" I said.

"Sneaked in here to hide what he'd stolen from us. After he died, and Mom and I learned there was nothing left, I understood. He hadn't killed that girl because she'd spurned his advances like he'd told me. She'd followed him in here, saw what he was doing and threatened to tell the world." He stopped and stared at me. "He was always a liar and ended up a thief, too. Stole from his own family."

"But you can explain all that to the police," I said. "They'll understand. You could maybe even get probation and—"

He pointed the gun at me. "You don't know what

you're talking about, so I suggest you shut up and let me think."

I closed my eyes. Why did I believe I could reason with a crazy, desperate man? But when I opened my eyes, he was no longer pointing the gun at me. He was doing his five-step walk one way and then the other.

And Boots had appeared. My little angel had come to offer comfort and I felt my speeding heart slow a little at the sight of her. She was sitting on the floor right near Stanley, her curled-up smiley mouth making me feel as if this would all work out. It had to. I loved Tom; I loved Kara and Candace and my three most precious babies. I had to get out of here alive. I *had* to.

I don't know if all ghost cats can read minds, but perhaps Boots could. She stood and ambled toward the feral shelter. She went away from me, her tail in the air. I squinted into the darkness and saw her find the little entrance on the side. She walked in.

The screech that followed startled me as well as my captor. But when three big cats came racing out of that shelter, they toppled Ward Stanley in their frantic race to escape. He dropped the gun and it slid away from him.

One cat had gotten tangled up with him and managed to swipe his face before disappearing. He yelped and I knew I had my chance. I snatched up the gun.

My two hands trembled as I gripped it and pointed it at Stanley. Candace had taught me a bit about guns and I knew this was a Glock, one of those automatics that didn't have a safety. I sure hoped it didn't go off, because if I hurt this man, even though he'd hurt me, I knew I couldn't live with myself.

"Get up and go open a door," I said. "I don't care which one, because you and I both know there are people waiting to help me no matter which one you choose."

I followed behind him, not getting too close in case he

decided to turn and fight me for the weapon. My hands were still shaking and I was glad he didn't know I could never pull the trigger unless the thing was aimed at his foot.

I suppose he decided he'd have a better chance with Tom than with the police. After all, the police had guns, too.

He was wrong.

The minute the door opened, Tom's fist landed on Stanley's chin and flattened him. He was out cold.

Thirty-six

The nice, warm police station seemed the best and safest place in the world to me. I was in the break room with Tom, a blanket around my shoulders and an ice pack pressed to my cheek. The memory of him holding me close in that kitchen would last for a lifetime. So would the scolding I'd gotten from Candace once she'd come in and handcuffed a dazed Ward Stanley back at the mill.

She'd just put Stanley in an interview room a few minutes ago, but she came in to check on me. That was when Tom, who'd driven me here, asked to speak to her—to talk to her alone—but only after asking if I'd be all right by myself for a few minutes.

"I'm not made of china," I said. "I didn't break and I don't plan to."

He grinned. "I'll be right back."

I grabbed a bottled water from the fridge and sat back down at the break table. I hadn't seen Boots after she scared those ferals out of the shelter, but I smiled at what she'd done. It was no accident—and it was something I could never tell anyone. The ferals got spooked and gave me an opportunity. That was my story and I would stick to it.

I took a sip and realized I wanted sweet tea far more than cold water, but that would have to wait. The cut inside my cheek reacted to the cold and I winced. *Pain is only a reminder you're still alive, Jillian. It's a good thing.*

Tom returned as promised and, of course, I had to know what he wanted with Candace.

He took my hands off the water I held and gripped them in his own. "I wanted to confirm something. Do you know you're a hero? That you took down a murderer tonight?"

"What? No. You knocked him out. Besides, his father is the one who killed Kay Ellen. Ward may be a bad person, but I believe him."

"I'm not talking about Kay Ellen," he said. "I'm talking about Penelope Webber."

I shook my head. "That doesn't make sense. Penelope was ready to vote through the condo proposal, just like Stanley wanted her to. She wanted to cash in on the deal, but someone found out—Landon Burgess, no doubt—and she was murdered to keep her from swaying the vote." I paused, considering this. "Stanley had to know which way she was leaning, so why would he want her dead? Once the mill was in his hands again, he could tear it completely apart looking for the money he believes his father hid."

"You mean the bearer bonds, diamonds and cash Dustin Gray helped Candace locate?" he said.

"No way," I said, smiling broadly. "They found it?"

"They found it thanks to Dustin's skill as an engineer," Tom said. "Who knows when that secret little room was constructed? Years ago, no doubt. But obviously son Ward knew nothing about it—nor did his mother."

I said, "But let's back up. You said he murdered Penelope. Why would he do that when she was about to help him get his proposal approved?"

"Here's the deal. I learned who the shadow investor was today. Penelope Webber had maxed out every credit card, drained her bank account and turned over her stocks to Stanley." He smiled. "That's how I found out she was the mysterious investor—because of the stocks she put in his name."

"That still doesn't explain why Stanley would kill one of his cash cows," I said.

"Your friend Dustin had a hand in that, I'm afraid," he said. "After he'd been to the mill, he voiced serious doubts to Penelope about the condo proposal. Told her the renovations for residential living would be far more costly, especially the insurance part. There wasn't enough in the condo till to cover it."

"Dustin did tell me something about that tonight. So, Penelope asked Stanley for her money back, didn't she?" I said.

"I think so, because she still had an investor offering up a real estate component—Landon Burgess. Penelope wouldn't cash in as quickly as with the condo project, but an urban village still could work for her down the line. She could become involved as a *commercial* real estate agent once the shops in the urban village were created," he said. "Candace and Morris will sweat the entire truth out of Stanley, I'm sure. Plus, that weapon he used— what's it called again?"

"A heddle hook," I said.

"It came from inside the mill. Who do we now know has been in that mill probably more times than we can count over the years?"

"Ward Stanley," I said, nodding slowly.

"A piece of circumstantial evidence, but it makes sense." He smiled. "Candace said I can take you home. What you told her in the car on the way over has given her plenty of ammunition to hold Stanley—but knowing her, she'll get him to confess. She said she'll get your formal statement tomorrow morning."

As we were walking out, Kara blasted through the

door in the waiting area. When she saw me, she pressed her hand to her heart. "I've never been so glad to see you in my life."

Tom held the gate open and she grabbed me in a bear hug. Then she gripped my forearms and held me back so she could look at my face.

"Did he do that to you?" she said, staring at what was probably an ugly bruise.

"It's okay. I'm fine. We were just going home and I'd love it if you came, too."

Tom told me he'd help me pick up my van tomorrow and we drove to my house in his Prius, with Kara's SUV on our tail.

The cats were lined up and I could tell they knew something had happened. All three rubbed against me and wound between my legs. When I knelt to pet them, Syrah sniffed at my swollen cheek and then rubbed his head against my biceps.

They followed on my heels, but once I'd poured myself a glass of sweet tea—the cure for everything, in my opinion—they seemed to know that the world was right again. Only then did they greet Kara and Tom.

I took my tea with me when I went to change. When I took off my clothes, I decided I never wanted to see them again. I tossed them in the trash when I came back to visit with Kara and Tom.

I curled up in the corner of the sofa with Chablis. My boy cats decided they weren't ready to rest, but they still needed to be near me, so they crouched at my feet, staring up at me.

After I'd filled Kara in on all that had happened since I'd last seen her at the restaurant, I said, "Did you talk to Morris about Earl Whitehouse?"

She nodded. "Related everything to Morris right after I dumped my *date*. I'd told Earl he wasn't my type. He was so drunk, I doubt he'll remember, so Morris said he'd have a chat with him about lying to the police and also promised to tell Whitehouse he wasn't to contact me ever again."

"Will they need him to testify about—" I stopped. "Oh. Kay Ellen's killer is dead. There won't be a trial."

"No trial for that murder—*if* Stanley is telling the truth," Tom said. "That guy is such a turd."

Kara said, "I'd love to see Earl Whitehouse get up on the witness stand, admit he dated a mill village girl and that the last place she probably went was to the mill to confront the intruder. And I'd like his father right there listening to him spill it."

"I have to say, I'm glad Jeannie won't have to face a trial," I said. "She's had enough heartache for a lifetime."

"What will happen to her?" Kara asked.

"There'll be a spot for her through UHP in a setting where she can learn new skills, maybe eventually earn money again. Plus they'll help her file for social security— something she probably knows nothing about."

"She's at the pastorium now, though? Until she recovers?" Kara said.

"Right." Sorrow came over me then. She didn't know how her daughter died; she didn't know her remains had been removed. I had to be the one to tell her. She deserved to know.

"What's wrong?" Tom asked.

"I'm just thinking about Jeannie," I said. "I've come to care about her." *And her little cat,* I thought. *The little cat who saved me.*

The next morning, I showered as soon as I woke up, even though I'd showered the night before. The hot water soothed my aching muscles. Stanley had shoved me, hit me, pulled me all over that mill kitchen, and my body made sure to remind me. But I'd be fine in a few days.

I put on jeans and a dark pink sweatshirt and walked

out to the living room, three cats leading the way. Tom was still asleep on the sofa. Last night Kara had to leave to write up the story for the *Messenger* and Tom had adamantly refused to leave me by myself.

I tiptoed past him into the kitchen and quickly fed my three amigos before they started meowing for their breakfast. I didn't want to wake up Tom. I couldn't grind coffee beans, either, I'd decided, but it all became moot when Candace's familiar knock sounded on the back door.

She took one look at me and said, "Ouch. That's gotta hurt."

"Not too bad," I whispered, hoping she'd take the cue and keep her voice down.

But Tom called out a sleepy, "Hi, Candace," and I turned and saw his hand raised in greeting.

"Hey, Tom." She looked back at me. "Glad you weren't alone last night. What an ordeal that lowlife put you through."

"I don't know about the two of you," I said, "but I need coffee. Then you can tell me what happened after I left the station last night."

Fifteen minutes later we all sat in the living room. After Candace took her first sip of coffee, she said, "He confessed. People would be amazed at how criminals fold when confronted with the evidence. He spilled everything—but then, he'd already admitted most of it to you. He thinks his confession will get him a reduced sentence. It won't."

I did a fist pump and said, "Yes. Go, Candace."

"He'll be charged with assault on Jillian, too, right?" Tom said.

"He will. He'll be charged with as much stuff as we can come up with along with the murder charge— multiple counts of breaking and entering, accessory to Kay Ellen's murder. It's a long list," she said.

"Tell me about what you found in the office," I said.

"Wonder boy Dustin led me to a fortune," she said. "He told me the small room we found had probably been there for decades—that old buildings often have secret spaces. A small door had been plastered over and painted—probably by the elder Stanley after he hid the bonds and jewels from his wife and son. There may have even been a safe in there at one time, though all we found was a steamer trunk filled with his fortune. We collected this evidence and we don't yet know the exact worth of what the elder Ward Stanley squirreled away. Of course, once the mill renovation got under way, someone would have found it."

"Who'll get the money?" Tom said.

"Beatrice Stanley's husband died before their divorce was final," Candace said. "I imagine it will go to her unless we find out she was complicit in either of the murders. Her son swears she knew nothing about any of it."

"Do you have any indication of her involvement?" Tom asked.

"Not a thing," she said. "Unless her son turns on her, she's free and clear. And will be rich again." Candace looked at me. "We have to go through the tedium of your formal statement. You up for that?"

"Sure. Down at the station?" I asked.

She said, "We can do it here. I brought my trusty notebook and tape recorder."

Tom stood, his coffee mug in hand. "In that case, since you'll be with Jillian, I'll head home to shower." He came over to where I sat and bent to kiss me gently. "I'll be back, though, making a pest of myself."

I laughed and found that laughter did hurt my face a little.

Candace spent an hour taking me through last evening's events step by step. I found myself trembling at one point as I relived it. She noticed, stopped and put her hand over my clenched fist. "You did amazing. And look who helped you? Cats, of course."

I smiled, thinking about Boots. I would always think of her not as a ghost, but rather as my guardian angel from this day on.

When we were finished with the statement, I told her I had to call Jeannie, see if I could come over and break the news to her about who had murdered her daughter.

Elizabeth Truman answered the phone and said I was welcome to come by. Jeannie would be back from her rehab treatment within the next half hour.

After I hung up, Candace said, "Do you want me to go with you?"

"You're in uniform," I said. "You know how Jeannie feels about that. Besides, Tom said he'd take me to pick up my van. I'll ask him to go with me."

Once Tom arrived, Candace departed after giving me a gentle hug. I told him the plan and after cat treats were dispensed, we were on our way to the mill village one more time. I was grateful for daylight and relieved a certain someone was locked up.

In fact, the morning was turning out to be bright and beautiful, the sun happy to shine on the truths that had been exposed.

Jeannie smiled when Elizabeth showed Tom and me into the parlor. She was sitting with both feet propped on a footstool and the quilt I'd made her across her lap.

Elizabeth said, "If we could make that quilt into a coat or a dress, I swear Jeannie would wear it all day."

"What's wrong with you?" Jeannie said, her voice filled with concern.

I said, "Nothing's wrong. Why do—"

"Your face," Elizabeth said. "I was wondering what happened, too."

"A bad man hit me, but he's in jail now," I said.

Elizabeth said, "He hit you? I read about the incident in the paper but it didn't mention you were assaulted. What a terrible man he turned out to be."

"Jail for him. Good," Jeannie said.

"I have some correspondence to take care of," Elizabeth said, "but I can make tea or coffee—"

I raised a hand. "We're fine. We need to tell Jeannie a few things."

Elizabeth nodded knowingly. "I understand. But if you need me or the pastor, just ring us over at the church."

Tom and I sat on the sofa across from Jeannie and I felt butterflies in my stomach. This wouldn't be easy. Tom sensed my anxiety and took my hand.

"He likes you," Jeannie said. "That's good."

"He does," I said, smiling at Tom.

And then there she was. Boots had crawled into Jeannie's lap, ready to be *her* guardian angel again.

"There you are, Bootsie. I been missin' you." She stroked the cat and I noticed Boots was translucent, not as fully visible as she'd been last night.

Tom shifted uncomfortably.

Jeannie said, "You don't see her. Just me and Jillian can."

I cleared my throat. "Many things have happened in the last week and a lot of them weren't good. The creepers you've been hearing all these years?"

She nodded vigorously. "Yup. Are they in jail, too?"

"Turns out it was only one person," I said. "Ward Stanley."

She paled. "But you told me he's dead. Don't go tellin' me I was seein' more than a ghost cat."

"His son. *That* Ward Stanley," I clarified.

Her mouth formed an *O*.

"But that's not all I have to tell you, and some of this might be difficult to hear," I said. "But you need to know."

In a soft, profoundly sad voice, Jeannie said, "I know she died by another's hand." Tears began to slide down her cheeks. "I don't need to know who done it. Don't want to."

"Are you sure?" I said.

"I am." She swiped at her tears with the back of her hand.

"There's more," I said. "They had to move Kay Ellen—so she can be put to rest in a proper place. So you won't have to stay by yourself and watch over her anymore."

Tom tightened his grip on my hand. He'd heard my voice crack and knew I was close to tears myself.

"They moved her when I wasn't there?" Her grief seemed even more magnified. "Why'd they go and do that?"

"You were in the hospital, Jeannie," I said. "But now, she can be put in the ground and you can visit her there. Isn't your mother in the ground?"

She waved her arm in the direction of the kitchen. "Right behind the church in the graveyard." She was quiet for a minute and then her expression changed. She began to smile. "I can lay my girl right beside my mama."

Just then we heard the kitchen door open and Pastor Mitch and his wife talking.

"Pastor Mitch," Jeannie called, "come quick."

He hurried into the room with Elizabeth right behind him.

"We can lay my girl to rest right by my mama, Pastor. And you and me and Miss Elizabeth can say a prayer for her every day."

He smiled broadly. "That's the best news I've heard all day."

Boots gave me one of her smiles, too, and then ever so slowly, she disappeared—at least to me. But I saw Jeannie's hand resting oddly in midair. It seemed the cat was still there for her.

I would miss Boots, but I was glad Jeannie would always have her precious companion.

Not long after, Tom and I left. As he drove me to my van, I let out a huge sigh of relief.

"People amaze me," I said. "She took the news far differently than I imagined."

"Because the person who delivered the news did such a beautiful job," he said. "One more reason to love you."

I looked over at him and rested a hand on his shoulder. "Know something? I love you, too."

He didn't speak until we were out of the car and he'd walked me to my van. "Last night was the scariest night of my life. I heard you scream from behind that locked door and I couldn't do anything, couldn't help you." He took my face in his hands, being careful to avoid the bruise. "Thank goodness you're okay, because I don't want to live without you."

I felt tears sting my eyes. "You know, when I was in that kitchen, I thought about you and Kara and Candace and my cats and all the love that surrounds me every day. I had to get back to you. I knew I would."

"You didn't panic. You kept your wits. You are amazing." He kissed me.

Then, in the shadow of a ruined mill and a culture I hoped this country would never revisit, Tom spoke softly.

"Jillian Hart, will you marry me?"

Read on for a look at the first novel
in the Cats in Trouble series,

The Cat, the Quilt
and the Corpse

Available in print and e-book from Obsidian

My cat is allergic to people—yes, odd, I know—so when I came in the back door and heard Chablis sneeze, I stopped dead. Why was she sneezing? This couldn't be a reaction to me. I use special shampoo, take precautions. Chablis and I are cool.

Besides, she hadn't been near any humans for more than twenty-four hours, since I was just arriving back from an overnight business trip to Spartanburg, a two-hour drive from my upstate South Carolina home. I'd left her and my two other cats, Merlot and Syrah, alone in the house, as I'd done many times before when I took short trips out of town. So how did human dander, better known as dandruff, find its way up her nose?

I released my grip on the rolling suitcase and started for the living room, thinking there could be a simple explanation for a sneezing cat other than allergies. Like an illness.

The thought of a sick Chablis pushed logic down to the hippocampus or wherever common sense goes when you have more important matters to attend to. I dropped my tote on the counter and hurried past the teak dining table. Since my kitchen, dining area and living room all blend together, the trip to where I'd heard Chablis sneeze wasn't more than twenty feet. But before I'd taken five steps, I stopped again. Something else besides a sneezing cat now had my attention.

Silence. No background noise. No *Animal Planet* playing on the television. I always leave the TV tuned to that station when I go away. If the cats were entertained by *The Jeff Corwin Experience* or *Heroes* or *E-Vet*, I'd convinced myself, my absences were more tolerable. Okay, I'm neurotic about my three friends. Not cat-lady neurotic. At forty-one I'm a little young for that. But cats have been my best friends for as long as I can remember, and the ones that live with me now have been amazing since my husband, John, died ten months ago. They take care of me. So I try my best to take care of them.

Could the TV be off because of a power failure?

Glancing back at the microwave, I saw that the clock showed the correct time—one p.m. Perhaps the high-def plasma TV blew up in a cloud of electronic smoke? Maybe. Didn't matter, though. Not now. I'd only heard from Chablis, and none of my cats had shown their faces. I was getting a bad vibe—and I can usually rely on my intuition.

"Chablis, I'm home," I called. I kept walking, slowly now—didn't want to panic them if I was overreacting—and went into the living area. "Syrah, where are you? Merlot, I missed you."

I breathed a sigh of relief when I found Chablis sitting on the olive chenille sofa, her blue eyes gazing up at me. Himalayans look like long-haired Siamese cats and Chablis was no different. Her gorgeous crystal blue eyes and her champagne fur were accented by deep brown feet, and she had a precious dark face and a fluffy wand of a tail.

Her nose was running and she seemed awfully puffed out—even for an already puffy cat. Was she totally swollen up by an allergen other than dandruff?

I knelt and stroked the side of her cheek with the

back of my fingers, ran my hands over her body, looking for the mass of giant hives I was sure I'd find.

Nothing. She was simply all bloated fur and loud purrs.

"I am truly sorry for leaving you overnight. Are you telling me you have feline separation anxiety?"

Chablis blinked slowly, opened her mouth and squeaked. How pitiful. She'd lost her voice. She *had* to be sick. With a virus? Or leukemia? Cats do get leukemia.

Quit it, Jillian. Call the vet.

When I stood to pull my phone from my jeans pocket, I heard Merlot's deep, loud meow and saw him perched on the seat cushions that line the dining area's bay window— a spot that provides a spectacular view of Mercy Lake. He knows the entire lake belongs to him, despite never having been closer than the window. But he hadn't been sitting there when I first came in, and he wasn't gazing out on the water. No, Merlot was looking right at me and his fur was all wild and big, too.

Since he isn't allergic to anything, dumb me finally realized that they were both scared.

And then I saw why.

Broken glass glittered near Merlot's paws—paws that could each substitute for a Swiffer duster.

My heart skipped. Broken glass . . . a broken *window*. "Merlot! Be careful." Fear escaped with my words. I attempted to mask my distress by smiling as I walked over to him.

Yeah, like Mr. Brainiac Cat would buy this fakery.

I petted his broad orange and white tiger-striped head while making sure none of his paws was bleeding. He seemed fine other than that he reminded me more than ever of one of those huge, shaggy stuffed animals at a carnival.

I hefted him off the cushions—he's a Maine coon, a

breed that weighs four times more than the smallest felines. Merlot stays lean, usually hovers around twenty
pounds. I was hoping to keep him clear of the glass, but
he was having none of that. He squirmed free and jumped
right back on the window seat and proved himself amazingly nimble by staying away from any shards. While I
examined the damaged window, he intently examined me
as if to ask, "How will you rectify this now that you're finally home, Miss Gadabout?"

The jagged hole in the lowest pane was large enough
for a hand to reach in and unlatch that window. And it
was unlatched.

"Someone's broken in. Someone's been in our house."
But stating the obvious couldn't help them explain what
had happened. Figuring this out was human territory.
For a millisecond, I wondered if this—this *intruder* might
still be here. I shook my head no. My cats are not fools.
They'd be in the basement or under a bed if any danger
still remained.

And exactly where was Syrah? My Abyssinian hadn't
made an appearance yet. I supposed he could have been
frightened enough to stay in hiding, but no. He was the
alpha cat of my little pack.

Okay, I decided. This break-in had upset him. That was
why he wasn't making an appearance. Either that or he
was so angry I'd left him and his friends to be threatened
by a burglar that he was hiding to teach me a lesson.

The thought of a thief frightening my cats produced
anger and fear and the sincere wish that I'd had a human
friend who could watch out for things just like this while
I was away. Since my husband's death, though, I'd been
caught up in my own troubles and too proud to reach out
to anyone. But making friends, getting to know my
neighbors, might have prevented this whole episode.

I inhaled deeply, let the air out slowly. *You can change
that, Jillian. But right now you need to find Syrah.*

That was what John would do if he were here. Hunt for the cat in a methodical, logical way. Solve this problem quickly. But I wasn't John and my calm began to crack like crusted snow before an avalanche. Between the silent TV, the scared animals and the absent Syrah, fear now claimed top billing.

"Where are you, baby?" I called, my voice tremulous. "Come here, Syrah."

I hurried toward the hallway leading to the bedrooms, Merlot on my heels. Poor Chablis would have been on his tail, but was stopped by a fit of sneezing. I began the search through all three thousand square feet of my house, the house that was supposed to be our dream home, the one John and I had designed ourselves.

But this was no longer a dream come true. John, at fifty-five, had been far too young to die of a sudden and unexpected heart attack. Though I was coming to terms with his death, letting go day by day, thoughts of him always seemed to flood my brain when I was stressed. And a broken window and a missing cat were certainly enough to produce that state of mind.

I rushed from room to room, but didn't find Syrah hiding behind my armoires or beneath the dressers or under any beds. He wasn't in the closets or the basement, either. I went outside and checked the trees and the roof for a third scared cat. After all, the intruder might have let him out when he made his escape. But leaves had been falling for weeks, and spotting Syrah's rusty gold fur against the reds, browns and yellows of the oak, hickory and pecan trees in my yard would be difficult.

Syrah, however, is my most vocal cat, and when I didn't hear any meowing in response to my calls, I was sure he wasn't nearby. Cats have such good hearing that they can detect the sound of a bat stretching its wings, and I was nearly shrieking his name.

I finally gave up, and when I came inside I found Merlot sitting by the back door. I was trembling all over as I crouched next to him. He rubbed against my knees and purred while I took my cell phone from my pocket, ready to report the break-in.

"Are you trying to comfort yourself or me?" I asked as I dialed 911. The last time I'd had to do that—when John collapsed—had been the worst day of my life. This event certainly wasn't as horrible, but punching those three numbers again made it seem like John had died only yesterday.

My big cat circled me lovingly as I stood, nudging me, trying to comfort me as best he could. He knew how upset I was.

"What is your emergency?" said the woman who answered.

"Um . . . um . . . my cat is missing."

The dispatcher said, "Ma'am, this line is for—"

"I've had a break-in. There's a shattered window and—" My mouth was so dry, the words wouldn't come.

"Your name, ma'am?"

"J-Jillian Hart. I live at 301 Cove Lane in Mercy." Merlot and I walked back to the living room and I picked up the cable and DVR remote. I hit the MUTE button to kill the audio before I turned on the TV. The Sony plasma worked fine and was tuned to *Animal Planet* as it should be. I jabbed the OFF button, wondering what kind of thief would break into my house and turn off my expensive TV.

"Ma'am. Are you there, ma'am?" It came out like "Ah you there, ma-aaam?" Very Southern, reminding me that I was far from our longtime Texas home and far from anyone who really understood what an emergency this was for me.

"Yes. I'm here."

"I see this is a cellular numbah, but are you callin' from inside the home?"

"Of course. My cat is gone and—"

"Officers are on their way. Do you feel safe or do you believe the intruder might still be inside or in the immediate vicinity?" Her South Carolina drawl was so thick and I was so distracted by worry that she might as well have been speaking a foreign language.

I closed my eyes, processed her question. "I-I've searched the house. No one's here but me and my two babies."

"But you do fear for your safety, ma'am?"

"I fear for my *cat's* safety and—" Tears sprang unexpectedly to my eyes and I bit my lip.

"Ma'am, is something happenin' right this minute? Is this intruder back?"

"No. It's just that . . . I don't know where he is. I can't find him." How pathetic I sounded. Syrah was a cat, after all.

"I fully understand your concern. My name is Barbara Lynne. May I call you Jillian?"

"Yes. Of course."

"Tell me about these babies you mentioned. How old are they, Jillian?"

"Chablis is about five and Merlot is probably around eight. They're fine. Well, not exactly fine because Chablis is having an allergic reaction and—"

"Oh my. Should we send an am-bu-lance?" Her previously unruffled tone was now laced with concern.

"I have medicine. She'll be okay in an hour or two. I haven't had time to give her an antihistamine. I've been busy searching—"

"Exactly where are your children, Jillian? I don't hear them, but I assume they're with you, with their mama?"

"Oh. Oh no. You're confused. Chablis and Merlot are my two other cats."

A pause, then, "Is that so?" Sweetness and concern had now left the building. She couldn't have sounded any colder if she'd been standing in a blizzard in North Dakota.

I stayed on the line as instructed—I was "ma'am" again—and no longer felt any love from the dispatcher. She offered only an occasional "Are you still there?"

Meanwhile, my panic worsened as I waited for the police. Possibilities ran through my head. The person who broke in obviously let Syrah out. My beautiful, wonderful cat could be lying dead by the road after being hit by a car. He could have fallen off the dock into the lake and drowned. He could have— *No. Stop this.*

I decided to do something constructive rather than continue to conjure up worst-case scenarios. To make sure Chablis and Merlot wouldn't run out the door if they got the chance, I put my cell on speaker and set it on the coffee table, then dragged their travel carriers out of the foyer closet. For once, crating them wasn't like trying to bag smoke. They were compliant, perhaps unnerved enough themselves to want the security of their carriers right now.

Not wanting them out of my sight, I kept them with me in the living room. I dreaded the arrival of sirens and uniformed strangers. It would only add to their trauma.

It didn't take long for the cops to show. Five minutes later I heard the cruiser's engine in my driveway, and the dispatcher quickly disconnected when I told her they had arrived. But the car had come without a siren—I guessed because this wasn't an emergency that required one.

Mercy is a small town—teensy compared to Houston, where I'd lived with John for the six years we'd been married. Seemed like you could get anywhere in Mercy in five minutes. I ran to the foyer and answered before the police officers could even knock.